George Robert Pembroke

South Sea Bubbles

By the Earl and the Doctor. Seventh Edition

George Robert Pembroke

South Sea Bubbles
By the Earl and the Doctor. Seventh Edition

ISBN/EAN: 9783337019020

Printed in Europe, USA, Canada, Australia, Japan

Cover: Foto ©Andreas Hilbeck / pixelio.de

More available books at **www.hansebooks.com**

SOUTH SEA BUBBLES.

BY THE EARL AND THE

DOCTOR.

SEVENTH EDITION

LONDON:

RICHARD BENTLEY AND SON,

Publishers in Ordinary to Her Majesty.

1895.

PREFACE.

HIS little work was composed originally of different sketches taken from my logs and put into shape, the aforesaid logs having been saved in a moist and pithy state from the wreck; they were then put into a rough kind of order to serve as a memorial of the cruise; but after our arrival home we were persuaded to publish them.

These excuses are tendered to any readers who may be driven into a mild exasperation at the occasional confusion of persons, the incongruous jumps from the highest subjects to the most solemn philosophy, or any other such slight characteristics, which make it, as Mark Twain said of his map of Paris, quite unlike anything of the kind that was ever seen.

THE EARL.

PREFACE TO FIFTH EDITION.

O the numerous members of the great Smell-fungus family I dedicate this preface. " South Sea Bubbles" was originally written under the magnetic influence of the scenes that it describes. Conventionality was temporarily dead in us, and innocence was rampant. Secure in our own good consciences, I fear that we entirely forgot that you would scarcely understand the possibility that our minds were composing, arrayed, as it were, in the costume of the country during the summer months. Our genuine innocence having now become partially corrupted by civilisation, we are able to perceive that one or two little paragraphs might as well have been omitted. These have been carefully expurgated in the present edition.

To you who say that it is not a fit book for a young lady to read, I answer simply, that though I believe that no innocent girl (not related to your family) would be any the worse for it, it was never intended for their perusal; and I have yet to learn that all literature is to be rendered adaptable to Miss Skimperton's academy. As for the rest of even your family consisting of the older women, the men, and the boys, I will only say, that if they cannot read a frank enthusiastic description of a cruise amongst pleasant places and pleasant people (startling though the frankness may occasionally be) without their minds creating prurient reflections, I am very sorry for them.

To the general public, for after all, my dear Smell-fungus, you are not everybody, we wish to offer our most earnest thanks for their warm reception of our humble effort to amuse them.

THE EARL.

CONTENTS.

SOUTH SEA BUBBLES.

CHAPTER I.

TAHITI.

AVE you never had a bad bilious fever?" says Tom Cringle; "then you have never known what it is to be in heaven or in the other place." I have had a bad fever and can testify to the truth of the remark. Physical, and worse still, mental agonies of indescribable horror, followed by visions of perfect peace, happiness, and beauty. There are certain places and scenes that are always blended in my mind with those glorious, strange, delirious dreams, filling me with a luxurious feeling of poetry and pleasure; yet utterly indescribable, because half their charm lies in the remembrance of the happiness they brought me. And so it is that, urged by

B

my fellow-labourer in this work, I sit down with a certain reluctance to write what I fear will be but a commonplace and colourless description of a place and time that will live for ever in my thoughts as some splendid dream of beauty and pleasure.

Such things will seldom stand the magic test of pen and ink, even when they are used by a master of the art of writing. I—and I believe I am not the only sinner in the world—sneakingly shirk descriptions of beautiful scenery in novels, except those in " Westward Ho ! " " Geoffry Hamlyn," and above all, "Tom Cringle's Log." What glorious masterpieces of word-painting they are, showing new beauties each time they are read—free and unconstrained, yet quaint and fanciful, filled with little points and touches seemingly minute and almost unnecessary in themselves, which, however, constitute the charm and perfection of the picture.

But this is above my hand. All I can do is to scribble down my dreams as they float before my brain, and please myself if not my readers.

I can never forget the scene that burst upon my astonished and half-opened eyes as I turned out of bed one morning and found myself entering the port of Papiete. Great mountains, of every shade of blue, pink, grey, and purple, torn and broken into every conceivable fantastic shape, with deep, dark, mysterious gorges, showing almost black by contrast with the surrounding brightness ; precipitous peaks and

pinnacles rising one above the other like giant senti-
nels, until they were lost in the heavy masses of cloud
they had impaled; while below, stretching from the
base of the mountains to the shore, a forest of tropical
trees, with the huts and houses of the town peeping
out between them.

The finest islands of the West Indies idealized, with
a dash of Ceylon, is all I can compare it to. And the
natives! How well they match the scene! The
women, with their voluptuous figures,—their unique,
free, graceful walk,—their nightgowns (for their dress
is nothing but a long chemise, white, pale green, red,
or red and white, according to the taste of the wearer,
which is invariably good) floating loosely about in a
cool refreshing manner,—their luxuriant black tresses,
crowned with a gracefully plaited Araroot chaplet, and
further ornamented by a great flowing bunch of white
" Reva-Reva,"—their delicious perfume of cocoa-nut
oil (it is worth going to Tahiti for the smell alone),—
and, above all, their smiling handsome faces, and singing, bubbling voices, full of soft cadences,—all this
set off by the broken, scattered rays of green light
shining through the shady avenues. Oh, that I were
the artist that could paint it! What pleasant places
those avenues are for a stroll in the evening, when the
heat of the sun is beginning to die away. To meet
the great, strapping, pleasant-looking men, in their
clean white shirts and parti-coloured waist-cloths, each
greeting you, especially if you are English, with a

ready smile and a hearty " Ya rana ! " which means all
kinds of salutations and blessings ; sometimes, even,
if they like the look of you, stopping to shake hands,
with no earthly object but kindly goodfellowship.　　I
have seen even small piccaninnies stop in their infantine gambols, and toddling up with their little faces
puckered into dimples, and their little puds held up to
reach your fingers, pipe out a shrill " How do you do ? "
And as for the young ladies ! the most bashful and coy
will never pass you without a greeting, a glance of the
eyes, and a slight gathering in of her dress with her
elbows to exhibit her buxom figure to full perfection.
Or else perhaps she will come up coquettishly, and ask
you for the loan of your cigar, take a few puffs at it,
and hand it back again gracefully to the rather astonished owner; and then, with a parting compliment,
which you most likely don't understand, let you go
your way in peace—or *not !*

The streets of Papiete at night are very pleasant and
merry.　　The first night we arrived the doctor and I
went for a stroll ; and, following the run of the crowd,
soon found ourselves in the principal grog-shop street.
There all was reckless jollity and good-nature.　Gangs
of French sailors careering wildly to and fro, singing
part-songs at the top of their voices, in capital time
and tune, all the natives within hearing joining in ;
native men and girls sitting about the doorsteps of the
shops, or strolling up and down together, some romping, some spooney.　By the bye, the proper way to

walk with your lady-love in Tahiti is as follows. You
put your arm round her neck, and she hers round your
waist, and hangs on your breast in a limply affectionate
manner. It is as much *selon les regles* as walking arm-
in-arm, and is much prettier to look at. But the man
should be tall, for to see a stumpy little French sailor
clawed in this way by the big brown object of his affections is a thought ludicrous.

At last we came to a place where two streets
crossed each other. Each corner house was a grog-
shop, where a lot of jolly Frenchmen were singing in
chorus, a crowd of natives standing round and joining.
Another knot was collected round the doctor, who
was holding forth about European politics (the war
between France and Prussia had just broken out) to a
learned native, who translated all he said to the eager
bystanders, while I was being addressed by a brown
lady in her native language, which edified me
exceedingly. Behind each bar the ideal French
barman presided, with the sleeves of his dingy white
shirt rolled up, brawny, bull-necked, black-haired, and
shaven. Here and there an unmistakeable Yankee
skipper might be seen amongst the mob, with an
occasional English Jack, or Scotch storekeeper. The
shifting crowd grew larger, and the singing noisier,
till on a sudden a native policeman appeared as if
from the clouds, and begged, prayed, entreated, com-
manded the crowd to disperse. Some one twitched
his stick out of his hand, which caused a roar of

laughter and a fresh torrent of eloquence from the brown bobby, which lasted till the mob good-humouredly did as they were told. Handcuffs have not yet been introduced into Tahiti, pieces of string being used as substitutes by the native constabulary when duty calls upon them to arrest a criminal or a disorderly person. If the offender is a person of active muscles and independent spirit, the capture becomes a very exciting and amusing spectacle for the bystanders.

The lighted shops and stores surrounded by the beautiful trees, and gaily dressed girls, the rollicking sailors, the pleasant smell, the perfect cleanliness, the universal mirth, civility, and goodnature of every one, the utter absence of quarrelling, jostling, or rudeness, made a very novel, picturesque, and pleasing night scene.

"Society Islandism" is very catching. In an incredibly short time you feel a kind of early Christian brotherly love coming over you, a delicious indolence, a refined gentleness of manner, and a blunting of the edge of your moral ideas. Tolerably virtuous and proper as I was, I always had a secret consciousness that I should not be the least surprised to find myself lolling about the groves after the manner of the natives, making lazy love, and utterly regardless of past or future. Things that would strike you any-where else as wrong and degrading, seem somehow only natural and beautiful in those lovely islands.

I feel that this aimless, pointless dreaminess, is pervading the chapter I am writing, making it utterly dreary to an incident-and-information-loving European reader. But if any such kind critic should come to me, and in the barbarous manner and language of the North inform me that my article was intolerably prosy and stupid, I should smile blandly, and say : " My dear fellow, don't be so horribly abrupt and angular ! As many poets have arranged their rhythm to suit and suggest the actions they were writing about, so I have made the style of my composition a reflection of the life and the people I was describing. It is just the sort of thing, too, to read in that country. Nothing startling, to make you fix your attention exclusively on its pages ; no deep thoughts or curious information to worry your brains with. Just the thing to dream over as you are sucking your coco-nut under the palm trees ; just the thing to go to sleep over at the end of every two sentences, while a native or half-caste young lady watches by your side with a fly-whisk or a fan to keep those abominable insects from settling on the tip of your nose.

By the way, those brutal flies are the only things that refuse to be Society Islandized. Under the most softening influences they still retain the tiresome energy and vulgar conceited obtrusiveness natural to their race. They are the Scotchmen amongst insects.

If you are wearied with the busy—I mean lazy— hum of men, you go out in a canoe on to the great coral

reef that forms the harbour, and dabbling your hands
and feet in the cool water, gaze dreamily down at the
gorgeous sights beneath you : the beautiful coral, with
its mysterious caves and fissures, from which you
almost expect to see real water-babies appear ; coral,
some of it like great crimson fans woven from the
most delicate twigs—some of a beautiful mauve or
purple—some like miniature models of old gnarled
trees—some like great round mounds of snow-white
ivory, chased and carved with a superhuman delicacy
—some like leaves and budding flowers—while all
about are scattered magnificent holothuria and great
red and yellow starfish, that look as if they were made
of leather, with horn buttons stuck all along their
feelers for ornament;[1] and echini, with their dense
profusion of long brown spikes, covering them so
completely as to make an unlearned person like myself
wonder how they can get at their food or mix in
society. Still more beautiful when they are dead and
their spikes are gone, and nothing remains but their
round white skeletons, splendidly embossed in long
lines with purple and pink knobs. Fish of every
shape and colour swimming lazily in and out of the
black-looking caves and fissures, or coasting round
under the overhanging edges of the coral precipices.
Some of the finest cobalt blue, some golden, some

---

[1] This is the "slate-pencil fish," a species overlooked by
Mr. Chas. Reade.

pink, some more like beautiful orange and purple butterflies than natives of the sea, with long white rat's tails, swimming or floating frontways, sternways, sideways, with apparently equal ease and partiality. Some variegated like harlequins; many, not with their hues more or less blending into each other where they meet, like Christian fishes, but mathematically divided by regular distinct lines, as if they had paid for their colours, and had them laid on by the square inch.

Oh, a coral reef is the thing to dream over! So gloriously beautiful, so wondrously fantastic, so treacherously dangerous, and so damnable to walk upon. In the first ten minutes your shoes are cut to pieces; then you step unexpectedly into a deep hole, and bark your shins against its edges. On getting clear of this, you most likely tread upon an echinus,[1] and with a howl of agony make a wild attempt to stand upon one leg and pick the spikes out of your injured foot, whereon you lose your balance and sit down violently upon some of his (the echinus's) relations. The only thing then to be done is to lie quietly where you are, like a stranded whale, swearing feebly, until some kind companion makes his appearance, and extricates the spines from the injured parts with his jack-knife.

---

[1] The species of echinus alluded to here can *thrust* its spines into the skin of its own proper motion. I have watched them most carefully, and have seen them do it.

And what glorious places for boating expeditions those Society Islands are. Threading your way between the patches, inside the outer reef, you can sail along the coast for miles in smooth water and beautiful scenery, with one picturesque bay after another to be explored. And though you be but a common sailor, with empty pockets, everywhere you are certain of a hearty welcome from everybody and everything, including those confounded mosquitoes. One man comes out to steer you by signs towards the best landing-place ; another, as soon as your boat sticks, trots out to her, and without more ado directs you to jump on his back, and carries you ashore, as if you were but a fly on his gigantic shoulders ; and on the beach you are received by the various members of the family, who set to work to entertain you, and supply your necessities as best they can. When you have had a short palaver, and have declined with some difficulty the various hospitable offers that have been pressed upon you, you return to your boat, and find in her a quantity of coco-nuts, bananas, bread-fruit, and similar delicacies; indeed, in one instance, I remember finding the paterfamilias in the act of lugging the last of his fowls, a tough-looking old cock, down to the beach by a string that was fast to his leg; I laughingly declined the present, at which he seemed a little hurt.

And then when all is ready for a start home, and even the youngest baby has been held up to lisp out a

parting " Ya rana," and you have shaken hands with
all the village, till you are tired, some stately matron
cries out, "John! just launch a canoe, and pilot the
gentleman out to the mouth of the bay, in case he
should stick anywhere," or words to that effect, which
John accordingly does, and you start away home; the
last thing you see being a kindly smile, and the last
thing you hear a cheerful God bless you!

It may be a confession of weakness, but I must own
I like this kind of thing. I like being petted and
made much of, as long as I am sure that there is no
affectation, humbug, or mercenary feeling about it.
"Bah!" cries the cynic, " their kiss-me-cum-cuddle-
me blarney is only skin-deep, they have made a prince
of Jack to-day, and will do the same with Bill to-
morrow." "Well, my friend," say I, "your feelings
may last a little longer than theirs, but are they im-
mutable and everlasting? and at any rate my brown
friends deserve admiration for their natural unsophisticated impulse towards kindness, affection, and unselfishness, shortlived though it may be, for it is a rare
enough thing in this world, especially where many
people of your sort are to be found."

When the nights are calm and dark, away go the
natives to spear fish by torchlight. They use several
kinds of weapons, according to the size of the prey
they are hunting, but the ordinary spear is like a
small metal broom, made of a lot of iron rods diverg-
ing outwards from the staff on which they are lashed,

between which the little fish become jammed without
being much injured.   Silently your canoe glides over
the coral reef through the clear shallow water, and
you stand up with the torch in one hand and the spear
in the other all ready for action.   A blaze of light
shines close to you and suddenly the figure of the
bowman in some other craft becomes revealed like
some splendid bronze statue, the torch lifted on high,
the form bent slightly forward, the eyes intently fixed
on the surface of the water, and the right arm raised
to strike, while behind you dimly distinguish the black
crouching figure of his comrade, noiselessly and almost
without motion propelling and steering the long
narrow pirogue.   Whish!   Down drops the end of
the torch—he's got one!   So he has sure enough, for
I hear the tap, tap of his spear against the side of the
boat, and the squatter of the fish as he drops into the
bottom of it.   I see one! and make a desperate
lunge, whereby I lose my balance and topple over,
luckily not overboard, dropping my spear into the
water, on one side, and the rather heavy reed torch on
the other, which leaves us in utter darkness, in which
I hear, not weeping and gnashing of teeth, but a
most unmistakeable gurgling and chuckling from my
native companion usually the most polite and dignified
of mortals.

We arrived at Tahiti just in time to celebrate the
feast of St. Napoleon.   The shore was thickly lined
with gigs and whaleboats that had brought in the

natives from all parts of the country, to say nothing of
the neighbouring islands. The festivities were about
to commence in full swing. Regattas, horse-races,
reviews, court processions, and hymns! ye powers!
to be sung for prizes by the different districts.
Hymns at that time were associated in my mind with
uncomfortable pews, swell bonnets, &c. and I wondered whether the judge would be low, church or dissenting, and give the prize to the choirs who sung
slowest and dolefullest, or whether he would be high
church, and reward those who could rattle out " Adeste
fideles " in the most triumphant style. Little did
I know what a South Sea hymn or " Himene " was like.
Little did I know that all styles of music, from the
most comic to the most sacred, came under the same
title, and that even dances more graceful than moral
were sanctified by the sacred name of hymns.

Aug. 16.—Bang! bang! Twenty-four guns at sunrise
in honour of the day, rousing me just as I had dropped
into a blissful slumber in the cool of the morning. I
repent it deeply, but I fear that the expression that
rose to my lips was more forcible than choice. However, I dozed off till about seven A.M., when I was
awoke again by some one coming on board. Such
was my pertinacity that I managed to get to sleep
again till eight o'clock, when another dose of twenty-
four guns, not to mention those of the frigate, shook
the vessel through and through and compelled me to
get up. At midday more guns as before.

After luncheon came the regatta, gig, whaleboat, and canoe races, the best of all being a great double-canoe-race, some fifty men or so in each craft. A glorious sight it was, all the way there was not five feet advantage to either, and they kept so close side by side, that a man could have jumped from one to the other. Every paddle caught the water at once with the regularity of clock-work, making the canoe lift and spring forward at each stroke like the rush of some great sea-serpent, while in the extreme nose stood or rather danced the chief or captain, yelling, swearing, stamping, and giving the time to the performers; at one moment whirling his long paddle over his head, and looking very much inclined to sweep the opposition leader in the rival canoe into the briny deep by a dexterous stroke, at the next making furious scoops at the water to add an inch or two to the speed of his vessel. Neck and neck they ran all the course, and when at last they passed the Astrée that was acting as flag-ship not a foot could have divided them. When it was all over and the cheering had subsided, they lay under the stern gallery of the frigate, where old Queen Pomare and her maids of honour were watching the fun, and beat time with their paddles against the sides of the canoes to the music of the band, producing a wonderful effect.

In the evening we went off to hear the rehearsal of the " Himenes " or native singing, which was to take place in the gardens of the governor's palace, where at the same time a swell ball *à l'European* was going on. Edging our way through the laughing, romping crowd outside, the doctor and I succeeded in getting in; but going out again to fetch Mitchell and the skipper we found ourselves in a fix, as the temper of the bullet-headed little French sentinel had completely given way under the continued fire of banter he had been compelled to receive without a chance of retaliation from the native young ladies, and he doggedly refused to let us re-enter the gates. So here we were stuck, feeling very much like the foolish virgins in the parable, or four male Peris gazing into Paradise; to all the doctor's logic and honeyed words the little brute only snapped "Montrez votre passe," to which we could only reply that we had an invitation from the governor himself which we had left on board, at which he only sniffed with the profoundest contempt for such a shallow imposition. We were beginning to have vague ideas of upsetting our Liliputian friend in the thick of the crowd and rushing the gate, when a swell naval officer appeared, and being struck, I suppose, with our respectable and ingenuous appearance, passed us in without more ado, and civilly fetched an A.D.C. to admit Mitchell and the skipper.

The scene that burst upon us was quite indescribable in its strange wild motley beauty; the gardens were lit up by countless lanterns hanging from the branches of the trees, the walks thronged by natives, French officers in full glory, white, brown, and beautiful half-

caste ladies in ball dresses, and a sprinkling of motley
civilians like ourselves, while all the rest of the space
was filled by the different native choirs, each, I should
think, several hundred strong. Each choir was divided
into two halves, one of which sat shoulder to shoulder
in long rows three or four deep, while the other half,
similarly disposed, faced them, leaving a long aisle
down the middle, where the chiefs of the district,
arrayed in old native dresses, consisting of short capes
with numerous many-coloured flounces walked to and
fro gravely directing the singers.

The effect of the music was quite indescribable.
Many of the tunes were, I believe, of European origin,
but so completely nativized, that their authors would
scarcely have recognized them.   They had a character
of their own utterly unlike and far finer than Arabic,
Turkish, or any savage melody I ever heard.   There
were many parts harmoniously arranged ; one set of
singers devoting themselves entirely to making a bass
" *boom* " something like the drone of a bagpipe, others
confining their energies to various long drawn high
falsetto notes, brought in at different times and varied
to suit the music.

The most striking features were the extraordinarily
perfect time, hundreds of men and women clapping
their hands together at stated intervals with a noise as
sharp as the crack of a stock-whip, and the strange
metallic ring of every voice, which though scarcely
beautiful in itself to an unaccustomed ear, had a wild

and curious effect, that was in perfect keeping with
the savage grandeur of the whole scene.

After doing the necessary poojah with the swells,
and being shown round by our good-natured consul
and a French officer, the doctor and I were left to our
own devices, and enjoyed ourselves to our heart's content, roaming from choir to choir as each struck up in
turn, and sitting down among the singers, who with
native politeness, immediately offered us a corner of
their mats to sprawl on. And very pleasant it was.
Wandering about among the merry crowd, speaking
whatever came into our heads to anybody we pleased
without fear of offending or being sat upon, squatting
down among the performers, and carrying on a broken
but laughing conversation with the ladies of the chorus
in the intervals of the music, listening to its execution
till the last sigh (Tahitian music always ends with a
kind of deep sigh) had died away, and the clear in-
spiriting chant of some distant choir rose suddenly and
ringingly in triumphant rivalry; watching the countless pretty little pictures of love and tenderness on all
sides, young men and maidens comparing souls, and
anxious mothers attending, when they had the chance,
to their remarkably patient and long-suffering offspring
that were rolled up in many-coloured handkerchiefs,
and strewed about the ground like bolsters in every
direction. How strange, and new, and beautiful it all
seemed, and yet, and yet—when I write it all down it
seems as flat as ditchwater—it is like exhibiting the

skeleton of some beautiful woman with the purpose of giving the spectators an idea of her loveliness. I think I shall head this chapter with a notice that no one but poets are allowed to read it, for none but a poetical imagination would be able to conceive the gorgeous colouring that gave birth to these dry pen-and-ink sketches. What seemed more odd to me than anything was, that scarcely any except ourselves were impressed with the beauty of what they heard or saw. Was it but an illusion produced by our too vivid imaginations ?

The French officers haw-hawed and pooh-poohed, and almost professed themselves bored with the whole concern, evidently considering that "better is the meanest café-chantant in the city of Paris than the most glorious festivity in the whole of the Pacific." Beauty of scene and even beauty of character lose much of their striking charm by their constant presence, and so it is less remarkable that the natives could not appreciate the loveliness of the picture of which they formed a great part ; but I shall not forget one woman, who, when I expressed to her that I thought the abominable brass-band that the swells were dancing to, a horrid nuisance, and not to be compared to the Tahitian "Himenes," gazed on me with an expression of shocked wonder, such as a Calvinistic preacher would direct upon a bold free-thinker, or the august Pio Nono on some more harmless freemason ; and then, having debated solemnly whether I was making fun of her or was only a harmless lunatic, she turned away without an answer, and gravely continued her singing.

Towards the end of the rehearsals Queen Pomare and the commandant appeared on the scene, and a dance was got up for their especial benefit. One division of singers stood up and made a circle, or rather oblong, and kept up a strange wild chant, while a boy and a girl performed their gambados much in the style of the Egyptian Ghawazee, twisting, wriggling, and undulating all over in a by no means ungraceful manner. After a little the girl pretended to be tired or out-danced and slipped aside. Instantly the music changed into a kind of satirical burst, and she reappeared. Then more performers joined in, and the singing and dancing grew faster and more furious to the end, when everyone cheered loudly. It was curious to see how the old queen's face, usually apathetic, brightened up. Her lips parted, her eyes glistened, till she looked as if she would have liked to kick over the old governor on whose arm she was leaning, and perform a *pas seul* on his prostrate carcase.

But the sight of the evening was the " Scratching dance." After a lively prelude all the singers threw themselves on to their left elbows and unanimously and violently scratched their right legs, and then *vice versâ*. What it all meant I don't know, but I fancy the words were a shade broad from the way the spectators laughed.

At last it all came to an end, the mats and bundles

and babies were gathered up, and amid much squeezing,
and laughing, and singing, the divisions filed one by
one out of the gates, to the sound of drums and other
barbarous instruments, to seek their night quarters,
while we went on board regularly bewildered with the
charms of all we had seen and heard.

Aug. 17.—In the afternoon we mounted some
strange little American carriages, and drove out to
see the races. The road was very gay and pretty;
natives dressed in their gala clothes, French officers
mounted on caracolling steeds, which they were teasing
and showing off with that absurd affectation of coolness
and nonchalance so common to them; jolly-looking
naval swells, some on foot, others crammed into little
buggies with their laughing, bubbling-voiced half-
caste friends; every large animal with four legs, and
every thing that could run upon wheels being put into
requisition.

Society in Tahiti is divided into two sects, between
which is a great gulf fixed; the first consists of the
white merchants and shopkeepers who have pale-
faced wives, and the second of the half-castes and their
friends. In a cynical temper I christened them the
mean whites and the dirty browns. The former have
all the virtue, and the latter all the charms, by which
they attract all the naval officers and distinguished
strangers into their circle, which causes the others to
regard them in a most unchristian spirit. They are
certainly very pleasant, nearly always handsome, and
with charming manners, simple without rudeness, easy

without vulgarity; free from the angular good qualities of their white cousins, and eke from their petty
meannesses; bubbling over with fun and good humour;
loving virtue, and I fear also vice, for its own sake
more than for any thing that may be got by it. If the
old proverb that "God made white men, and God made
black men, but the devil made half-castes" be true, all
I can say is that when his Satanic majesty was at Tahiti
he showed a very pretty taste in creation.

On arriving at the course we were placed in the
grand stand, a splendid erection, capable of containing
at least thirty moderate-sized people, and soon after
appeared Queen Pomare, to whom I was introduced by
Mrs. Miller, our consul's wife, together with her relations and suite. I never saw anyone look so thoroughly
bored as she did; and I fancied she seemed half inclined
to resent being made a puppet of by the French officers, who kept telling her what she had to do and say.
Poor old lady! would that the imperious "Oui-oui"
had never placed foot upon your sacred shores! The
French officials complain that she is very obstinate
sometimes, and small blame to her, say I.

The racing was of course execrable, but very amusing.
Races with saddles and without; a trotting race, in
which the sole competitors were two horses too far
gone to be able to gallop; and a human running race,
in which all but two shut up at once, leaving them to
make an exciting finish at the pace of seven miles an
hour.

After the races we were invited by a hospitable

civilian to his house among the palm trees, to partake of beer and lemonade. There we found a lot of visitors, naval and military, male and female; and after a pleasant chat we drove home along the shady broom-road.[1]

At seven in the evening we joined the Millers and went with them to the garden of the queen's palace, where the " grand himene " was to take place. This erection I have christened the Tower of Babel, as it is always building, is never finished, and, they say, is never intended to be. The French use it somewhat like the man in the pictures, who is always represented galloping on a donkey with a bunch of vegetables at the end of a long pole, which he keeps dangling just in front of the donkey's nose.

There the whole population of Tahiti and the neighbouring islands, with the exception of the sick and aged, were assembled. The bare stone verandahs of the palace were filled on every story to suffocation, and the open space below densely crowded. All

---

[1] Not properly a specific name for any particular drive. Nearly every village in the Society Islands consists of a long row of houses stretching round the bay about sixty or a hundred yards from the beach, behind which is a dense belt of foliage backed by precipitous mountains—the wide smooth path between the houses and the beach is invariably called the broom-road. This word is simply the native word " purumu," and describes the purpose to which the slopes are put after dark. For the meaning whereof overhaul the Church Catechism, or Williams' Maori Dictionary.

shades of beauty were represented, from the swarthy
Tahitian to the washed-out white. All dressed much
alike, in the long, loose, cool-looking chemise of white
muslin or linen, their luxuriant tresses set off by
brilliant flowers and masses of snowy reva-reva, a
gauzy white stuff, looking like strips of silver paper,
made out of the shoots of young cocoa-nut trees—
(ah! well I remember who first taught me to make it,
but never mind that now!) —and their flashing,
melting eyes, directing their fire here and there, for a
Tahitian lady well understands optical effects! Alas,
that they should so often prove optical illusions!

Most of the choirs this night were arranged in dis-
tinctive dresses; one in particular I remarked, where
the performers were decorated with green boughs,
like the pillars of a church at Christmas, the chiefs
and directors wearing the ancient costume of the
country, as before described, the general effect being
rather marred by a pair of black cloth trousers from
some Yankee store, which were added for the sake of
decency.

O that I could give an idea of the exquisite time
and harmony of their wild part-songs! Each choir
sang in turn, the auricular committee, with the commandant and admiral, attending the singers; and at
the end of each performance the directing chief of the
district yelled out " Vive l'Empereur! Hurrah! Vive
l'Imperatrice! Hurrah! Vive le Prince Imperial!
Hurrah! Vive la Reine Pomare, Monsieur le Com-

mandant, le Commissionnaire, l'Amiral!" "Vive, tout
le monde," in fact. One of these directing chiefs, the
leader of one of the most crack companies—for there
were degrees of excellence amongst them—took my
fancy amazingly. He was evidently a South Sea Michael
Costa. As soon as his "*divas*" had struck up, he
appeared to take no more notice of the performance,
but strolled gently up and down, gazing calmly at the
twinkling stars, with an expression of countenance,
as if he were calculating the distance between the sun
and the moon, or analysing the theory of light, until
the cantata was finished. Then he looked quietly
round on the spectators, as if to say, " See what
perfection I have trained them to," and gracefully
condescended to set an example of loyalty by leading
the cheering.

We strolled about the gardens all the evening,
carefully stepping over or picking our way between
the numerous babies that were scattered about the
ground in such profusion as to make it very difficult
to walk without committing infanticide, receiving information from the civil naval men amongst whom we
had already an extensive acquaintance, and inter-
changing ready laughs and symbolical compliments
with the young ladies we were jammed against in the
crowd. They were so clean, graceful, good-humoured,
and merry, that I would have defied the most sour-
hearted Methodist preacher to have kept up a cool
dignity amongst them long. At one time we were

standing close to two of them, when one turned round to the doctor with a smile, and asked him for his cigar. He presented it with great civility, and the young lady, after a few modest sucks, handed it back with the utmost grace. I grinned in spite of myself, but the doctor made an elegant bow, and puffed away coolly, saying that there was nothing like falling in with the customs of the country. We soon got accustomed to this little courtesy afterwards.

After the merits of the different performers had been settled, the captain of the " Entrecasteaux " took us to see a dance, and introduced us to a little French gentleman well versed in the language and customs of the country. After a spirited burst of singing, half-a-dozen girls rushed out of the ranks, and did the wriggling business, a dance common all over the world, from the Irish jig to the nautch of India. We were standing just inside the oblong space, and presently one of the girls came and danced to the little Frenchman, who, much to my amusement, accepted the challenge, straddled his legs, twisted his body, and went through the regular rigmarole till the close of the performance. Then Mr. B—, the interpreter, made a speech on behalf of the governor from the verandah of the palace, while I took a last stroll under its bare walls, and soon after the natives began to file out of the gates, the lights died out one by one, the crowd dispersed, and the whole scene faded away like a beautiful dream.

On arriving at Tahiti we heard the news that war had broken out between France and Prussia, but we little thought that we were about to witness the last *Fête Napoleonne* that would take place in the South Seas. *Eheu, fugaces, &c.*

Aug. 18.—To-day I went with our kind consul, Mr. Miller, to pay a visit to Queen Pomare, who had graciously consented to accord me an interview. Not being a Yankee, and hearing besides that her majesty was as apt to be bored with these formal introductions as I was myself, I did not look forward to it with any great amount of pleasure. But it turned out better than I anticipated. On our way to the palace we picked up Mr. B—, who kindly consented to act as interpreter; the Queen, though she can speak a little English, disliking to use any but her mother tongue. We were shown into a long low room detached from the rest of the building, with seats round the sides, and some tolerable pictures on the walls, including one of Pomare herself. At last she appeared, a very quiet, but dignified and good-natured old lady. There is something that carries respect with it to my mind in the name of Queen; an early prejudice radicals will say, but so it is. And she was a fallen Queen, more or less; and this it was, I suppose, that brought the most quixotic part of my nature to the surface, for it is a fact no less strange than true that I, usually the most rough-mannered and brusque of mortals, bent down respectfully and kissed

her hand, whereby I retained a not unpleasant smell
of coco-nut oil in my nose for the rest of the day,
and caused no small astonishment and amusement,
I suspect, among the lookers-on.   Anyhow, she was
pleased, which was the main thing.   We talked about
my cousin, Lord G——, whom she remembered very
well at Tahiti; and I went my way, after a short time,
much gratified at having seen the famous savage Queen
I had read and dreamt about in my childish days.

In the evening we went to hear the band of the
Astrée play opposite Government House.   It was very
pleasant and pretty, as the natives are invariably fond
of music and thronged round in crowds, laughing,
talking, romping, and spooning.   I fell in with some
naval acquaintance, who, in the sublime innocence of
perfect immorality, showed me a good deal of the
manners and customs of the Society Islanders.   Then
I met with my dancing friend of the night before,
who distributed his favours among the crowd with a
most amusing fervour and impartiality, and a superb
conceit of which only a Frenchman is capable.   He
introduced me to many of the swell chiefesses of the
districts, who were very cordial and promised me a
reception if I would look in upon them at their country
places ; the warmth and earnestness of which Jawley-
ford himself could barely have surpassed.

But at last I began to say to myself, " This society
is not improving, young man ; if you don't steer clear
of what's-his-name you'll go to thingummy."   So I

sought out the doctor and the Millers, who invited us
to tea, together with the admiral and his officers.

The threshold of a kindly host is " *tapu*," and it is
bad taste, or something worse, to describe or criticise
what passes within its walls ; yet I cannot refrain from
mentioning the many pleasant evenings we spent with
our good-natured consul, Mr. Miller, and his charming
wife.   Every night there was an unconventional re-
union for everyone who cared about agreeable conversation : the kind-hearted, shrewd old Admiral Cloué
and the officers of the French fleet, a few French residents, official and non-official, with an occasional stray
missionary, or a half-caste young lady formed the usual
party.   All subjects were discussed with good-natured
freedom, our host and hostess—with a natural tact un-
common enough in the highest society—putting no
restraint upon their visitors, but showing a trust in
their manners and taste.   And as for the languages
spoken—the tower of Babel is all I can compare it
to ! each person used the tongue in which he fancied
he was most likely to be understood.   K— and I
first addressing the more gifted of our audience in
English, and then laboriously translating our metaphysical ideas into the most canine French, and receiving our answers perhaps in that language, perhaps
in Spanish.   It was confusing a little, but it had all
the exciting pleasure of putting together a child's
puzzle.   What good-tempered chaff and wit there
used to be ! what strange South-sea stories used to be

told ! One man describing how the savages used to feel the insides of his thighs in a perfectly easy and familiar manner to see how they would "eat." Another, relating how a whole ship's crew had been devoured in the Pomotou group ; and how when a man-of-war was sent to avenge the outrage the natives all dived into the caves in the coral, and though they could be heard, could not be got at, until the widow of the murdered skipper fitted out a small schooner that took them by surprise, and obtained her the satisfaction of beholding the chief that had eaten her husband and two children. Another informing us that in the Fiji a slave had been fattened on purpose to be killed and eaten on the visit of Prince Alfred ; but whether they allowed him to try Banting when his Royal Highness did not make his appearance, or served him up to a select party to reap the reward of their care and trouble, deponent sayeth not.

One learns little odds and ends by strolling about the streets of Papiete. It is curious to think that the unique garb of the women, that has such a tropical appearance, is nothing more or less than the " *sacque*," the old dress of English and French women some generation and a half ago, immortalised by numerous caricatures of the time, but now only to be seen in the slow changing Pacific Ocean, where it was introduced by the earliest missionaries.

It is not wise to hold conversation with an English-speaking native for more than ten minutes ; during that time he will talk Shakespeare and the musical glasses, so to speak, or discourse on any subject you please, but in the end he invariably comes round to one proposal which is apt to be offensive to one who is not yet completely Society-Islandised—simply to provide you with a native wife from amongst his relations, temporary or permanent. The natural, innocent, kind-hearted creature means nothing but kindness and hospitality by his offers, but quite unintentionally he is apt to bring a blush to the cheek of the young person, who is not yet sufficiently naturalised to have shed his breeks and adopted the blue and white *sulu* or kilt of the country. When this metamorphosis has taken place, the back-sliding individual is looked upon, not without reason, by the more religious and decent of the community as little better than one of the what's-his-names. I remember seeing a fat, pallid greasy Frenchman, clothed in nothing but the aforesaid garment, a large grass hat, and a pair of gold spectacles, looking like a study of Silenus in the nineteenth century.

The chief occupation of the natives is gambling. When a man has lost his whole fortune, probably some five or six dollars, he simply goes up into the mountain and brings down a load or two of fruit, with which he begins life afresh.

Aug. 19.—Louey and I took a sail down the coast inside the reef; the lagoon was crowded with boats and canoes of all sorts and sizes, full of laughing,

singing natives returning to their homes, every kind
of sail being hoisted, from new white canvas to the
under garments of the lady passengers. We noticed
many acquaintances of the preceding evenings, and
many and loud were the " Ya ranas," and the offers
of drinks out of bottles, which we wisely declined,
though we were fearfully hot and thirsty from pulling
in the blazing sun.

Racing, laughing, and chaffing, we travelled along
the coast for some ten miles ; canoes and boats as far
as we could see ahead and astern, when a tempting
shady bay opened out, and we picked our way into
it through the coral, intending to lunch and recruit
ourselves in peace and solitude. Soon, however, appeared a strange, dried-up old native whom I had
met at the Himenes, and, through my greenness and
ignorance of native manners, had put down as an unmitigated old scoundrel. In a queer mixture of
English and Portuguese he asked us to come up to
his house, introduced us to his family, who set to work
to get us shells and coco-nuts, wanted to cook us
some dinner, and behaved like a courtly old gentleman,
in fact. When at last the time came to go on our
homeward way, we received an affectionate shower
of farewell blessings from him and his wife, and his
daughters, and his sons, and his brothers-in-law,
and his aunts, and his uncles, his first cousins, and
his second cousins, &c., as if we had been intimate
friends for five years at the least.

It would seem or be thought strange in Europe if a young lady whom you had seen scarcely ten minutes and had not spoken ten words to, were coolly to propose deserting her kindred and friends, and accompanying you bag and baggage to the other end of the world, but in the South Seas it is but an ordinary occurrence, scarcely deserving of mention.

I remember at Samoa two ladies of high degree, fat, brown, and forty, paying their court with such irresistible ardour, that after telling most shameless lies about a ferociously jealous wife in England, by way of making a polite excuse for not taking them, I was fain to bolt ignominiously for fear they should win their end by sheer persistency, like the widow and the unjust judge in the parable.

Aug. 23.—This day we went for a pic-nic at Point Venus, so called because it is the place where Cook observed the transit of the planet, but many in Tahiti seriously believe he discovered it there, as it were some strange beast, while others declare the name is derived from a worship of the Heathen goddess that the ancient mariners used to celebrate on that spot.

We met together at the consul's, who with his wife and children, the admiral, and his secretary Mr. M., Mrs. B., the doctor, and I, made up the party.

We then bundled ourselves with some difficulty into some extraordinary uncomfortable little Yankee carriages, my companions being Mr. M. a very agreeable amusing young man, and Mrs. B. a half-Spanish, half-American widow, whose husband was eaten some time ago. A merry little soul she was, with eyes that always twinkled, and a tongue that never stopped talking except to laugh, always in a blaze of fun or feeling, and discussing everything as if her life depended on it.

What a jolly drive it was! Arguing in a circle on every subject under heaven, talking the wildest nonsense. (How rare and pleasant it is to meet any one who can talk good nonsense and understand it, instead of getting up and knocking the wind out of you with a boring fact.) Hearing the histories of various people as we passed their houses—and Tahitian life-histories are usually strange and chequered—and enjoying the beautiful scenery all the more for the high pitch of our animal spirits.

The road ran for a long way parallel with the shore, under the shade of the trees, crossing innumerable little streams, mostly filled with native girls washing themselves or their garments, for the Society Islanders are the most cleanly race I ever met, very different from their Maori cousins.

Then the road wound up the sides of the steep mountains. Precipices above and below it; in fact, a South Sea Cornice, but far grander, and more beautiful, for here the most perpendicular hill sides are covered with a luxuriant vegetation. Perhaps we should have enjoyed it more if we had not been in some danger of going over the said precipices, owing

D

to the imperfection of our harness, as we descended on the other side. This consisted of a pole, with a cross piece of wood at the end, to which the horses were attached, and which, being only fastened to the pole with string, kept sliding first one way and then the other, as soon as the strain came on it, jamming one horse inwards and shoving the other right away. There being only one trace, and no splinter bars, the vehicle twisted about in an exciting and uncertain manner.

At length we finished the descent, and having arrived at our destination, strolled about the native settlement. In the chief's house we found a party of French officers surveying. Most of the native houses are built of hybiscus poles, planted in the ground about two inches apart, giving them the appearance of enormous birdcages. The roof is ingeniously constructed of plaited palm leaves. When you retire for the night you fasten up a shawl or blanket against the side to keep the wind off you; but the natives suffer much from cold or rheumatics, at which I don't wonder.

In the more considerable villages there is a large building of this kind which is public property, and where the mayor and corporation, the local board, or whatever answers to those things in Tahiti, hold their meetings, and where also the people collect together to perform Himenes.

Then we were shown the chapel, by the priest

thereof, close to which was the old Protestant one in
ruins. "Un clou chasse l'autre," remarked the
doctor. After this we proceeded to the tamarind tree
planted by the immortal Cook, where we rested while
some of the party went off to go up the light-house
that has been built here. What hidden feeling is it
that makes humanity desire to get to the top of everything—spires, lighthouses, pyramids, and what not?
And it is curious that the two things that tend to
make men most unbearably conceited, are getting to
the top of something or seeing a sunrise. I would
give any man who wilfully committed either of these
acts, solitary confinement for forty-eight hours.

Then we had luncheon in the chief's house, followed
by a pleasant stroll about the village. We noticed
that all the fowls had feathers on their legs right
down to their toes, and the doctor started a theory
that they were bred so by the missionaries for the
sake of propriety.

We came upon a curious little hut with a kind of
door at one end, which, when opened, disclosed
nothing more or less than a coffin. It is a custom
among the natives to keep them above ground for a
time, to be visited by the relatives of the deceased, a
sensible and decent practice enough compared to the
ghastly ones that may be found in some places in
Europe. I remember in Sicily, when a young lady of
good family died, she was dressed in ball clothes and
stuck up at the end of the drawing room, to receive

all her friends, who paid her a visit in evening dresses to bid her a last farewell. I don't think this case was exceptional.

Then, after a very merry drive home, we dined on board the "Astrée," where we were shown some very ingenious breechloading cannon; and then, after a short stroll ashore, to bed.

Aug. 24.—Up before daylight in the morning to drive to Mr. Stewart's plantation at Atimaono. He had kindly sent over a carriage for us, and dragged by two little mules, driven by a sturdy Scotchman, we were soon rattling along the road, bound for the other side of the island. We met lots of natives bearing fish, mostly mullet, to the morning market, as long as we were within three miles of Papiete. There is no way of going *through* any Society island, as they are all a mass of great mountains, gorges, and precipices, so our road lay all the way along the shore, amid groves of bananas, plantains, &c., amongst which the huts of the natives were sprinkled. Some appeared lazily in the doorways as we galloped by, some we saw gnawing pensively at pieces of bread fruit which served them as an early breakfast, others performing their toilettes in the little rivers that we were continually splashing through, nearly all looking up to give us a cheerful "Ya rana." I won't answer for the spelling of any native words that I use, but what does it matter? The Missionaries made it a written language, and I have just as much right to spell the words after my own fancy as they had.

The scenery was splendid. Wherever there was a break in the glorious tropical forest, we could see on one side the barrier reef line of great white breakers curling over without ceasing, though the deep blue sea beyond seemed as smooth as glass, while between us and it was a line of bright pale green water in which an occasional man or woman might be noticed wading or poling, fish-spear in hand, in search of a dainty breakfast, and then some ten miles off the picturesque island of Eiméo rising fantastically from the bosom of the horizon, its ruggedness and grandeur set off by a gigantic and distinct hole bored right through the centre of its loftiest peak, while on the other side of us a mass of splendid cliffs and mountains would be revealed, hanging almost over our heads, with deep narrow gorges running up between them into the very clouds.

About every hour we stopped to change horses, when we took the opportunity to stretch our legs, chat with any people who might chance to be about, and ornament our hats and heads with crimson hybiscus flowers; for you will find if you go to the Society Islands, that unless you are a wooden idiot, you will do things quite naturally that you would look upon as stark staring lunacy any where else.

Soon we began to feel the fresh trade wind in our faces, a great relief, after the stifling atmosphere of Papiete, and the third stage brought us to the boundary of the plantation, after which we drove through a long avenue of bananas with cotton fields behind them till we came to Mr. Stewart's house, a fine building on the shore, built with large rooms, and well suited for a hot climate, where we were very kindly received by its owner.

Mr. Stewart and the plantation of Atimaono have a strange history, too long and complicated for me to attempt to give a full or judicial account of, especially as every one tells a different tale on the subject. I have heard him bitterly abused, but with so little sensible reason, that I strongly suspect that the jealousy of the smaller white merchants and settlers is the chief motive of their virulent attacks.

He came out here as agent to a company with a grant of land, and his troubles seem to have begun at once; the grant was delayed, so he set to work to buy land from the natives out of his own pocket. A report was then circulated that the natives were forced to sell to him, which, whether true or not was peremptorily denied by the governor. As soon as the plantation was fairly under weigh specimens of inferior cotton were sent to Europe as the produce of Atimaono. Infamous libels were circulated in the American papers, describing the horrible cruelties of Stewart and his myrmidons on their unfortunate workmen; the sick were left to die, the dead left unburied, the men cheated out of their pay, &c.

Mr. Elea, the overseer, in particular was represented as a most bloodthirsty monster. He had hung women

with child up and flogged them, he had roasted Chinamen alive, &c. Mr. Stewart was a perfect wicked
baron of the middle ages, brutally assaulting every
one who came too near his castle; to all these accusa-
tions Mr. S. answered by demanding a public inquiry,
which was granted. This cleared away the whole
cloud of lies, every thing being found and reported in
the most perfect order, every regard being paid to the
health and comfort of the coolies. The only serious
complaint made by the Chinese was a curious one—
that they were not allowed to hang themselves as payment for gambling debts.

But the troubles of Atimaono were not yet over.
Certain men, amongst them the Juge Imperial, for-
merly a blacksmith, entered into a conspiracy to ruin
the plantation, for which Mr. S. is now bringing an
action against them. He has won his way in spite
of all opposition, and little heeds the snarling of his
enemies. *Vive le succès!* Of course I do not know
enough to be able to judge exactly of the fairness of
what I have just written, but I must say that a
happier, healthier looking set of men than the fifteen
hundred workmen I saw at Atimaono could not be
found in a long day's walk among the manufacturing
classes of England.

K. was lodged in a little room built right out in
the sea, so that he could catch fish out of his window
if it so pleased him. The other day when the plantation doctor was lodged in this place, it came on to

blow heavily, and one night the bridge between it
and the land was washed right away by the sea; the
medico turned out of bed and was rather horrified
to find himself alone in his glory on a desolate and
rather shaky island.

We spent the day very pleasantly, reading and
loafing about till dinner-time, when Mr. Stewart
treated us to some native dishes, which I did not
appreciate so much as his capital French cookery.
Besides the admiral, who had also driven over from
Papiete, our dinner-party was made up of several
people employed in different ways on the estate, and
very pleasant company they were. Some good types
of what I call the cosmopolitan Micawber, men whom
one comes across oftener in the Southern than in the
Northern hemisphere, who try their hands at every
kind of wild speculation in strange places, generally
clever, energetic, and brave, but often too restless,
too dreamy, or too sanguine to meet with permanent
success; men whom you may meet one day living
in affluence, and next month earning their bread by
the work of their hands, waiting for another chance
to turn up. I delight in these fellows; more often
than not they are gentlemen by birth and education,
whose chance of success in life has been ruined by the
very qualities that make them so charming, their good
nature, love of freedom, independence, and wild adventure. Some that I have met are the most
delightful companions in the world. They have tried

every thing, know every thing, and have been every where. They are vagabond adventurers, respectable English society may cry. So were Sir Walter Raleigh and Francis Drake, say I; but it is this class of man that macadamizes the world; and I don't think they are worse as a rule than nine-tenths of the respectable men in white chokers and faultless boots that one meets at an English dinner-party. I have known specimens who could set an example that would make society blush, as far as kindness, unselfishness and honour go. There is one appearing before my mind now, known but for a short time, yet not easily forgotten. Well do I remember his massive well-shaped head; nearly all these men have fine heads; his *worn* yet handsome and merry face, so full of humour, kindness, and fun, that it used to warm the cockles of my heart, would brighten up the dullest physiognomy in a room when he entered it, and produce a good-humoured laugh at the first word he spoke. A man with the mark of the "vagabond dry rot" plainly written upon him, yet one that few could help loving and even trusting. Often he used to tell me in his quaint, laughing, philosophical way the stories of his many wild speculations in different parts of the world, and how they had ended in his becoming "flat broke" as he used merrily to call it. Full of wit, kindness, cleverness, energy and courage, yet unable to make or at least keep his own fortune, and consequently worthless in the eyes of the great mass of the world,

which judges mankind a great deal more by the rule
of the "almighty dollar" than it is willing to own.
One who would share his last sixpence with a friend, or
risk his life without hesitation for a noble purpose ;
one still young, yet in spite of his never-ceasing fund
of mirth and humour evidently broken and worn out.
He used to give me an inner feeling of sadness and
pity, even while I was laughing at his exuberant fun.
And the next door neighbour to a man like this, or
perhaps even his chum, living in the same hut on terms
of equality, may be an old whaler or run-away man-of-
war's-man of the worst type, who is utterly devoid of
all feelings but the basest, and has broken every one
of the commandments, not to mention committing a
few other crimes scarcely comprehended in that interesting catalogue.

Ye worldly old philosophers of the London clubs,
who fancy you know life, should make a trip to the
South Seas to study it in its vivid incongruities. Here
at Atimaono, a comparatively speaking civilized spot,
the book-keeper was an infantry major, the store-keeper
a captain in a light cavalry regiment, and the barman
the son of rich parents and grandson of the mayor of
a great town in the British Isles. There are ups in
this world, and there are downs, as Mr. Plornish
wisely remarks. Such is life south of the Equator !

Aug. 25.—In the afternoon we drove down to the
cotton mill, and I was much interested in watching
the work. The cotton was brought in in baskets and

thrown into a kind of trough which, by an ingenious process, winnowed it through the bottom, cleaning it of all the black berries, or whatever the proper name of them may be, and coarse stuff. Then it was poured into the top of an enormous strong box, stamped down, and shut in; then it was compressed by machinery as tight as possible, and on the great iron clasps which fastened the sides of the box being unfastened they swung open on hinges, disclosing a square white compact mass of cotton; a few split bamboos were lashed round this to keep it in shape, and then, being sewn up in strong canvas, it was all ready for exportation.

All the labourers were Chinese or Hervey Islanders, the latter strong, healthy, savage-looking people, who build their huts on a platform of poles and enter them by a ladder. There would be a fine case of hereditary instinct for some naturalist or philosopher to work out. Doubtless, there was originally a purpose and a reason for this peculiar style of architecture, but though that has now disappeared the practice it gave birth to still remains.

In one place the labourers were employed repairing carts, making wheels, and doing carpentering generally. In another they were building a ship; while in one of the buildings we came upon an ingenious old Chinaman making a beautiful epergne of silver and mother-of-pearl shells. I could not help being struck with the universality of Stewart's genius, and his wonderful power of finding his men's spécialité, and setting them to the right work; and he seemed to be one who had the rare gift of combining justice with strictness.

I saw at once the absurdity of the libels about cruelty that were published against him and his overseer, Mr. Elea. That two men might torture and tyrannise over the same number of negroes in the old slave states might be possible, because in the case of a rebellion they would be certain of support from their fellow planters; but here, where the slightest scandal or disturbance on the estate would be hailed with joy by nearly every white merchant in Tahiti, and the mass of people to be managed are not negroes, but clever, desperate Chinese, proverbially careless of life, such a system would be impossible.

I saw a list of the regulations of the plantation, the heaviest punishment being imprisonment for five days. The ordinary penalty for small offences is, I think, twenty-four or forty-eight hours of drudging labour, during which time their pay is stopped.

I was much amused by observing two Chinamen in disgrace doing penance by carrying ballast into one of the ships, watched by a big Hervey Island savage with a stick; the unutterable disgust visible in the countenances of the two prisoners, and the pompous grin of their temporary commander, as he followed them to and fro and kept them up to their work, were very ludicrous.

Down by the sea was an enormous yard, full of pigs,

and such pigs! Of all sizes, from a guinea pig to a
Shetland pony; of all colours, from a zebra to a negro.
And as for shape! They were thin where they ought
to be fat, long where they ought to be short, more
like great wedges with the sharp end uppermost than
anything else I can think of. Such gaunt horrible
monsters were never beheld; the scene was like the
nightmare of a dyspeptic farmer.

There has only been one serious disturbance among
the labourers since the commencement of the plantation, when they quarrelled about some gambling debt,
and set to work stabbing each other, and so on. One
of the ringleaders was guillotined as an example.

Whilst we were here the overseer came in, bringing
some forged notes, very cleverly made, that had been
uttered by ingenious John Chinaman for the purpose
of swindling the simple natives. These last get on,
however, with the Chinese more amicably than might
be expected, which is chiefly owing to the low moral
feeling of the Tahitians, who get money from the
Chinese by the aid of their female relations.

As the afternoon wore on the Hervey Islanders—
men, women, and children—began to flock round the
store, and on a bell ringing each came up to receive a
spoonful or two of molasses, of which they seemed in-
ordinately fond. It was served out by the storekeeper
from a great tub, and the whole operation reminded
me forcibly of Mrs. Squeers and her brimstone and
treacle.

Then we drove through the cotton fields and re-

turned to dinner. The next morning we bade farewell
to our kind host, and drove back to Papiete.

Swiftly, too swiftly, the days passed away. From
the natives, the French, and, above all, from Mr. and
Mrs. Miller we received the greatest kindness. In the
mornings reading and dreaming on board, or talking
lazily with friends on shore ; sailing or paddling about
the reefs when the heat of the day was passed ; and
when the cool night had cast its veil over the island,
strolling about the quiet paths in the dim moonlight,
or enjoying the pleasant society that could always be
found at the house of our hospitable consul. What
is the use of trying to describe dreamland ? Its beauty
is that of the dead calm ocean, unbroken by a rugged
or prominent line, and much of that which its loveliness consists in seems always to my mind too sacred
to be painted or written.

If I were a mendacious mendicant, I might have
enlivened this chapter with hairbreadth escapes, romantic adventures, fights, love stories, &c., *ad libitum*,
after the manner of most books of travels, but, in spite
of my several years of voyaging and the time I have
spent in the South Sea Islands, I have not yet become
utterly demoralized on the score of veracity. I don't
know how it is, but I never, or very seldom, do meet
with any romantic adventures. I did at last manage
to get shipwrecked ; but even that disappointed my
expectations as far as romance was concerned. I

suspect they are like miracles, not common to those who don't look out for them and meet them half way. However this may be, I consider I am hardly treated about such matters. I don't, as I said before, get a proper share of romantic adventures. I never see ghosts; I never have mysterious prophetic dreams that come true; I can't get mesmerised, nor even turn tables successfully, and as for miracles! if I were in one parish they would be sure to take place in the next one. I once went to the church of S. Januarius in Naples, thinking that at last I should succeed in witnessing a miracle, or an imitation of one; but when it was performed, I could not make out that anything happened at all, and so went home disgusted.

Soon, too soon, the time came for us to leave the South Sea Capua. I was so happy there, that I verily believe I should have been content to dream away my life, without care or ambition. I was Society Island-ised, in fact. It could not be, and it was best for me as it was. Perhaps after a time a man's feelings and thoughts would become degraded and numbed by such a life; he would lose that power of enjoyment that made it at first so charming and pleasant to him. Peace, and quiet, and perfect freedom, are useful medicines, but not a wholesome diet. Their charm lies in contrast; there is no spark without the concussion of the flint and steel; there is no fine thought, even no perfect happiness, that is not born of toil, sorrow, and vexation of spirit.

"Be virtuous and you will be happy," is an old English proverb, which in Tahiti should be rendered, "Be happy and you will be virtuous." And the latter version is as true as the former. To be *perfectly* happy, you will find that sympathy is necessary; you must make others happy too, which is the essence of virtue. You cannot sin against God except by sinning against your neighbour *or yourself*, and so I hold that my brown friends are a good and happy people, in spite of what stern Judaical moralists may say to the contrary. It was with a heavy heart that I put up the wheel, to let our little schooner go bowling and tearing out through the narrow channel, and it gave me pain to look back and see the dear old island growing fainter and dimmer as each minute passed.

I wonder if I shall ever see it again. I promised and vowed that I would, and was sadly answered: "You say so now; but when you go home, you will find new duties, new pleasures, and new friends; you will never come back again."

Truly we are often compelled, bitterly against our will, to write "finis" under the pleasantest pages of our life.

> One day I was watching a boat .
>   Borne on by the wind and the tide,
> And into the rushes 'twould float
>   That grew 'neath the bank on each side.
>
> For a moment perhaps it would stay,
>   But their arms could not hold it for long,

They broke, and the boat swept away,
    For the wind and the current were strong.

As down the swift stream it was hurl'd,
    I fancied I heard these words spoken,
" Few partings there are in this world
    In which friendly ties are not broken.

" All are hard at the best to burst through,
    Some are bitter and painful to sever,
While some, but alas ! very few,
    Will stand time and distance for ever."

Chapter II.

EIMEO OR MOREA.

August.

IMEO, as seen from Tahiti, is a wonderfully beautiful island, peaked and jagged in a way seldom seen. Some of the isolated peaks may be rivalled by those of the Dolomite Gebirge (as little visited when I first knew them as Eimeo is now), but there are some which are nearly unique in their forms. But we must make comparisons now-a-days with bated breath, for fear the "Alta California" should be down on us with some fresh discovery of strange loveliness. If photography is to be trusted the scenery of that part of Western America must equal if not exceed in beauty, any in the world.

We easily found our way into the western harbour, through the fringing reef, though there are one or two nasty lumps and patches to be looked for in the passage. The reef gives one generally the idea of a fringing reef which is being gradually changed into a barrier reef by subsidence. Inside the harbour the water is tremendously deep, and you have to run a long way up to get an anchorage.

The harbour is a " gorge," and one of the noblest gorges I have ever seen. Green precipices rising upwards of two thousand feet, sheer from the water, fringed round their feet by cocoa-nut, and orange trees—trees not bushes; I think I never saw any so large elsewhere.

Far up on the green cliff side may be seen the large leaves of the " Faïes " or wild plantain, a never failing source of food, but one which often requires no little strength of limb and steadiness of head to gather, and still more to bring down to the sea-shore. A sort of vegetable chamois over which many a life is lost.

A charming little boy of a good half-caste breed (his mother being an English woman and his father a Frenchman), told me a legend, in good biblical English, anent a great red scar on the green cliff side. How that " a man went gathering Faïes on the sabbath, and God was angry with him, and he fell down, and made the mark on the hill side."

These " islands of the blest " are not without their drawbacks ; even Faïes, though it grows wild, sometimes grows very wild indeed. The plants we can see from the deck of the yacht would require a sturdy climb to reach; I should think they are at least 1,500

feet above the water's edge ; pleasant for the father of
a family, with a sore foot, or a swelled leg—two very
common complaints in these parts.   Better a store of
potatoes and a keg of salt fish after all, though it may
require more sustained labour to obtain them.

The trap dikes are very grand here, running
positively like walls and towers from above to the sea,
through the mass of green.   By moonlight it is almost
impossible to believe that they are not ruins of some
old fortification.   Some are as regular as that old
stepped wall which runs up the Rock of Gibraltar.

One of the highest and most acute peaks is per-
forated right through, just below the summit, which
aperture we can plainly see from the ship, and might
walk through if we were so minded, which we are
not ; a climb of 2,000 feet, with the thermometer
at 120°, being no joke.   This aperture can also be
seen from Atimaono in Tahiti.   Of course it was
caused by an ancient hero throwing his spear through
the mountain peak.   This sort of thing always is.

The upper end of the harbour softens into a pretty
bit of delta, backed by high green hills, and with a
sparkling stream running through it.   This is cultivated with great success as a sugar plantation, and the
white walled, red tiled building connected with the
establishment, comes in very prettily.   It seemed
rather a dead season with them, but the resident representatives of the company, a cheery Italian doctor,
and a more grave *ex-colonel de la ligne*, did not seem
much depressed on the subject.

When a European meets you in one of these out of
the way places, he either sulks and says nothing, or
else gives you at .once a slight autobiographical
sketch of his previous career, and is most careful to
explain the circumstances which brought him there,
as if his presence required some explanation. Mighty
queer histories some of these worthy beach-combers
have, I have no doubt.

On the shore were certain gigantic baskets, or
rather wattled buildings, consisting of two sides, a
bottom and one end, some twenty feet by twelve,
which puzzled us very much. Our young friend tried
to explain that they were to catch fish and sharks in,
though he so utterly failed to explain how, that we
concluded that they were ladies' bathing machines, so
contrived to shield their beauties from the impertinent
gaze of the 'long-shore loafers. Having, however, by
this time some little insight into the proprieties of these
islands, we merely accepted the theory provisionally,
and for want of a better.

The time came when we found, as usual, that our
theory was wrong.

Sitting on deck one day, we observed a deal of fire-
lighting, singing, and general hustling and bustling,
under the orange trees on the shore, and forthwith
paddled across to see what the fun was. It needed no
interpretation of the cries of welcome to tell us, for,
looking over the side of the boat into two or three
feet water, we saw that the bottom was literally paved

with small fish, omething between a dace and a char;
they were po tively in myriads.   Unable to resist
the temptatio , we took a throw with the casting net,
whereby we got nothing but an ugly lump of old
coral, the bottom being much too broken for that style
of thing.   Our ill success was greeted with derisive
cheers from the opposition, who then invited us to see
how they did the trick.

Three or four women walked into the water with no
small merriment, bearing an aboriginal kind of seine,
made of the leaves of the pandanus thickly interwoven in a line of coir.   Making a long sweep, they
drew it cautiously in a semicircle to the shore; and
when at the proper distance, they inserted a small
edition of the big baskets and swept in the beauties
by hundreds, a most original and successful way of
going to work.   Had they tried to land the fish, they
would certainly have succeeded in wriggling away
under the leaves.

I think amongst all the fish glories I have seen, this
was the most glorious one.   These thousands and
thousands of silver-green backs and crimson bellies
all flickering in the sun! It was like looking at
bushels of diamonds, emeralds, and rubies, all being
shaken together, and one fairly winked with their
brilliancy.

Not only are these " fishlets," known to the natives
by the name of " *urio*," most beautiful to the eye, but
they are most pleasant to the taste, being even as a

mixture of whitebait from Greenwich, fresh char from the König Sea, and—the best other fish you can think of. Scale them not, clean them not, cast them into the frying pan, and continue eating, not till you are satiated, for that will never be, but till there are no more to eat.

It is a curious fact, which I *have* noticed myself, and so can*not* warrant, that the only singing bird on this island is a kingfisher. (Why fisher? They hardly any of them fish, and even the English one is a poor hand, wounding more than he catches.) Day and night he pipeth pleasant notes, not unlike the beginning of the thrush's song, " che-whi-schew."

Sitting on board in the afternoon, we saw Admiral Cloué and his tender, the " d'Entrecasteau," slipping quietly to leeward on some private expedition. The admiral seemed, when we left him in Tahiti, to be by no means easy about the war. " Men in plenty we have, and our men are brave, but where are our generals?" He is a fine old fellow, and scorned the idea of taking German merchantmen out of Samoan ports. " No ; we will make neutral ports of them, and perhaps help to civilize the native rulers by showing them that we respect their authority."

I always expected that the native of the Isle of Piner, or the New Caledonian would eat me if he could, they looked so like it. But these folks grin and laugh whatever I do, right or wrong. And somehow it puts me in mind of the two Australian

crows at the Kawau, who were found dancing and
laughing joyously round Miss Annie's pet canary,
which they were slowly pecking to death. 'Tis but a
vain fancy, however.

Saturday, Sept. 3. Along the channel inside the
reef, to the eastward harbour, which is very lovely, but
I think not equal to the one in which we are lying.

Sept. 2. Called on Mrs. Simpson, the widow of the
late missionary, a most agreeable and lady-like woman,
whose mere presence and example must have been of
infinite use.   She speaks the purest Biblical English ;
which may be accounted for by her having lived forty
years of the seventy of her life in this island, with few
books but her Bible.   Her grandson, a boy of some
eight or ten years old, being a private and particular
friend of my own, took me a long walk by the Broom
road, bearing with him his fish spear, composed of a
light shaft of hybiscus, with a brush of iron wires,
little larger than netting needles, lashed round the
larger end.   Indeed, our walk was principally under-
taken for the purpose of procuring similar instruments
from a cunning man who dwelt at the far end of the
big village.   We beguiled the way by trying to spear
the landcrabs, as they popped sideways into their
holes in the road ; a difficult and delicate task, requiring much skill.   We rested the shaft on the tips
of the two first fingers of our left hands, and projected
it with those of our right ; but the crabs were very
shy, and though we made some beautiful shots at the

entrance, the crab had always retired into his back parlour, before the missile reached him. Wearying of this we tried the sea-shore, and there the sea urchins and holothuriæ, being more passive targets, suffered severely. I also think that, quite accidentally we speared a fish, but he was so spiny that we had to knock him off the spear on to the rocks, and he fled again to the sea.

Then we came to the village, consisting of neat wattled whitewashed cottages, raised above the ground on stone supports; a practice which though it favoured ventilation, oddly enough at the same time encouraged dirty habits. The cottages themselves seemed cleanly and well kept, but their inhabitants seemed much of a muchness with those in the next harbour, who live in huts made of interwoven coco-nut branches. · They were particularly indelicate in their habits; they were, however, most friendly and kindly, and it was very pleasant to see how fond they were of my boy companion, and how confident he was of their affection.

The spear maker was from home, but there was something to repay us for our walk in the shape of certain large canoes hauled up on the strand, each of which had a large forked spar, some twenty feet long, projecting from its bow. My young friend informed me that these were used as a sort of Anakim fishing-rod; lines being fastened to the end well baited, and the canoe kept well up to the bobble of the sea. "And they catch fish, so large—so large!" quoth

he, indicating a size as large as, or larger than himself.

Under his guidance I walked into the old missionary
house, once a commodious slab building, but now, I
fear, on the high road to ruin.   It was curious to see
how every small household article, glass, table, basin,
ewer, had remained exactly in the place in which they
were left, when the missionary's widow had closed the
door behind her for the last time.   The place was evidently strictly " tapu."   I was puzzled to find amongst
a quantity of low church divinity some very incongruous French books, such as drill books for such and
such a " Regiment de la ligne " and Jasmin's poems.
It was not till I returned to head-quarters that I learned
that the missionary's daughter had married the gallant
French ex-colonel, and that my young friend was the
consequence.   As we returned, a native woman gave the
boy a gelatinous matter of a pearly grey colour, made
from arrowroot, and wrapped up in a banana leaf,
which he thought very nice, and I, luckily for him,
very nasty.

P— and Louey, the suspected Russian Fin, went
exploring inside the reef to Cook's Harbour.   They
represent the passage as by no means clear or pleasant,
and as the wind was dead a-head they had to down
sail and pull.   Where the reported " Ship Channel "
is, is by no means clear.

It seems to be difficult to decide whether Cook's
Harbour or the one in which the yacht is lying is the

most beautiful. Possibly the difference between a handsome woman and a pretty one. "I landed," says P—, " close to the head of the bay, near a small creek. All round the harbour was a beautiful shady avenue, close to the water's edge, brightened by the crimson flowers of the arrow-root, the fresh green of the banana, and the richer, redder green of the taro plant.

" Here we ate our luncheon and the mosquitoes ate us, and it is a question whether the latter had not the best of the bargain. (These infernal mosquitoes and the flies, says P—, are the real cause of the demoralization of the white settlers in these parts; it would be impossible to live without keeping some one to brush away the plagues, and as male labour is difficult to obtain—you have to run into danger.) Then approached a jolly old dame, who talked and laughed at the top of her voice for ten good minutes. I could not understand much that she said, except that her strong point was that she hated the French (an almost universal sentiment in these parts) and that, in order to avoid them, she should intensely like to accompany me back to England—a proposition which I firmly, but I hope politely, declined. Then we landed at another point of the harbour, where there was a benevolent old gentleman, and a woman and child, who (with the exception of the last, who howled) greeted us with the usual ' Ya rana.' The old man, in the usual broken English of the island, asked me about the war, and when the English were coming back to

the country ? All which I answered as well as I could.
At the mention of the French he made a very wry face.
After a little conversation he said, ' Come, I give you
coco-nut;' and calling a boy, he shouldered a long
bamboo and a stick sharpened at both ends, and
marched off towards the feathery cocoes. In spite of
my remonstrances he insisted on knocking down
dozens before he could find any he considered good
enough for me. On deciding he placed his sharp stick
in the ground, and proceeded to peel off the outer shell
by striking it against the other sharp point in a very
workmanlike manner, though one fancied every moment that he must impale his own old paws. In very
young coco-nuts you have merely to cut through husk
and shell with a knife when out springs the cool water
as briskly as champagne when the string is cut.

" When he had placed the nuts on board, he seized
a tough-looking old cock who was looking very melancholy at the end of a piece of string, and proceeded to
add him to the cargo. I laughed and told him that I
had no money. ' I no want money,' quoth he, a little
offended, still dragging along the unfortunate cock.
However, at last I got him to understand that I did
not want it, having plenty on board, and we embraced
and parted excellent friends.

" We ran back under easy sail, picking our way between the coral rocks, without accident, but I don't
envy the man who tries it, in a dark night, blowing
fresh ! "

Sept. 3.—Tempted by P—'s description of Cook's harbour the "Dingey" and the "Fish Fag" were commissioned to pull round the point, and a hard pull it was, as it blew half a gale of wind dead against us all the way, the rough coral bottom creating a nasty short sea, which nearly stopped the little dingey altogether. At last we turned the corner and discovered the location of P—'s old friend of yesterday, who kept up his reputation by giving us unlimited coco-nut-water. There was a Kanaka who spoke very good and forcible English, having served on board a whaler for several years. He informed us, amongst other important facts, that all their pigs had been killed by "those dam rascals of Frenchmen." "Ouis-ouis," said P—, whereupon the old lady recognising the slang, kept on repeating "Oui,-oui," over and over again, like the dormouse in "Alice," and they all laughed till they were hoarse at the new and exquisite joke. "What are these sticks in the holes for?" asked P—. "Kill those dam crabs, make their dam holes everywhere," quoth our enlightened friend; and certainly, if saying it would do it, he would have d—, I mean stopped a river in full flood.

Hillo! Walker's original! or the Aboriginal Walker, the twopenny postman! and up shambled a uniformed Kanaka on a stumbling pony, with an enormous letter-bag with one letter in it, which he ingenuously showed us, and would, I believe, have given us, if we had asked for it. The baby of the establishment was given him to nurse on the pommel of his saddle, I suppose because he was imagined to have a share in it, which the babe appeared to deny with the most strenuous howls.

On our return, we landed on the reef, and "floundered" about in the water, sometimes up to our ankles, sometimes up to our waists. We saw an infinity of fish, many large ones in the very surf itself, and I think if I had had my young friend's spear I should have made a good bag; having only the common "grains" with me, I got nothing, not even an enormous squid which I speared through and through two or three times, but which always forced itself off again, and escaped eventually into a hole. Those horrible, lidless eyes, and nothing else of the squid, always struck me as uncanny, especially when you suddenly come upon one staring at you out of a dark hole.

The real principle for catching reef-fish is compression, not penetration, pinching the fish between the wires, not boring a hole in him. Of course with the larger fish, penetration must be resorted to, the weapon growing larger and larger, till it becomes a veritable harpoon, which will hold most things, except perhaps a porpoise, which we have never yet managed to get on board though we have been well into many a one. When a porpoise is wounded he dashes away with the whole herd after him—whether to eat him, or to see what he had left them in his will, I have

never been able to determine. The ordinary " grains"
is a very valuable and firm-holding weapon, but cannot be thrown far. You want to be over your game
to handle it properly. In this way I once, after a
tremendous fight, killed a black scowling trygon, or
"stingaree," which weighed one hundred and thirty-five
pounds. I really think that these black trygons are the
most repulsive and ruffianly-looking of created beings.

The grains will not do everything. There is a
legend of P— and Louey having tried to kill a wild
pig with them, and failing most signally.

At low tide day or night all hands go on to the reef
and get fish for food and squid for bait. Scalken
would have been the man to paint the night fishing.
The torch gives a ruddy glow to the skin of the holder,
which is very rich and warm, more especially when
standing out against a jet black sea and sky, as is
generally the case, a perfect calm and dark night being
indispensable to good fishing.

A Society Islander, with his feet firmly planted on
the sides of his canoe, and bending over the water in
act to strike, would make a grand study for a sculptor.
The roundness and development of the upper part of
the back and arms, from constant use of the spear, are
most beautiful; and when not disfigured by elephantiasis, which is too often the case, the lower leg and
ankle are perfect; as superior to the coarse limbs of a
Maori, as the fetlock of a thorough-bred is to that of a
cart-horse.

Chapter III.

HUAHINE.

September 5.

SAILED for Huahine. Saw a very long-flighted flying-fish, with large red pectorals like a gurnet, which possibly it was. Flying-fish *do* fly, moving their pectoral fins with extreme rapidity, like a pair of twin-screws. Moreover, they raise and lower themselves over the tops of waves, and do *not* dip into them to wet either their whistles or their wings. I do not think that their flight is necessarily the proof of submarine persecution; of course they fly if the bonito is after them, but I suspect that, often as not, they fly for the mere fun of the thing. Why else do they make such wild dabs at the bits of light in a ship's side at night? I remember, between Panama and Rapa, I used to see the cabin "bulls-eyes" surrounded by a circle of scales every morning, left there by flying-fish, attracted by the light within, and possibly asking for a passage.

I should consider two hundred yards a very good flight for a flying-fish, and very few there be who do it, twenty or thirty being the general range. It seems limited, in some degree, by the difficulty of keeping the body horizontal. The tail droops more and more and more, and at last, splash! he goes into the sea. It struck me that as the flying-fish grew scarcer they grew larger, as if only the very big and strong individuals could reach the outside of the circle. Whenever I have seen them in the New Zealand seas, they have been large and solitary. The largest I ever saw (twenty-two inches, if I recollect right) flew on board the "Tauranga," a small steamer, in which I was taking a passage to the Bay of Islands, in New Zealand. It went slap into the engine-room, and smote the engineer a smart rap on the cheek. He, supposing that his stoker had assaulted him, used language which I need not repeat, and threatened reprisals. On explanation being given, however, the fish was discovered, and handed over to Dr. Hector for preservation in the Colonial Museum, where it may now, I have no doubt, be seen by the curious.

From Panama to Wellington, from New Zealand to New Caledonia, from Auckland to Tahiti, and back again, a fair number of miles, I have watched the flying-fish carefully, and I never saw one seized by a bird in its flight. Nor have I ever seen such an occurrence in the Atlantic or West Indian seas. I cannot doubt that it happens somewhere, because I

F

have seen pictures of it, but in the seas *I* know it must
be rare.   Possibly other lands, other manners, and
likely enough other flying-fish and sea-fowl.

I should as soon think it possible for a kiwi to catch
a rifle ball in full flight, as for any real sea bird to
seize a flying-fish on the wing.   The albatross I dis-
miss at once, his chances of trying are too few to bring
him into question, as far as the South Pacific is concerned.   The frigate bird, or man-of-war hawk, decidedly the swiftest flier amongst sea birds I have ever
seen, seems to have given up fishing on his own account altogether, and makes use of the tern as his fish-
monger.   The tern, if the sea be smooth, has a neat
little way of picking up small morsels from its surface,
and, if necessary, makes a very respectable gannet-like
splash ; never, however, as far as I have seen, im-
mersing himself, and always keeping his wings in
motion, to get him up again.

The gannet, a splendid yellow-headed species of
which is common in the South Pacific, is, I think, the
finest of all fishing birds from John o'Groat's House to
the Chatham Islands.   But even he could never catch a
flying fish, his strong point being the " perpendicular,"
not the horizontal pace.   Soaring high he marks his
prey beneath him, and shutting up his wings (like a
wood pigeon darting into cover) he plunges downwards with a splash that makes one's head ache to look
at, and after a semicircular dive of five or six yards he
emerges, sneezing and flapping, with his prey safely
lodged in his throat.

I have seen a good deal of gannet life, both domestic and public. On Nepean and Philip Islands, in the Norfolk Island group, I used to find the fond gannet mother sitting affectionately by the side of the snow white fluff she called her child (paterfamilias having made himself scarce long before we reached the party) till I was within two or three yards of her, when she solemnly disgorged the two fish she had cooking in her throat for her darlings' supper, and followed her mate's example. These two fish on Nepean Island were nearly always a species of anchovy, with the brown line of flesh, or fish, strongly marked; they were closely pressed together, and had evidently undergone a process of maceration if not of digestion. The New Zealand " Sula," like his Maori fellow countryman, is of a more warlike nature and fights fiercely for the sanctity of his nursery.

I once saw the most stout-hearted of British skippers fairly driven off a rookery of them with his breeks in rags and his legs in holes, positively obliged to retreat and arm himself with a big stick before he could make his ground good. Even after the old birds were driven off we had to walk warily amongst the sharp-billed powder puffs, as they never missed a chance of giving us a sharp prod if we came within their reach.

I have watched the osprey fishing carefully, and never saw him swoop at a flying-fish; if he did I would back the fish.

One rarely sees him on the flying-fish ground, generally contenting himself with beating the shallow water
inside the reef; generally, as far as I have seen, grab-
bing his prey in a very slow, hovering fashion, without
any of the murderous lightning dash of the falcon.

I have seen the sea in the Indian Ocean alive with
big fish, and sea-birds darting down to secure their
prey. But I suspect that it was a case of the flying-
fish chasing the brit and the seerfish, and the bonito
chasing the flying-fish, and the birds picking up the
wounded brit, not the flying-fish, in full flight. I
must repeat that I never saw a bird, a real sea-bird,
capable of bagging a "rocketing" flying-fish; if I
knew the bird that could, and could tame him as
John Chinaman tames the cormorant, what glorious
fish hawking I would have !

Sept. 6.—As soon as it was light we ran down for
the land, rounding the northern corner of the island.
The skipper, aloft on the foreyard, soon made out the
opening in the reef and we stood in for it, opening out
a beautiful bay with trees and white houses sprinkled
along its shores. The wind was dead out, and the
channel very narrow, and the first board we stood on
a little too far, and the little ship shooting a head in
stays we looked for a moment very like landing on the
top of the reef, which would have been mighty unpleasant with the surf there was on.

But even this momentary uneasiness could not prevent our remarking the beautiful effect produced by

the fresh breeze catching the top of the breaking roller, and sending it up in a long wavy wall of sparkling diamonds.

As soon as we were well through the pass the brown pilot came on board, and disdaining to explain why he had not appeared before, merely remarked to the skipper, "You too much savey the reef," as if he suspected him of trying to do him out of his dues.

Our friend, to prevent our pleading ignorance, in case of our committing any little peccadillo on the island, presented us with the penal code, elegantly written in an ancient copy book. It struck us as having been compiled more for the sake of the rulers than the ruled. After studying it carefully, we came to the conclusion that it was all a matter of dollars, and that having dollars you could do what you liked, just as at home. Some one proposed that we should "square" the authorities with a five-pound note, and go in for an unlimited "scoop" as long as it lasted, begging them to tell us when we had sinned to the full amount. It is not dear; a man could be frightfully wicked for a ten-pound note if he confined himself strictly to crime. If he threw his money away by paying the queen ten dollars for a deserter, or two for making a man go ashore against his will, or another two for stopping on shore after nine o'clock at night, and luxuries of that sort, why then the thing would come more expensive. Of course you do not pay unless you are found out, but in order to prevent that you must

be very careful, as there is a set of disreputable beings
here who prowl about at night and peer through the
bars of the houses with an eye to dollars.

The island is governed by a queen (now in Tahiti),
she is governed by a prime minister, and they by a
house of peers, who bully them both and have all the
real power in their hands.

Went on shore and called on Mr. and Mrs. Saville,
the missionaries. I consider that the missionary's wife
is a missionary herself; and, in a large number of
cases, the most efficient one of the two.

The well-filled book-shelves showed their owner to
be a man of education and culture. He is also a
doctor, not a mere *dilettánte* but an ex-student of the
London University; I think it is an excellent thing
for a missionary to pass at least one session in the
wards of a hospital before he starts; that is if he have
a fancy for it, if not he is likely to do more harm than
good.

He accompanied us back to the yacht, and gave us
the island news. How they had " revolushed " the
other day (pardon the slang, there is a species of
lingua Franca in the South Seas wonderfully catching),
and he fears will shortly do so again, which will be a bad
thing for his people. There is the rub; Christianity
is the religion of peace, but as men will and indeed
must go to war we must have a religion to suit both
states of existence. A *coup-d'état* is also expected at
Raiatea, our next island. Some fiend in human form

tried to console him by saying, that even that was better than a " riot-here," but he was punished by his joke falling utterly flat. Here a revolution is a purely political affair; there it generally causes a heavy fight, so we may come in for some fun.

All the morning the schooner was crowded with natives, many of them ill, coming to be doctored. " Elephantiasis is very prevalent here, even amongst the European residents. The early symptoms are—" Here the doctor was stopped, this not being a medical work. Queen Elizabeth having a spite against a youthful rival would have banished her to this island, had she known of its existence; a horrible revenge, for her ankles would have been clean spoilt in a twelvemonth perhaps.

After luncheon we cruised inside; the lifeboat, I suspect, making an experiment or two to test which was the hardest, her mahogany planking or the coral. The results were in favour of the coral, which cuts like a knife.

In a lovely cove we found a number of women and children immersed to their middles, like a graduated row of Pandæan pipes, fishing with the rod and line in a highly artistic manner. The bait was a little pounded crab, a very small bit of which was used. They cast their line very deftly, and when they hooked a fish paralyzed it by a most crafty swing round their heads, and pouched it. I never saw better fishing; no, not even amongst the bank fishers of Thames or

Trent; their striking was perfection. The amusement
seemed to be entirely confined to women, and the
immature of the opposite sex; as we gazed at them a
feeling of shyness and an inclination to giggle seemed
to come over them now and then, but the latter most
of them could not indulge in with safety, as they carried
their bait where the Eaton boy carried his "wums;"
altogether they looked singularly like a row of brown
herons.

On our return called and gossipped for an hour with
Mr. Saville and his family. It is hard to say how
thoroughly refreshing the sight of his two darling
little children was, even to the bachelor half of us;
even a brown gentleman who came in evidently sub-
mitted to the same influence. I do not know why,
but there is always something curious to me in the
relationship between the coloured man and the white
child. The child invariably assumes an attitude of the
most intense superiority over her brown friend, patron-
ising whilst loving him. Whilst he as invariably bows
down and worships with a tenderness and courteous-
ness which is very beautiful.

More island gossip. The missionaries having taken
the power of performing legal marriages into their
own hands, the natives have ingeniously contrived to
hold their own by assuming that of civil divorce, and
some curious cases arose in consequence. There is a
white man living here, called Mr. What's-his-name,
whose wife being, I suppose, tired of nursing got

divorced from him one fine day when he was ill and
unable to appear in court. Having now got well, he
has appealed again and again for a fresh trial, but in
vain; and is likely to remain a divorced man to the
end of his days. Now this is not a question of White
v. Brown, for the ex Mrs. What's-her-name is a full
blooded Lima Spaniard, real *sángre azul.* Is it not
quaint to find a brown society divorce court deciding
a case of White v. White.

The natives here insist on choosing their own
" sacred " music. A most pious effusion of the lower
school of divinity was " offered up " to the tune of
" So early in the morning."

Sauntered back along the shore, amongst the native
warrés. They are built as usual of upright bamboos
or hybiscus sticks, supporting a roof which forms one
large room.

" Come in; you need not be afraid. They are all
my own people," quoth our friend, to our slight
amusement. If he had an idea of the queer places
into which we had poked our noses during the last
few years, he would not have fancied that we needed
encouragement.

And so, shaking hands with everybody, we went
on board.

September 17.—At ten o'clock in the morning we
made ourselves tidy to go to a " school inspection,"
and with the recollections of similar inflictions at home
we pulled ashore in a very low state of mind.

School inspection! it was a *fête!* a baccanaliad! On the very beach we were received by a perfect torrent of muslin, smiles, and laughter, which swept us into the school-room—a large, open, cool, well planned building, with all manner of kindly greetings.

As they all settled down, we found that there were three classes of scholars. Girls, boys, and grown women, all got up in their best clothes to do us honour, and not only that, but crowned one and all with the most beautiful and tasteful wreaths it has ever been our lot to see; there was not one single wreath round the forehead or neck of a girl or boy which was not admirable, in the judgment with which the flowers were selected and arranged, and the scent! Orange flowers being used in profusion; "'twas as a bridal!" They had been employed since early dawn in gathering and arranging them. It is not always that this flower wreath-wearing is permitted in school. They may wear them to the door but must leave them outside. The naughty little dears have invented a flower language for themselves, and make love under "teacher's" very nose without a word or a glance passing.

After infinite wrigglings, gigglings, and whisperings it was proposed that a song should be sung in P—'s honour. Songs of this sort are sung to impromptu words like the "Schnada-hupferl" of the Tyrolese, and it required no little encouragement to induce the shy little prima donna to begin. At last she commenced in a wild high-pitched key, and was gallantly seconded by an elderly lady in spectacles, who had a private and particular " skirl " of her own, which was supposed to be very perfect; it put me much in mind of the strange falsetto notes, so common in Arab songs: altogether it was most pretty and pleasing, and their idea of time seemed absolutely perfect, and though different possibly from our own, they evidently seem to have a decidedly musical talent: in fact they can sing anything, even the alphabet, out of which apparently dry subject they have made a really pretty song, a sort of " A with an A with a B-A-Ba " ballad, which, when closed with clapping of hands and joyous laughter, is by no means to be despised. Every now and again one of the more advanced pupils would give us her slate filled with monstrous sums, and retire to her place blushing and giggling, which struck us as being the most original form of flirting we had ever seen. Unfortunately we were bad arithmeticians, or I firmly believe that we should have discovered that there was a way of making love in a rule-of-three sum. There is nothing the darlings could not do, I am firmly convinced that they could dance the Multiplication Table if they tried.

Another pretty song they had was descriptive of all manner of employments—digging, weaving, &c.— accompanied with appropriate motions; arms, hands, and legs being freely used. The one they delighted most in was the rowing song, in which they pulled with ever increasing vigour, till at last they tumbled one a-top of t'other, with shrieks of joyous laughter and infinite innocent romping.

There was one wee brown boy in a chair who was as good as a play in his way. To watch how thoroughly he threw himself into the spirit of the thing, gracefully waving his arms and legs in time to the singing, was delightful ; I do not think that he could have been more than two years old, but he evidently had the old spirit in his very blood.

Some of the young princes and princesses were presented to us, all of a decidedly high-caste type, and very well mannered. They all had almost flaxen hair, and their complexions were not darker than those of Marseilles children of the same age, if as dark. Amongst them was the ex-king of Raiatea, a nice bright-looking lad, dressed in white shirt and trousers, who seemed to trouble himself mighty little about his lost grandeur.

The school inspection being over, the whole of the scholars, little and big, passed before us, every one as they passed giving a pretty shake of the hand, and depositing his or her wreath at our feet, till we were knee-deep in flowers. It was the prettiest, newest, freshest, thing that either of us had ever seen. The dresses, flowers, and cheerful laughter gave a sunshine to the whole affair which it is impossible to describe. We loaded ourselves with their beautiful wreaths, wherewith to decorate our cabin, and strolled down to the beach, like heathen deities out for a walk, attended by their worshippers.

Just as we pushed off from the shore, our eyes were simultaneously attracted to a most lovely vision; a tall and graceful girl, dressed in a long white muslin sacque, leaning on the shoulder of a brown girl. Her whole form undulating with grace as she walked, her eyes were full and swimming with light, her beautiful lips full, red, and rosy; her hair, as poor Heine says,—

> " Like a warm moonless night
> Stream'd from her braid-crown'd temples down,
> And curl'd all dreamily beautiful,
> Around her sweet pale face."

Oh, such a beautiful creature! such a real, ideal Cleopatra!

We thought that we had discovered a new race of Kanakas, and wondered what island had the priviledge of producing such beauty. We asked, and found, alas, that she was only the divorced Mrs. What's-her-name from Lima!

In the afternoon P— and Louey started in the life-boat, on a voyage of exploration inside the reef, their point being a strait which divides the island into two halves. After a long sail with baffling winds, we reached what appeared to be an enormous bay, with a small island across the entrance. Beating through the channel between it and the land, we

found ourselves in a mighty basin, surrounded by
towering green mountains.   At the opposite end one
could see a narrow channel winding in and out between them.   It was a perfect fairy-land !   Working
up through the channel, we found ourselves in another
deep bay on the weather side of the main island, and
after beating out to seaward for some time, reached a
little village.   A kindly native waded out into the
shallow water and piloted us in.   As soon as the boat
was made fast, he carried me ashore as easily as if I
had been a baby.   The people were kindly and hospitable as usual, offering to load the boat with fruit to
any extent.

   To my great delight they showed me the often
described, seldom seen, manner of making fire by
friction.   One of the boys took a long dry hybiscus
stick, about an inch and a half in diameter, cut a piece
of bark off it to get a flat surface, squatted down upon
it to keep it steady, and worked away with a little
pointed stick till a groove gradually appeared, at the
far end of which the dust produced by the friction
collected.   This soon began to smoke, and in about a
minute caught fire, showing that the savage had
practically understood the "correlation of forces,"
long before Mrs. Somerville or Dr. Tyndall.

   Meanwhile, Mr. Saville, a most intelligent native,
and I, with a native rejoicing in the name of Riti, or
Rice, had been on·an excursion in another direction.
Our friend Riti had obtained his name from having

attended one of Queen Pomare's children during its
illness. It seemed that the child asked constantly
for rice; and so, after the fashion of these parts, the
name of the thing brought descended on to the bearer
thereof. There is a gentleman here whose name,
being translated, means merely "a drop of tea."
And the great name Pomare itself, which has passed
through so many generations, means simply " he who
coughs in the night." The great object of our expedition was to examine some very extensive and sacred
" marais," a few miles down the bay in which we were
anchored.

A very pleasant walk through the scrub on the
raised coral beach at the foot of the older hills,
brought us to the edge of a lagoon, which was separated from the sea by a wide sweeping reef, covered
thickly with cocoes, bread-fruit, and iron trees. We
took canoe, and paddled a mile or so, to a large and
curious village, a real " Phal-bauten " affair, built
principally over the water on piles and large stones.
Some of the houses were of considerable size, the
walls (?) formed of hybiscus or bamboo poles, with
sufficiently large interstices between to admit of a
very free current of air, which the inhabitants seemed
to enjoy exceedingly. The floor was covered with
sweet-scented dry grass and bright mats, the general
effect being very clean and tidy. The mats seemed
to be used as some sort of separation between the
different branches of the family. Each set being

evidently distinct from the other, and having its own
little objects of use or luxury grouped upon it.   The
general impression was really a very pleasant one.

The opening of this lagoon into the sea is the
Thermophylæ of Huahine, the scene of the defeat of
the French by the islanders in 1847.   Headed by a
tough old Scotchman, they fought very bravely, killing
a great number of their adversaries, and even captur-
ing a gun, at least for a time.   Our friend Te Riki,
who was in the fight, pointed out all the principal
points of interest, and even the identical stones behind
which his men sheltered themselves.   The gun seems
to have been excellently placed, so as to command the
narrow path from the village ; but the natives made
a flank movement over the ridge, and killed every
artilleryman.   "Here stood the officer behind, and
when all his men were killed, he advanced and fired
the gun himself for the last time, being instantly shot
down."   Almost the only ammunition the Kanakas
had was composed of the heads of nails, extracted
from barrel hoops, a mighty nasty sort of thing at
close quarters.

They gallantly buried the dead Frenchmen with
the greatest care on the reef outside.

To and from Thermophylæ, the village girls and
boys followed our steps in a small crowd, and evidently
carefully treasured up Te Riki's descriptions of the
great fight.   Passing a bush of tea-tree, whose leaves
had the proper brown red colour, they made a rush at

it, and in a moment had woven themselves all
manner of head dresses, collars and ceintures, after
the ancient manner. These wild leaf dresses have a
great attraction for me, and great taste is always
shown in their arrangement. Seeing that we took an
interest in the affair, they began to weave, and twist,
and twine all manner of adornments for us and clicked
and screamed with delight when we put them on.
The people of this village are the most natural and
unsophisticated of any I have met with in all my
wanderings; I fancy that it is a rare thing for them
ever to see a white man, except the missionary.

The great "Marai" on the hill side above the
village is now overgrown with scrub, but one can still
make out its principal features. It consists of a series
of terraces of stone, placed without any particular
regard to regularity, against the hill side—lanes being
left between them. They were partly places for
religious rites and partly places of meeting for the
discussion of public affairs. Along the edge of one
of the principal terraces is a row of upright stones,
said to have been placed there at the first subdivision
of the land between the emigrant tribes, and still
called " the stones of dividing." Te Riki assured me
that the history of each of these was perfectly well
known to the chiefs at the present time, and he
pointed me out the particular stone which referred to
the land possessed by his tribe. I wonder whether
the Maori Meri-Ponamu, which is often connected

G

with land titles in New Zealand, is a relic of this custom ?

I asked about human sacrifices. Te Riki denied that they had ever taken place on this large public Marai, and pointed out a pecular deep lane, walled in on each side, up which the pigs used to be driven long, long ago : he said that human sacrifices were offered up occasionally in times of great national distress, on the smaller private Marais which are very numerous along the shores of the Lagoon. He repudiated the idea of their ever having been eaten, with disgust and scorn.

One large and very sacred stone resting on three others, apparently as it had fallen from the neighbouring hill, was pointed out to me as having been the high altar, and possibly was the cause of the Marai being built around it. It was exactly like the so-called Druidical altars of Brittany, and Cornwall.

Wherever a savage race finds a big stone supported by others, they believe at once that it has been so placed by supernatural means, and worship through it the tremendous forces which did so. Then they try and propitiate these forces by giving presents to their representative. In time comes a man more crafty than the rest of his tribe, or possibly slightly mad, and declares that the Forces have come to him in his sleep, and told him to take care of their representative and its presents. At first the priest and

chief squabble on the subject, and the chief is apt to
get the worst; sometimes, however, the priest gets
clubbed, and as civilisation advances, both see that it
is to their mutual advantage to pull together to a
certain extent. Population increasing and food becoming scarce, part of the tribe have to migrate,
taking with them a priest who, finding no sacred stone
in the new country (probably a rich alluvial plain)
builds one, and so wags the world! From the storm
dropped stone at Huahine you get the gilded dome of
St. Paul's.

We crossed the lagoon in a canoe to the reef, which
was densely wooded, and inspected some more Marais.
One very large one was built of enormous slabs of
coral rock set on their edges, and the interior filled
up with smaller stones. It was built on the flat
ground and regularly terraced. I should think it
some thirty feet by fourteen feet high.

Here a big bunch of the fibre of the coco-nut at the
mouth of a hole, told of the presence of the coco-nut
robber-crab, or rather del lobster. We worked hard
to get him, and I am sorry to say brought down a
good deal of the Marai in the excitement of our hunt;
however, he was either not at home or had a bolting
hole, and we got him not. He climbs here and cuts
off the coco-nuts: some say that he comes down on
the top of the coco-nut; others that he comes down
the way he went up. Who is right I know not, for I
never saw him. Oh, it was hot! and what whirlwinds.

of poisonous flies whizzed around us.　In sheer des-
peration we burst through the jungle, and emerged
mosquito-bitten, sweat-bedabbled, on to the hard white
sand, and into the roaring, tearing fresh trade wind,
that sent the blue sea foaming to our feet.

Besides the Marais, we visited a very remarkable
cyclopean causeway, said to have been built by a
numerous tribe in a single night, in order to procure a
famous beauty as the wife of their chief; it being supposed proper to do something heroical and out of the
common on these occasions, to show the lady the
value placed on her charms.　The Duke of Bridgwater
is said to have devoted himself to canal cutting because the woman he wished to marry refused him.
Had he cut his canal first and proposed afterwards, the
case might have been different.

Returning home in the dusk, my friend Mr. Saville,
who was sitting in front of me in the canoe, nearly
had a severe if not fatal accident from a curious
cause.

There is in all these waters a gar or guard fish
(Hemiramphus ?) some two feet long, with a hard and
sharp prolonged lower jaw.　This fish has an unpleasant custom, when suddenly startled, of leaping
out of the water with such extreme velocity, as to
transfix any soft substance which happens to be in his
way.　Cases of severe wounds, even death, from this
cause are by no means unknown.　In this case Mr.
Saville was saved by the fish striking him obliquely

(as I plainly saw, not being a foot from him), had it
hit fairly end on between the ribs, the consequences
would certainly have been serious. As it was he was
quit for a thump and some fish-scales on his coat. I
have often observed the same power of making a
strong rush amongst the small gar-fish of New Zealand, a rush strong enough to bring them into a boat.
These latter fish have a wide distribution; I have
caught them in the harbours of Suez, Auckland, New
Zealand, and Tahiti.

Our walk home, pleasant enough in itself, was rendered still more so, by the evidences of kindly feeling
between my companion and his flock. If any good is
to be done here by religious teaching these new missionaries are the men to do it. They have most
certainly gained both the affection and respect of
the people, and are looked upon as friends, not as
tyrants.

Beguiling the walk with gossip, my friend Riti, a
most grave and proper man, confessed to have just
married his eighth wife, some of the others being
dead and some divorced, but he does not seem quite
clear which is which. The real history of this marriage and divorce question cannot be entered upon
here, it being fitter for the pages of the "Lancet"
than for the drawing-room. Though for that matter
it seems by no means impossible that that excellent
medical journal may find its way into every lady's
boudoir, if things go on as they are going. There

are many social " questions " of this sort, which are
often discussed but never answered, because a feeling
of natural decency forbids those who really understand the subject from airing their knowledge in
general society.

Arrived on board, Mr. Saville's " boy " (here as in
the Indies all male servants are boys irrespective of
age), demonstrated the art of fire rubbing to us
again, and we carefully preserved the sticks as
curiosities.

In early times there arose difficulties in the infant
church at Huahine very like those hinted at by the
fathers of the early church of Corinth.

The " communicants " would drink far too much
sacramental wine, and wink in a highly improper
manner after having done so. This sort of thing
could never answer, either one way or the other, being
in fact both improper and expensive. So the wine
was stopped, and a mixture of coco-nut water and
molasses (why molasses ?) was substituted, to, I should
imagine, the infinitely increased confusion of a question quite intricate enough before.

Possibly, however, they had read their " Faust "
and knew that

> " Wine is grape, and grapes are wood,
> The coco-nut yields wine as good."

September 8.—Mr. Saville came on board at breakfast time to tell us that the Regent, the Queen's

speaker, and some of the principal chiefs requested
P—'s presence on shore, in order to present him with
a gift, as a token of their kindliness and good will.
On shore we found a large portion of the population
waiting to receive us, and accompanied by them we
walked up to the Queen's house, and were solemnly
introduced into her reception-room. We were there
received by the chiefs, and our flaxen-haired friends
the princes and princesses, and better behaved and
better mannered princes and princesses it would be
hard to find. We shook hands all round and pelted
each other with the flowers of compliment through
the kindly medium of Mr. Saville.

The present consisted of about two boatloads of
yams, bananas, coco-nuts, &c., besides three small pigs
and half-a-dozen fowls. P— thanked them, and invited them on board in half-an-hour, during which
short time Mr. Saville bundled off to his school to tell
his young people to be ready to join whatever might
be going on a little later.

The Regent and chiefs, with the royal children,
came on board at the appointed time, and evidently
admired our pleasant little craft immensely, having
never before, I fancy, seen anything but small coasting schooners, in which the captain's cabin is anything
but "all same one house." What delighted them
most was the galley below, and they could not make
out how we could keep a fire in it without burning the
ship ; and though one would have supposed it hot

enough in all conscience on deck, they positively enjoyed the extra heat : I believe that the way to deter
these people from being naughty would be to preach
a future eternity of ice.   It is a great mistake to
suppose that the idea of the " fire punishment " must
necessarily have arisen in a hot climate ; I have seen
the natives of hot climates suffer from cold but never,
if I remember, from heat.

The Queen of Huahine's speaker is as unlike Mr.
Denison, as far as personal appearance is concerned,
as it is well possible to imagine.   He is most fearfully
diseased and distorted.   In other respects, some re-
semblance might be discovered, as he is a most courteous, and, we are given to understand, talented man.

Our visitors were mightily tickled at the care we
had taken of " the boy's" fire sticks, marvelling how
men who could command countless matches, could be
interested in such relics of barbarism.   P— presented
the ex-king of Raiatea with a striped blue rowing-cap,
and his brothers and sisters with infinite pots of jam,
which were highly appreciated.   A sack of flour was
placed in the boat for the chiefs, a great treat for
them, and with much hand-shaking they went on
shore.

Then there was peace on board till two o'clock,
when a fresh rumpus began.   The school children,
and very fine grown children some of them were,
collected on the beach, and the boats were sent to
fetch them, the lifeboat and the " fish-fag " being

loaded to the water's edge; the lifeboat on one occasion bringing off no fewer than thirty-seven very strapping young ladies. Luckily the water was smooth, or even *she* might have capsized; not that it would have made much difference, they would have swum on board singing. They were evidently in a high state of delight, laughing, cheering, and clapping their hands in ecstasy, at the prospect of an outing.

P— and the skipper received them at the gangway, and stevedore Mitchell "took tally" as they came on board; a hundred and twenty-two regulars, besides some thirty strange sheep, who came off in private canoes.

First they explored the cabin, pouring down one hatchway and surging up the other; and when they had exhausted the marvels of the lower world, they seated themselves on the deck in close ranks and began to sing. What a wonderful picture it would have made! and what a pity it was that there was no one to do it justice, either with pen or pencil! The dense mass of merry faces and flashing teeth and eyes; the gay wreaths and flower crowns; their bright, pure, graceful dresses; the lithe swaying of their bodies and movement of their limbs as they sang; and the occasional unanimous clap of their hands from one end of the ship to the other. Captain Cook himself never saw anything better!

To get from one end of the schooner to the other,

one had to climb "outside," so closely packed were
they; and the mighty bunches of green and golden
bananas which festooned the rigging added no little to
the picturesqueness of the general effect.

After giving us half-a-dozen songs, each prettier
than the other, .they began to leave the ship, pouring
over the side like a snow wreath, laughing, singing,
and decorating us and the sailors with their beautiful
flower wreaths.   P—'s right arm fairly broke down,
with the repeated, or rather uninterrupted, hand-
shaking.

Surely such a school feast was never seen before;
and I know not where you could find such a set of
well-behaved, affectionate children to make another.

The pigs presented to us turn out to be hideous
little animals of some aboriginal breed, at least one
third head, and very ugly head too.   They gave one
the general impression of having been squeezed from
their youth up between two tight boards.   And their
manner corresponded with their appearance; wickeder
pork, for its age, I never saw alive !   When stevedore
Mitchell civilly offered one a banana, it flew at him
and barked like a dog, to his no small discomfiture.
Then it dropped on its fore knees, and seemed for
some time to be wrapped in religious contemplation.
After fortifying its soul with prayer, it suddenly, and
quite *à propos des bottes*, attacked one of our little
Maori porkers, who was poking about the deck thinking no evil, and a tremendous fight ensued.   Maori

was so fat and round that for some time the new
"chum" could not raise a bite out of him, more
particularly as he steadily presented the fattest and
roundest part of his person to his adversary. At last
a new idea seemed to strike the latter, and he took
poor Maori by the tail and made him squeak again.
Maori, paralysed for a time, retired into a quiet corner, thought the thing over, and his native fighting
blood gradually rising to boiling point, he came out
with a rush, and with many a prod, and poke, and
bite, finished off his slabsided assailant in one last and
decisive round.

He turned out a clever and original pig, but never
became really civilized.

Idled away half an hour watching a young man and
some boys (amongst whom was my young friend the
ex-king, now dressed in nothing but the "paréu")
practising spear throwing at the stump of a coco-
branch, stuck into the sand. The spear here is
thrown rather underhand, the shaft resting on the two
forefingers of the left hand, and propelled by the tips
of the two first fingers of the right. They threw up
to ten or fifteen yards with fair accuracy, the young
man nailing his palm branch at nearly every throw;
but it seemed more adapted for fishing than fighting.
They are not to be compared with the New Caledonians or the Pine islanders, who drive light spears
of hard wood with tremendous force, by means of a
"hitch" made of the wool of the flying fox. By the

way, their best spears almost always have a head with
a nose and chin like Punch's carved on them, as also
have often their canoes. I wonder where they got
that ideal face, so utterly unlike their own, from?

The west Australian blacks, however, with the
throwing stick, would give them both points and beat
them hollow. I have seen them make very fair shots
at swallows on the wing, without of course killing
them, but going mighty near them.

Seeing a mighty bustle of folk on the reef, paddled
up, and found them preparing a labyrinth of fish traps
for an expected high tide, making leads and *cul-de-
sacs* of coral as artful as any set nets for salmon.
Curious to see how crafty the natives were not to lift
a lump of rock out of water, but to carry it along
beneath it.

An evening here at Huahine is a mighty pleasant affair. From the moment we land a cloud of
light infantry attend our steps; running, jumping,
spear-throwing, and larking generally. Now and
again as we lounge along in the bright moonlight, a
dusky beauty, with a charming shyness, gives a
sweet-scented flower, and then subsides amongst the
feet of her young companions, overcome with the
sense of her own audacity—very much! They may
be a little naughty, but that is no reason why you
should be naughty, and there is no doubt that the man
who wishes to pass through these islands pleasantly

and with the love and respect of their inhabitants,
cannot do better than show that he is above the mere
profligacy of the whaler or the beach-man. Apart
from other considerations, by doing this you find that
you are trusted by women who would never have
approached you, had they fancied that you were a
mere idle voluptuary. And really I have met few
women who appreciate the mutual trust system more,
or who are more worthy of it.

It really seems to open up a new life to them when
they are talked to as reasonable beings, and nothing
more.

To compare the "Broom-road" of Huahine with
the streets of an English town after nightfall, would
be a most infamous libel on the former. What immorality there may be, is infinitely less immoral in
Huahine than in England, as one might easily prove
did one care to go into the foul subject.

Sauntering along attended by our train of dusky
beauties, we met our Cleopatra of yesterday, Mrs.
What's-her-name? What's-her-name? Why, what
should it be but Maria Dolores! and a very pretty
name, too. And gentle and kindly, and speaking a
soft and pleasant form of English was Maria Dolores!
And, moreover, quite ready to have any amount of
baskets full of the flowers of compliment, showered
over her in that stiff tongue. We rambled and
scrambled together over the hybiscus fences, and in

and out amongst the houses, without the slightest
regard to the laws of trespass; and peeped and peered
about without much regard to those of domestic
privacy.   Cleopatra enlivening the walk with many a
choice bit of island scandal, which would have done
good service in a St. James' Street club; but generally
rather too highly flavoured to be admitted into the
pages of this proper and decent chronicle

A pretty little girl and boy coming up to kiss
P—'s hand, he asked her who was supposed to look
after the royal children? " Oh, nobody," she answered
with a graceful carelessness; " they look after themselves."   And I must say they seemed to do it very
well.

The whole beach was alive with fish scraping and
fish cooking, the products of the artful arrangements
we had watched in the afternoon.   And we might
have loaded a boat with the cheerfully proffered
presents.   The cookery was carried on in the real old
" Maori" way, by means of hot stones, and any one
who can find a better (barring the mystery of the wet
newspaper) let him tell it me, and I'll do what I can
for him.

Hearing a rub-dub-dubbing approaching, we feared
that our 'long shore cruise was coming to an end, and
meeting the princes beating the " rappel," we expressed
our sorrow at having to go on board so soon. " Oh ! "
quoth Cleopatra, with her loftiest air, " laws were not
made for *you*."   And we continued our saunter with

ever increasing satisfaction, every patch of bright moonlight or dim shade producing some fresh group of prettiness; but we are not going to tell you *all* we saw that evening!

Farewell Huahine! surely you take your name from " Wahine "—γυνη—woman!

Chapter IV.

RAIATEA AND TAHA.

Sept. 9.

ALAS, alas! That abominable invention of civilisation called time has decreed that we shall tarry no longer at Huahine, the woman's island. It is, indeed, a perfect little Garden of Eden; plenty of Eves, but no snakes. They have not tasted the tree of knowledge of good and evil as yet. Nature is almost their only law, hard as the missionaries have tried to elevate them to a sense of sin.

Kind little Mr. S— came on board at nine to say good-bye; and, in spite of many assurances that we should find Raiatea not nearly so pleasant, we weighed anchor at ten, and exchanging farewell salutations with the royal flag, stood out of the cozy little harbour. It seems to me that I can't leave one of these islands without feeling low and sentimental. I know each time that another leaf of the pleasantest part of my life-book is past and finished.

At about one o'clock, steering by the directions
we had received from Huahine, we found ourselves
off the N.E. end of Raiatea, where a pilot came off to
show us the passage through the reef. And a strange
reef it was; like a great necklace, enclosing both
Raiatea and Taha, the neighbouring island, while to
complete the simile, a quantity of gigantic emeralds,
consisting of most lovely little islets, were threaded
at regular intervals upon the white surf line. Looking through the passage between Raiatea and Taha,
we could see in the far distance the splendid peak
of Borra-Borra, rising like some giant's castle out of
the sea.

I noticed that the little reef islands lay generally
in couples, with bold water between them, giving
them the appearance of poetical gate-posts, placed
there on purpose to mark the entrances to the lagoon.

We shot through one of these narrow gaps, and ran
down towards Uturoa, the chief settlement, where we
came to an anchor. Immediately, as at Huahine, the
penal code was handed to us by the pilot, this time in
a washing book; given to us as it were some criminal
bill of fare, the exact price of the most delightful offences being stated to half a dollar. The laws read
horribly strict, but they are seldom carried out to the
letter, unless the king happens to be short of spirituous liquors, and wants to raise his revenue, when he
has only to put into force the one relating to every
one being in their houses by nine o'clock P.M. to screw

a couple of dollars a-piece out of half the population.
When I asked Queen Moé whether I should have to
respect this rule, she gave me to understand that I
might be as naughty as ever I liked with impunity,
which was very nice.

I had been entrusted with some letters by Queen
Pomare, the directions on which would fill Bedlam
with post-office officials in six months, besides a letter
of introduction to Queen Moé from her cousin in Tahiti,
and soon after our arrival we proceeded on shore to
deliver them. First we reported ourselves to the missionary, Mr. V——, a most agreeable and kind hearted
gentleman, whose wife has suffered terribly in health
from the heat of the climate. Having no children of
their own, they have adopted a charming little native
girl, after the custom of the country. The Society
Islanders are death on adoption, as a Yankee would
say. Nearly every one has four parents, their real
ones and their feeding ones; the second couple being
responsible for their bringing up and education, which
consists chiefly of teaching them to spear fish, the crabs
which infest the shore and dig it into holes, representing their A.B.C., and are considered in the eye of the
law as being nearer relations than the real papa and
mamma. It must be rather hard on the young native
to have to keep the fifth commandment double. The
children are often bespoken before birth, and handed
over as soon as they are weaned. I don't know what
this custom originated in, but I have a fanciful theory

that it was introduced by the fond fathers to check that engrossing, offensive, and boring pride which possessed their helpmates whenever they had produced, and were engaged in rearing, a child of their own. A woman with a new baby, or a man with a new book, is a monomaniac and a bore.

Relationships in these small islands are intricate and confusing enough, but when this adoptive element is introduced they become utterly maddening and hopeless.

Then we went down to Queen Moé's, with her letters and a parcel from her cousin Moetia. We were shown into her reception-house, a large birdcage room on a platform about two feet from the ground, while some one went up to her private house to announce our arrival. These buildings have one great advantage worth introducing into civilised society, which is that you can always look through the bars to see who is at home before paying your visit.

At last she appeared, a tall, graceful, wonderfully pretty girl. She had rather a large but well shaped head with an unusual amount of forehead, under which were a pair of the biggest, roundest, shyest, gentlest, quietly laughingest (bother the adjectives!) eyes I ever saw, a small *retroussé* nose, and a most lovely little mouth that puckered up her cheeks into cozy little dimples whenever she smiled ; the ladylike gentleness of her manner, and the quaintness and *naïveté* of her words and ideas were most charming.

Tamatoa, her husband, is a most awful sweep, committing the most fearful extravagances when he is drunk, which is his normal condition. The other day, when slightly elevated, he took a Snider rifle, purporting to polish off a minister or two by way of a lark. Having loaded it the right way he thought to increase the effect by shoving a lot more ammunition down the barrel, by which exploit he nearly succeeded in blowing his arm off. This the queen told us with the greatest coolness and gravity.

But like most men he has his good points, the chief one being that when he is drunk he goes away on the loose; and when he is sober, shuts himself up altogether. He is the son of Queen Pomare, but instead of taking after his sainted mother, imitates the noble example of his father, a very naughty old man.

Outside the house I was introduced to several native lions. Amongst them Queen Pomare's mother, a wonderful old lady with an eye as keen and piercing as a hawk, old as she was. We have just arrived at a political crisis in Raiatea; Taha (the next island), the Ireland of this kingdom, has demanded a separate government, because King Tamatoa wastes so much of the revenues on orange rum and other spirituous liquors. No one knows how it will be settled, and a war is looked upon as more than probable.

This orange rum drinking is a regular and elaborate ceremony—no light casual intoxication. Large parties of men and women go up into the mountains

for the sole purpose of drinking themselves drunk and
enjoying the sensation. It is a weak vinegary stuff,
I believe, about two pailfuls or so being required to
make a man jovial. They keep on brewing and
drinking for a month or six weeks, till at last some one
gets killed, or drinks himself to death, when they return to their villages and are penitent until their diges-
tions are restored.

A good deal of intoxication, said Mr. V——, arises
out of connubial differences. There is a quarrel, and
the weaker vessel gets drunk and takes up with
another man out of spite. On this the injured
husband drowns his sorrows in the flowing bowl,
and solaces his spirit by consorting with some friend's
wife. On this the woman gets sober and, with that
faithful cleaving to her first love for which her sex
is so remarkable, forgives his iniquities, and goes for
advice to the missionary, who makes up the quarrel
and sends them off reunited with a blessing.

They remember my cousin, Lord G——, very well
here, and call him "the silver-arm." Nearly every
one, even the missionaries, are nick-named in these
islands; my title being, I believe, "the coco-nut
tree." I noticed a small schooner aground near the
royal mansion, with her hull, masts, and rigging all
falling to pieces; this, I was told, was the chief line-
of-battle ship or crack frigate of the Taha navy that
had been taken in the last war.

Sept. 10.—L—— and I sailed away in the lifeboat

in search of adventures in the direction of Taha.
We picked our way along inside the barrier reef with
some difficulty, owing to the numerous shoal ridges.
In the court-house of Raiatea, the principal chiefs
were still vehemently discussing; boats and canoes
kept crossing and recrossing between the two islands,
and as no one knew at what moment the signal for
war might be given, and the peaceful passengers
turned into desperate pirates and privateers, it was
all rather good fun.

In about an hour we had crossed the channel between the two islands, and soon after passed the
principal village on the south-east end of Taha; and
stretching still further on opened out a fine bay,
some three miles deep, nearly cutting the island in two.

Then, seeing a large boat ashore on a beautiful
little island on the coral reef, we stood out towards
it.   We found there were two islands with a deep
channel through the reef between them, and beaching
our boat close to the stranger soon came upon two
natives roasting bread fruit.   They explained that
there was a great fishing business going on on the
other side, which we proceeded to see.

Sure enough appeared about twenty natives on
the reefs, up to their necks in water, attended by
a few small canoes, all shouting and bobbing round
a kind of circular net which they were gradually
dragging towards the shore—rather, I should say,
lifting, for you cannot drag a net over a coral reef.

At last they brought it close to us, into about three
feet of water, when the two men who were standing
with us, respectable clerical-looking old fellows,
began to get violently excited. One seized a huge
faggot of stakes, with which he ran violently down
toward the sea, while his friend did likewise with
a bundle of spears, three-pronged, two-pronged, but
more often long single harpoons with a barb on
one side. The stakes were planted in a circle to
support the net that was hung upon them, and
then each native seized his weapon, began spitting
the fish inside with the most extraordinary skill
and precision, and dropping them into the canoes
alongside. There was wild excitement, and how
they avoided prodding each others' toes I know
not. Some of the men, evidently the masters
of their art, stood a long way back from the mass as
if they were fielding at cricket; and when a fish
escaped from the net chased him in the shallow
water, shying their spears at him with nearly in-
variable success, a feat that Louey and I applauded
tremendously.

Then the haul being over, and half a canoe full
being secured, they came back to where their simple
dinner was cooking, laughing, shouting, and racing
through the clear water like a lot of mad mermen.
Bread-fruit is a delightfully simple thing to cook.
You make a lot of hot ashes and pitch it amongst
them, and then go for a walk. If there are any

little pigs about, they go and scratch their little sterns
against it, which turns it round and round, and when
you re-appear your dinner is ready. All the little
pigs at the isle of Pines had bald sterns and tails
in consequence of this practice.

The natives presented us with some fish, and we
sailed across to the other island to lunch, in defiance
of mosquitoes.

I was very much struck with the big sailing out-
rigger canoes, and the pace they run. They carry
one enormous sprit sail on a mast stepped far forward,
and raking tremendously.   A great cross-piece of
wood is lashed across the canoe where the mast is
stepped, to which three or four shrouds and stays are
fixed.   One man, or two, according to the strength
of the breeze, stands out on the weather side of this
cross-piece, which keeps the canoe upright.   A pole
like the tail of a passionate cow runs outward and
upward from the stern, which gives one the idea that
the builder was drunk, and had put the bowsprit on
the wrong end of the vessel.   A rope runs from the
end of this to the point of the sprit, to keep the great
sail from swagging over too much.

They are of enormous length, with no more draught
or beam than a racing wherry, all their stability under
sail being effected by the leverage of the great out-
rigger and the additional effect of the men on the
cross-piece.   These peculiarities give them a speed in
running quite incredible to anyone who has not seen

them, and they work to windward better than one
would expect, to look at them. Of course in the case
of a sudden calm they inevitably capsize; but the
natives are amphibious, and don't care about that.
The steerer holds his paddle perpendicularly against
the lee side of the canoe.

Then we ran back among the fishing-canoes for the
chief settlement of rebellious Taha. I managed to get
pretty close in shore by the help of the signals of the
people on the beach, and as soon as the boat stuck
fast, a brawny native waded out and transported me
to the beach on his shoulders, to the amusement of
the population, who gave me a very kind reception.
After a little broken conversation and the usual present of fruit, they asked me if I should like to see
a white man who lived there; and I was guided to a
nice little cottage, where a pretty half-caste woman
asked me to come in and make myself at home. Soon
after the owner of the house arrived, a man of the true
pakeha-maori stamp, brown, restless-eyed, plausible,
civil, and good-for-nothing; and we sat down for a
talk, surrounded by a group of admiring natives.
" You're rather in difficulties with your king, I believe," said I, by way of starting the conversation.
" He's an awful scoundrel, isn't he ? " Whereon my
friend replied, in a mysterious whisper: " He is all
you say, sir, but I mus'n't say nothing; these natives
understand more than they pretend to very often, and
I might get into trouble." So politics were barred.

How unlike the glorious freedom of my own country, where any foul-mouthed rascal, with the gift of the gab, may get up and abuse Her Majesty in public with impunity. Speak not of the king in thy chamber, lest a bird of the air carry the matter; a proverb that should be slightly altered to suit modern times, when it is not the bird of the air that carries the matter, but the beast of the area.

My friend declared that there was no way of getting any money on these islands, as the natives would neither sell nor let their land; and even if they would no labour could be got. " They've got their grub hanging over their heads, and their water at their feet; and when they want fish they can go out and get it as soon as they like. If I could only get two nights' frost, to make them work for their breakfast, I might do what I liked." Then I said good-bye, and he asked us how we intended to pick our way home through the reefs. I got the bearings and directions by heart, as well as I could, and went down to the beach. Then I was carried aboard again, solemnly attended by the chief people of the town—all out of good-nature, for I was not known, and to all their questions about myself and the schooner returned vague and mysterious answers—and one of them said he should like to come with me and show me the way, if I would let him. " Jump on board," said I. And a very pleasant passenger he proved, showing us all the short cuts through the reef, giving us lessons in the native language, and learning English in return; expressing his hopeless inability to speak words with many consonants by laughing, shaking his head, and touching his tongue, to explain that he could not spit it out.

As soon as I got on board I heard that the queen had been enquiring for me; and hurried ashore, where I was introduced to King Tamatoa, a powerful, bullet-headed, but not very ill-looking man, very decently dressed in Européan clothes. Like Mr. Bob Sawyer, except when he's elevated, he's the quietest creature breathing.

After a short conversation, with her majesty as interpreter, I departed, promising to come again to-morrow to be taught to make reva-reva.

Sept. 11. After luncheon the doctor and I went ashore to the queen's. Close to her reception room was another bird-cage building, the House of Parliament, only yesterday the scene of a stormy and critical debate, but now occupied by the peaceful votaries of music, five or six of whom were squatted in a circle performing native ballads, while a young man accompanied them, melodiously playing a flute through his nose. Men, women, and children, lolling around on their mats, lazily enjoying the performance. A Pan and Dryad effect. Then the queen showed us how to make reva-reva, from the shoot of a young coco-nut tree, an operation simple enough when seen, but very difficult to describe intelligibly. She then tried to teach me to do it; but my fingers were too clumsy, and I generally managed to tear the delicate stuff. She would have made a wonderfully pretty picture, engaged in this work; and when she asked me wonderingly what I wanted to see it done for, I felt inclined to give that as the reason.

Then appeared Tamatoa, and in his right mind, who signified his desire, through the missionary, to make me the usual present of pigs, fruit, and fowls, while the queen gave me a beautifully-worked araroot crown, decked with reva-reva, besides many fine plumes of the latter article.

I think I shall introduce Society Island manners into England, with some slight omissions.

When visitors call on me at W— on their departure, I shall put into their carriage a couple of sacks of potatoes, ditto of flour, cloves, &c., a dozen bunches of grapes, half a dozen melons, peaches, &c., a few fowls, and some fine young pigs from the model farm; and perhaps a housemaid to make the thing quite complete.

In return for this my lady-visitor will present me with her bonnet, shawl, jewels, or perhaps her boots, or my gentleman-visitor with his best shiny hat, watch, walking-stick, shirt-studs, or metal buttons if he has any.

Then the king, queen, and the Bismarck of Raiatea, a handsome, intelligent, jovial man, came on board with us, and we had some amusing conversation on

all kinds of subjects, Her Majesty interpreting. "Do
you bathe much here?" said I. "No," replied she,
"I fear the beeg fish. I see the Frenchman bathe in
Papiete, and the sharks bite their legs," for which she
didn't appear to be the least sorry. They were very
anxious to know all about England, whether there
were bread-fruit and coco-nut trees there? what kind
of houses were built? and how the people lived?
Carriages drawn by horses, great fast-running pigs
they call them, they could understand, having seen
specimens in Tahiti, but we broke down at the description of a railway train; the only definition by
which we could convey the idea, was a man-of-war
that ran along the shore upon wheels.

In the evening we went for a stroll along the shore,
and fell in with a party of exceedingly intoxicated
natives, who begged my cigar, and would have retained the doctor's pipe, a proceeding he objected to
decidedly. But drunk as they were, they were perfectly good-tempered and civil. These, and a few
ladies of shady character were the only people we
met. Unlike Huahine this is not a nocturnal place,
for it is constantly exposed to the trade wind, which
the natives consider cold, and which moreover produces a most unpleasant smell of rotting coral-stuff.

Sept. 12.—The doctor and I went ashore to church.
It was a very pretty sight to see them all in their
best clothes, neat little hats, and fresh flowers.

They didn't seem to care much about the service

except the hymns, occupying the rest of the time by reading the hymn-books, whispering little jokes to each other, and laughing and telegraphing with their eyes. A good part of the congregation kept outside the doors, looking in occasionally to see how things were getting on. The sermon was in the native language, and Queen Pomare's mamma after taking a note or two on a piece of foolscap paper with great gravity, curled herself up on a bench and went fast asleep; as did also the Missionary's big dog, which I considered wrong and rather too cool in an animal of his associations, so trod on his tail to wake him up.

I did once know a bishop's wife who always took a nap during her husband's sermons, and I always felt an intense respect for her moral courage.

In the afternoon the doctor and I went for a stroll, and walking along under the pleasant shade of the bread-fruit trees arrived at the further end of the village, and sat ourselves down on the sad sea shore, surrounded by a group of admiring natives of all ages and sexes. I can quite understand and sympathise with the feelings of the brindled gnu in the Zoological gardens, who always charges furiously at the visitors who come to stare at him. It requires a long training to be able to think and talk comfortably and unconsciously under the steady gaze of twenty or thirty eyes.

Sometimes one of the girls would get up and pick an orange, present it slyly, and retire giggling about twenty yards, sit down again and stare as before. I was particularly struck with a lively baby of an observant and humourous tone, who seemed delighted with our appearance, and crowed approvingly and continuously, until we attempted to draw nearer to make his acquaintance, when he changed his note, and howled till we ceased to advance.

As we walked back we met the whole congregation coming out of chapel with a broad grin on, and much hand-shaking ensued. "These are some of his Riverence's servants," said the doctor, when I heard "Good afternoon," behind me, and turning round saw "his Riverence" laughing at us, and we proceeded to his house.

He told me that a war does some good here by killing off the bad characters who are usually foremost in getting it up. As there are no prisons here, and no punishment but a nominal fine these fellows accumulate till they become quite a drug in the market.

Waterspouts are very common about these islands; not long ago a large one came into the lagoon, ran all along the water close to the shore—the natives shying sticks and stones at it—ran up the beach, smashed all the venetian windows of the chapel, and took the roof right off, leaving an old woman saying her prayers in the middle of it, very much astonished, and half expecting she was going to be taken straight up to heaven.

While we were at dinner the pilot came off to me with a note from the queen, rather a curiosity in its way. The address was charmingly simple, " For the lord ! " the writing was good and the spelling tolerable, only there was not enough of it ; the words being run into one another in a most confusing manner. The substance of the epistle was that she had heard that I had been out last night walking, and had been insulted, or assaulted, by some drunken people ; if it was true I was to tell her, and the king would put them in the law, as she expressed it. This is very delightful, to have a real live queen to watch over my safety and keep me out of mischief.

I fear it will be long before Queen Victoria will exercise a like maternal protection over her humble servant—God bless her !

I wrote back a warm, civil answer, saying I had met with nothing but kindness from her people ; for which, perhaps, the king won't thank me, it being two or more dollars out of his pocket.

The royalties of the Society Islands are all, more or less, members of one family, connected by various mysterious and confusing relationships. I have been very much struck with the tone of perfect equality in social life observed between the royal families in these islands and their subjects. It seems to me essentially unbarbaric, and is one of their numerous marks of high-bred feeling and unsnobbishness, to coin a most awkward word. Yet in spite of this social equality, there is a powerful instinct of loyalty amongst them, even in connection with such a man as King Tamatoa.

And what is still more strange, and shows still more what thorough gentlemen and ladies they all are, is that though the king and queen talk and live with the meanest of their subjects naturally and apparently without any feeling of superiority, yet all · have the greatest respect for high birth or, rather, good ancestry. No matter how poor and insignificant a man may be, if his pedigree is good he is the social equal or superior of the highest dignitary of the land.

As England is getting so radical now, and professing to be so much above that kind of thing, it would not be a bad idea for the Heralds' Office to remove to the Society Islands.

They treat idiots and madmen here with great respect and consideration, which perhaps is the reason that—Never mind! There is an " old foolish man " here, as Moé calls him, who has got into his head that I am his grandson, and comes to her perpetually to inquire what time I am coming on shore. He is very proud of me, she says. Lord help him, he must be mad indeed !

An American brigantine, "The Timandra," came in to-day from Tahiti. She carries a three-cornered mainsail without a gaff, the gaff-topsail sheets going right down to the end of the main-boom.

The population of Raiatea is, I believe, about fifteen hundred souls ; Taha is rather less.

I

When the men go to war their lady-loves gird up their loins and accompany them to battle to take care of them and carry their ammunition; sometimes, I believe, they take part in the fighting. These lazy, good-natured folks appear to be no cowards.

Sept. 13.—The morning was wet and cloudy, so the school people, who were to have paid us a visit, had to wait till the afternoon, when it cleared a little. Soon we saw them coming along the shore in an apparently endless string, two and two, like the beasts going into the ark, chattering and laughing furiously, and singing their wild choruses; all dressed in their best, with new crowns and reva-reva on their heads instead of the wreaths of fresh flowers they sported at Huahine.

All our boats were soon engaged as transports and off they came, cheering and singing and making the boat roll, utterly regardless of a capsize, which I momentarily expected.

They came on board to the number of one hundred and seven, not so many as at Huahine, but much bigger. I took a lot of them down into the cabin. "You sit there," said the principal pupil teacher, laughing and pointing to the divan, which I did, and held a regular *levée:* they poured down the after companion, and each girl was presented in turn, shook hands, and gave me the crown from her head beautifully worked and plaited into various devices, and decked with reva-reva or flowers, and then passed on through the galley and up the fore companion. It was a wonderful skylark; the slightest mistake, such as a young lady shaking the wrong hand, or dropping her garland, was greeted with screams of laughter from her friends, while the abashed maiden would flee swiftly and hide her diminished head amongst the crowd.

Oh Lord! thought I, if my friends and relatives could see me now, seated in state and a flannel shirt and trousers, receiving homage from the nobility and gentry of Raiatea, what would they think?

Then we proceeded on deck, and a lot of the small boys began clambering about the masts and rigging. " They won't do any mischief," said their pastor. " Not unless they break their own necks," replied I, as I observed one infant of tender years slide right down a stay from the masthead. " Oh, there's no danger of that, they can all climb like cats or monkeys;" and directly after two little brats, certainly not more than eight or nine years old, were on the trucks. Then we had some singing—everything has to be altered to suit the temperament of these people—the multiplication table, always connected in my mind with a fusty Colenso or a slate, was here a dance and a song combined; the alphabet was sung to the tune of " Auld Lang Syne;" one hymn to that of " Jolly Dogs " nativized, and another to that of " Ho, Susannah! don't you weep for me!"—" Green Sleeves moralized " was nothing to it.

Then a gang of them began quietly to perform a

little dance, Mr. V— consenting to wink at it. Two
little imps of girls came out of the mob, wriggled
their bodies, and waved their little arms, after the
approved fashion, while the rest of the girls formed
round them and sang. It was very amusing to see
the way they all dried up whenever Mr. V— looked
over his shoulder; though occasionally they became
so inspired by the performance, as to require a gentle
tap on the head with an umbrella to call them to order.

Then they all departed in high good-humour,
laughing, cheering, and skylarking, from the prime
minister's wife to the housemaid's baby. And for
years after they will keep up the tradition of their
visit to the ship that was a house inside, and had a
fire to cook with below deck; and a place that when
you touched it poured out water that came from the
other end of the vessel, and so on, *ad libitum.*

The beauty of these people's faces improves with
age, a rare thing among brown races. The ruggedness of their strongly-marked faces looks natural and
fine when they begin to grow old, and sets off the
bright, healthy-minded good-humour of their expression.

Sept. 14. The doctor went ashore in a medical
capacity, and had a look at all the incurables of the
island. Elephantiasis is fearfully common, both among
the whites and natives, and is an intermittent disease.

He also visited the school, and found that the text
for the copy books of the upper classes was "Lord

P— and Doctor K—." This is, I think, the first time I was ever made use of for educational purposes.

After luncheon I went ashore to see the queen, and found that the whole population were away picking oranges for the Timandra; but the king had ordered them back, fearing that the Taha natives might seize the opportunity for an invasion. The poor little woman said she was very frightened ; and indeed she seems far too gentle and civilized to live in such a savage state of affairs.

I gave her two tortoiseshell head ornaments from Ceylon, while she presented me with her pretty little araroot hat, &c. &c. "Compliments pass when gentlefolks meet." These hats are made from the dried leaves of the araroot tree, washed and rubbed in some peculiar way, which gives them an appearance far brighter and more delicate than straw. The devices and patterns into which they are worked are very beautiful and ingenious.

Tamatoa, as I have said before, is not a model young man. One of his latest exploits was to borrow, without leave, the missionary's whale-boat, to go off on an orange rum-drinking excursion. It was delightfully wicked to go for such a purpose at all; but how much more so to do it in a missionary's boat! And then he and his friends, returning from the orgie in a jovial frame of mind, took it into their heads that it would be a most delightful spree to ride the boat right over the coral reef through the surf. The natural consequence of this was, that the boat was considerably damaged, and the oars lost.   When they reached home I believe Mr. Vivian was not pleased.

Not long ago, this naughty king had an attack of conscience, or perhaps indigestion, and he resolved to amend his ways.   Great was the rejoicing even in this world over this precious sinner who had repented, and an account of his conversion was sent by the pleased missionary to their magazine at home. Alas, alas !

> " When the devil was sick, the devil a saint would be ;
> When the devil got well, the devil a saint was he ! "

Soon, too soon, he relapsed into his evil courses, and the account of his repentance in the missionary magazine came out to Raiatea just after the performance of some of his most abominable bestialities.

Sept. 15.—The doctor, Louey, and I, escorted by the native pilot, set off in the life-boat to see the " marais," or sacred stones, the last vestiges of the old religion of the country.   The sail along the coast inside the reef was very beautiful. On one side of us the many coloured coral-water in long streaks of green and yellow and purple, bounded by a long snow line of breakers, broken at intervals by fairy-like little islands covered densely with bread-fruit trees, screw palms, and coco-nuts ; beyond, the deep blue sea— bluer than the Mediterranean—looked at through sun spectacles, and on the far horizon the peaks of Huahine mingled with the summer clouds.

On the other side, the beautiful bays, and grand mountains of Raiatea changing every minute as we crept along. The wind was very light, and the heat was awful. I could feel the skin crackling and pealing off my nose; and I must confess, that in spite of the beautiful scenery all around, the subject of my meditations was beer—beer—nothing but beer.

At the end of some seven or eight miles we arrived at our destination, and ran ashore close to an extraordinary little hut, built right out in the sea, and communicating with the land by a plank, perhaps the hermitage of some old priest?

A short walk through the forest brought us to the " marais "—strange places they were; built of enormous slabs of rock or coral, arranged in an oblong shape, and the space inside them filled with shingle and coral, so as to form a platform about eight feet high. I think the largest was about fifty yards long; we scrambled up on to it by help of a tree, and stood on the spot stained with so much blood shed in the *name* of religion. What horrible stories these stones could tell if they could speak!

How strangely universal this devil-worship, this low and blasphemous doctrine of God getting angry with the beings of his creation, and requiring sacrifices to appease him, is.

It was, I suspect, a creation of the priestly mind, that mind that has extended, through all ages, from the earliest times down to Doctor M—; and is so singularly alike at this day all over the world, from the Maori Tohunga to the presbyterian minister. They invented it, first, because they used to get the benefit of the offerings that were presented for sacrifice; secondly, because by representing God as a terrible vengeful monster, that they knew how to manage better than the rest of the world, they got and held their power over the people. This second reason is the main one for keeping up the sacrificial, vengeful, part of Christianity now-a-days, though in the Roman church the first cause is by no means extinct.

Lord! to think what thousands and thousands are paid every year to the priests for " persuading God " to take people's souls out of a horrible place of torture called Purgatory, latitude and longitude unknown.

If a man were to get the true statistics of the amount of money expended in English law courts to obtain justice, and the enormous quantity of men who lived and thrived upon the same, people would cry what a monstrous shame!

What should be said to the thousands of men who live well and make money by professing to make peace between the Omnipotent and Allwise God, and the beings that he, knowing what he was about, I suppose, created. It makes me mad to think of it. All honour to the simple clergyman who devotes himself merely to the care, education, and welfare of his people; he earns his salt as well as any man in the world. It is the priest who sets up for supernatural powers, who claims for himself or his profession some superior share in the favour of the Almighty; and thus works upon the superstitions of the foolish, the ignorant, and the cowardly, that excites my loathing and contempt. When will men have courage and energy to destroy this many-headed hydra? Not for a long, long time, for there is a considerable leaven of fools in this world, and men who have never known freedom cannot feel the vile chains that bind them, and are even afraid of being loosed.

But at least, thought I, a great step has been made in the right direction, and no longer can Samuel hew Agag in pieces *before the Lord!*

What made the human sacrifices of the Society Islands so strangely ghastly and horrible, was the fact that the wretched victim was always chosen from one of certain families, set apart for that special purpose for generation after generation for ever. How this caste originated I do not know. Many of these families used to put to sea secretly in canoes, preferring an almost certain death by drowning or starvation to the terribly uncertain fate that was always hanging over their heads.

When a man came to the priests to beg some heavenly, or rather infernal, favour, they would tell him, either from whim, malice, or some reason best known to themselves, that the God required a human sacrifice, and naming the victim, present the supplicant with the death warrant in the shape of a sacred stone. He hides this carefully somewhere about him, and collecting a few friends, seeks out the doomed man. At last they find him sitting lazily under a tree or mending his canoe, and squatting down round him begin talking about the weather, fishing, or what not. Suddenly a hand is opened — the death-stone discovered to his horrified view. He starts up terror-stricken, and tries to escape — one short furious struggle and he is knocked down, secured, and carried off to the merciless priests. Ugh! it is an ugly picture.

Sometimes these men have succeeded in shaking off their captors, and fleeing to the mountains, have lived and died there unseen and undiscovered.

It was too hot to shiver, but the very shady green quiet beauty of the place made its history the more horrible.

There we saw traces of the great coco-nut eating crabs; they run up the trees, nip off the coco-nuts, and inserting one of their powerful claws into the eye, tear off the husk, and eat the nut. The natives put things like small crinolines on the trees a few feet up to stop their ascent.

Then, after refreshing ourselves with luncheon and coco-nuts, we set off home. Mr. Vivian dined with us and told us a great many interesting things.

Sept. 16.—After luncheon the doctor and I went ashore to bid farewell to Beauty and the Beast, as we call their majesties. But the Beast was away on

political business at Taha; so, after giving Queen
Moé notice to finish her mail for Bora-Bora, we ad-
journed to Mr. Vivian's house. The doctor and Mrs.
V. went into the next room to see a half-caste girl,
who had something the matter with her foot. Meanwhile Mr. V. gave me a discourse on the subject of
half-castes, describing them as the most whimsical,
provoking, inconstant, mendacious, and immoral of
women. Presently Mrs. V. came back, and her husband went out with the doctor to talk medicine. Mrs.
V. sat down with her back to the door that led into
the interior of the house, I being at right angles to
her on the sofa, and we began talking. In the passage behind the door-way some natives were sitting
and staring. Presently appeared the head of the
doctor's half-caste patient, who began smiling and
making little signals of like kind, rather to my confusion under the circumstances. It was almost beyond
the powers of humanity to talk to a female missionary,
and respond to the smiles of a beautiful young lady at
one and the same time. But I couldn't help looking
that way and laughing occasionally, especially as Mrs.
V. was descanting to me at the moment on that young
lady's unusual steadiness and sobriety.

Very soon Mrs. V. perceived that something was
going on behind her, and kept turning sharply round,
thinking to catch the native servants in some impropriety. Whenever she did so Miss Toe dodged out
of sight, which made me grin all the worse. And so

the farce went on till the doctor and Mr. V. returned,
when we took a cordial farewell of the good kind
hearted people, and left them.   As we went down the
steps the missionary made us an earnest, but rather
parsonical, little speech, ending with "you will meet
many dangers before you reach home, but you must
remember that there's a Power above you," &c.   I
felt dreadfully tempted to say that we should either be
providentially saved or providentially drowned, but
refrained from criticizing a speech that was so kindly
meant.

Just as we were going to dinner I got a note from
the queen, saying that the king wanted me to show
him how to fix the gun I had given him, and I went
ashore.   We should have made a strange picture,
Beauty, the Beast, and I, sprawling on the floor of the
birdcage house, putting the gun together, and ex-
plaining the use of its appurtenances by the dim light
of a solitary lantern.   The king wanted to buy my
life-boat, but I did not see it, especially as it would
have cost the greater part of his yearly revenues, and
perhaps caused a rebellion.   The queen asked me to
spend the evening with them, but I foolishly refused
on account of dinner.   If we had done so we should
have seen some fun as Queen Moé's attendants are of
a lively and saltatory disposition.

The captain to-day took the life-boat and sailed
round to examine the channel through the reef, on the
lee side of the island through which we purpose sailing
to-morrow.

Sept. 17.—Mr. Vivian came on board to say good-bye, bringing with him a mat as a farewell present from Queen Moé, their majesties' mail for Bora-Bora, a native bible for me from himself, and some hymn books for the doctor. I gave him a copy of George Herbert's poems as a souvenir. He said that the queen had asked him to ask me whether I would give her one of our "little round pigs," as she expressed it, which of course I did, with many expressions of goodwill. I have often been asked for a photograph on leaving, or, perhaps, a lock of my hair, but never before for "a little round pig." These Society Islands are certainly original places.

Then we got under way, and running down without accident between Raiatea and Bora-Bora, we slipped out of the reef on the leeside of the former island, and stood away for the great peak of Bora-Bora.

P.S. I have since heard that Queen Moé's husband has been shot, and has left her an interesting widow, with only one infantine encumbrance. I deliberated whether or not to go back and propose for her, but reflected that most likely she would have dried her tears on somebody else's shirt-front before I could make my appearance, and that on the whole, perhaps, my over-fastidious relations might object to the connection. So I didn't.

Chapter V.

BORA-BORA.

ORA-BORA at a distance seems split into two, a tower and a steeple; but as we approached, the two blended into one, and one has a ruined cathedral, with a stately grey tower above it. Shattered naves and transepts, and here and there a flying buttress still standing. But such a cathedral was never raised by human hands, for size or beauty. The tower, viewed as it is, seems a good three thousand feet high. The reefs about it are very extensive and dangerous, and we had to keep off a long way to avoid one of them; but being almost entirely wooded, they make a gorgeous fringe at the foot of the grand grey rocks. We had a long work up through the opening, disturbing flying-fish innumerable; but though there were abundance of sea birds of all sorts about, I did not see one sweep down upon them. Amongst the flocks were divers very gurnetty specimens, the motion of whose pectorals was not nearly as pronounced as in the real flying-

fish. We were boarded by a quaint old pilot, the most
curious specimen of his profession ever seen. He
coolly walked about the ship, peering through the
skylights and down the companions, making little
grunts of approbation when anything took his fancy,
and evidently perceiving that the yacht was something
out of the common line. "Are we going all right?"
roared the skipper from the fore-yard as we began to
get into the narrows (and very narrow they were).
"Oh, yes! O'right," answered the old gentleman with
such perfect coolness and indifference that even the
iron-faced Jim burst into convulsive laughter, enough
to break his face. Presentl he condescended to go
forward and give his directions, which he accompanied
with wonderful spasmodic yells that almost incapaci-
tated the sailors with laughter. He had another slight
failing (considered from a nautical point of view). He
could not say "Keep her off!" The nearest he could
get to it was "Keep your duff," which he used instead,
thinking, I suppose, that such a slight difference in
sound did not signify much. This little mistake naturally caused some slight confusion at first, but, fortune
favouring us, we gained our anchorage safely. The
harbour is most magnificently beautiful, overhung by
a mass of rock, three thousand feet high, and looking
in the moonlight as if it was hanging almost over our
heads, and noble basaltic cliffs, standing out from a
perfect cascade of verdure. Nowhere but in these
islands have I ever seen, positively, richly green cliffs.

If one of the smallest, Bora-Bora is most certainly one of the most beautiful, if not *the* most beautiful island we have visited in the South Sea.

Sept. 18.—A walk on shore, to deliver our mails at the missionaries' house. The village was delightfully green and fresh, the bread-fruit, with its magnificent leaves, being very luxuriant. Mr. Pierce has not been long on the island, and has not yet mastered the language, but a few weeks' work may do wonders. As the missionaries invented a good deal of it—certainly all the writing and reading part—it is but fair that they should be able to learn it easily. We had a highly-pleasant stroll along the beach under the cool shade of the trees. The women seemed fairer in complexion than in the other islands, and are fine great animals, apparently averaging ten or eleven stone, and the men are proportionally large. There was a good deal of coco-nut oil being manufactured in old dug-out canoes, a manufacture most decidedly more profitable to the pocket than pleasant to the nose. In our walk we were accompanied with the usual admiring tail of light infantry, and it came into our heads suddenly to turn and go back, whereon they all scattered as if a shell had burst in the midst of them, and one little girl was seized with a most horrible panic, rushing away screaming as hard as she could to the arms of her papa, and refused to be comforted. I am sure I don't know why we should frighten the children; we are anything but pale-faces, and brick-dust-red is as pretty as brown any day.

Mr. and Mrs. Pierce called on board, and also a
flaxen-headed boy, brother to the fair little princes
and princesses at Huahine, and related in some mysterious way to Pomare, Moé, Tamatoa, the King of
Bora-Bora, and all the rest of the South Sea Island
royalties.

Every island, though it possesses a distinct government, is always under a member of one great royal
family, and the relationships are more confusing and
intricate than those of the Bourbons. The king here
is brother to darling Queen Moé of Raiatea; his wife
is the sister of Tamatoa, Queen Moé's husband, Tamatoa is the son of Queen Pomare, who is related to
Queen Moé, who is cousin to Moitea and Mrs. Bran-
don, who are also related to Queen Pomare. The
flaxen-haired children are the children of the Queen of
Bora-Bora, who is daughter or some such thing to
Queen Pomare, and are also cousins to Tamatoa, Moé,
and the King and Queen of Bora-Bora? Can anything
be clearer?

Sept. 19.—*Our* Monday—Sunday in these parts—
and so to church. The said church being a most excellently planned building, capable of receiving five hundred people in comfort and coolness, and thank Heaven
as utterly unlike the popular idea of what a church
ought to be as one could well imagine.

The wall all window, the roof lofty, the shape oval,
and the ends of the white hybiscus rafters, prettily
ornamented with coloured tappa, wrapped round them

K

to conceal their juncture with the wall. The floor was covered with comfortable benches, but the greater number of the female population preferred lounging about on the mat-covered floor, exactly like a herd of great soft-eyed brown seals. They were dressed in the long soft muslin sacque, but the most popular ornament was a soft rough-fringed bathing-towel, with a red border, one end twisted round the neck and the other thrown over the shoulder in a particularly graceful way.

I do not think that I ever enjoyed a church more in my life ; it was really delicious to sit near the door and listen to the wind whistling through those glorious bread-fruit trees, and watch the strange green stemmed silk cotton trees and the quaint huts, and the quaint things going on in and about them, to the land side, and to the other the glorious blue sea, with the white foam of the barrier reef for the edging of the picture. I am the less to be blamed for these distractions, as the service was conducted in " Maori " by a native gentleman in spectacles (spectacles are always great " medicine " in these parts, though even without glasses) and even the missionary was obliged to content himself with giving out the hymns ; the singing was very good indeed, and I am given to understand that they consider themselves *nulli secundus* as far as that is concerned. Their great prima donna was not however in church to-day, being engaged canticling on the other side of the island.

Some of the women were very handsome, and there was a great deal of quiet fun going on here and there. We saw the white hat of the skipper glancing about outside, and once or twice he evidently attempted a slight flirtation through the window, but the native beadle soon settled his hash, going out boldly to him, and bringing him as "meek as a maid" into the sacred edifice, where he sat for the rest of the service looking as if butter would not melt in his mouth, to our great edification.

The babies were charming, jolly, merry little brown things who crawled about the mat-covered floor, playing and crowing, without a squall in a ton of them; the elderly women all *began* to take strict notes of the sermon with a pencil and paper, just as we used to do at school, and I should not much wonder if the greater part of their notes ended as ours used to do. However, there is, I believe, a sort of examination held on the subject once a week, and there is a certain amount of emulation in remembering as much as possible of the sermon.

The people were civil and kindly beyond all praise, and "yer hannering" and hand-shaking was incessant.

After sermon we went up to Mr. Pierce's, to have tea and to meet the king and queen. The title of *Her* Majesty is Taupoa-Wahine. The king is a splendid young fellow, six feet three inches and a half in height, and wonderfully well grown and proportioned, with a well poised, antique looking head, not unlike a male edition of his sister Moé.

Conversation was difficult, as none of the European party could speak Kanaka (or rather Maori) and neither the king nor the queen spoke English. Ultimately we found a means of communication through the former, who had spent three years in France and spoke a remarkably good and idiomatic French. He is a most gentleman-like and intelligent young fellow, with a strong spice of fun in him.

We are given to understand that he is not king in his own right, but merely a species of king-consort, as it were. The queen on the death (?) of her first husband picked up with this young gentleman on his return from France and married him; I think I *did* hear that she had not waited for the death of her first husband, but had simply sent him about his business.

Her Majesty is stout certainly, very stout, and though only twenty-six, looks quite old enough to be the king's mother, but it has been whispered to me that she has lived very *hard,* and that in these parts means something very hard indeed. At tea, she did not shine much in conversation, but philosophically concentrated her faculties on sardines and cake. But Lord! to see how civil we were, and how upright we all sat on our chairs though hard and hot!

We are informed on the "highest" authority that the Bora-Boraborians will eat goats, but will not eat the "long woolly-haired pig," the sheep; which seems strange.

Sept. 20.—A guard of honour from the king to show us round the island, consisting of the king's Portuguese servant (Joe, of course), a very smart fellow, and a fellow pilot, in the shape of a remarkably handsome, intelligent, fine-faced native, who was no less a personage than a full colonel of the king's troops. We had the colonel to show us the way, and Portuguese Joe as an interpreter. He was a most civil and polite man, but from having picked up his English on the beach, always addressed us as "You fellows," which, when done in the most intensely respectful manner, had a certain smack of quaintness in it. However, we made a very pleasant cruize of it, sailing between the island and the barrier reef; the latter, almost uninterruptedly clothed with hybiscus, coco-trees, and iron-wood. But eh! how hot, how hot! with just enough breeze to steal us through the calm water, but not enough to cool us.

To our right soared the grey tower and buttresses, and sheer green cliffs, every turn showing us some new beauty. I think that altogether it is the most magnificently beautiful piece of rock-scenery I have ever seen. The tower seemed utterly inaccessible, but we were told that it has been ascended, God knows how! But these natives have a wonderful power of climbing, developed by their researches after the wild plantain.

We landed on the barrier-reef to lunch, and the old colonel fitting his feet into a kind of noose of green withes, skipped up a tall coco-tree like a remarkably well-preserved old brown grasshopper, without touching the bare stem with anything but his feet and hands. Louey slipped the noose on to his feet and tried it, but active little monkey as he is, he could make nothing of it, and after getting about half way up with extreme difficulty, and barking his shins in the most unpleasant manner, he was compelled to give it up and come down again, ignominiously.

There were a good many small birds amongst the bushes, one of which was a small whistling parrot, with a purple back and white throat, which I am told is the king's favourite gibier.

After leaving Bora-Bora, I was told that there was a sea-bird peculiar to that island and found nowhere else. It builds on the highest cliffs, and carries its young down to the water on its wings. It is a great delicacy, and reserved entirely for the royal table. It is a great pity that we did not know of this before we left the island.

After a lovely sail right round the island, being within the reef the whole time, we reached the yacht late. The colonel and the portingale were given a glass of grog apiece, and P— gave each half-a-sovereign, blushing ingenuously, for it is rather difficult to know how to tip a real live colonel.

Wednesday, 21.—The king and his prime minister

came on board, bringing with them two beautiful
crowns and an ancient native dress, from the queen,
together with the usual boat-load of fruit.   P— presented the king with a revolver, with which, let us
trust, he has shot neither himself nor any one else.

He remained chatting on board all the morning,
and is a very sensible and well-behaved young fellow.
He has the character of being a " good boy " amongst
his people, and really seems to deserve it.   Amongst
other bits of gossip, he told us that when Gilley was
here he practised at an island and mowed down many
coco-trees, to the no small disgust of the natives.

The people are not as well off as they look, which
may be the means of inducing them to introduce some
local industry, as cotton, &c.

When the fruit season is over, they stow the ban-
nanas in great pits, and continue to feed on them till
they are all rotten, a custom which produces much
sickness.

Climbing the cliffs for the faies, generally ends in a
broken neck or two in the course of the year; and no
wonder.

There are very few oranges on the island, so it is
comparatively free from the abominations of orange
rum-drinking.

The doctor went fishing in the reef opening, with
Portuguese Joe.   The fishing as usual amongst the
coral was very poor, and requires much skill and
patience.   One of their ways of fishing is worthy of a

Thames barbel-fisher. They saw off the convex side
of a large spotted cowry, fasten a hook to one end and
a line to the other. They then fill the shell with a
large lump of roasted bread-fruit, and bait with a
smaller lump ; in fact much in the way balls of clay
and worms are used at home. Whilst sitting in the
canoe, something passed us swimming about a foot
under the water, which I took for a turtle, but which
Joe declared to be a sun-fish. I have often seen sun-
fish basking upright in the water, but this one was
swimming, not quite on its side, but at a certain angle
in the water, and the wavy motion of its fins gave it a
very remarkable appearance quite unlike any fish I
have ever seen. Unluckily we had no heavy spear in
the boat or we might easily have secured it. Joe tells
me that about a month ago a very large one was killed
in the harbour, and that it had three live young ones
in it, so much alive that they began to swim as soon
as they were put into the water. I cross-questioned
him on the subject, but he declared that there was no
mistake. There were three live little sun-fishes in the
old one. I do not remember to have heard before
that the sun-fish was viviparous. The flying-fish were
darting about us in swarms, and I had an excellent
opportunity of watching their manner of flying.

Getting wearied of our bad sport, we landed on a
small wooded island, on which is the Windsor Castle
or rather Balmoral of the island, represented by a large
open shed, one end being closed by interwoven palm

leaves. The royal bed was on the mat-covered floor. Two or three mattresses, one on the top of the other, and plenty of blankets neatly tucked over, more for show than use, I should fancy, in this climate. At the bed-head were his personal knick-knacks, gun, accordian, &c.; round the post were hanging numerous coco - nuts of fresh water, the holes being neatly stopped with green leaves. The principal furniture consisted of fishing-tackle of various sorts, fish-spears and long bamboo rods. And here comes the king when wearied by affairs of state, fishing and shooting parrots with his private friends, whilst the queen remains in regal splendour on the main island.

P— took a farewell stroll along the village road under the shade of the beautiful bread-fruit trees, certainly one of the handsomest leaved trees in the world. They make a very little settlement go a very long way here as there is no back to it, the strip of land between the sea and the mountain being very narrow. It is nothing but a long single row of scattered huts, with a clean smooth road between it and the beach, made rather unsafe for riding, by the way it is undermined and filled by the great land crabs. These " broom roads" are quite a characteristic of the Society Islands, and have been formed by the " utilisation of naughtiness" system—all minor improprieties being punished by the penalty of making so many yards of road. I am informed that in old times road-making was carried out in exceeding good company.

Guided by a confused noise of loud singing and screams of laughter to the neighbourhood of the church, we found the greater part of our crew, and the whole of the younger part of the population, playing a kind of foot-ball with round things made of the husks of coco-nuts rolled up tight. Their way of kicking was entirely different to ours, they threw the ball into the air and kicked it with the sole of the foot in the oddest manner. An oddity which was heightened in the case of the young ladies, whose long white dresses were rather in their way and had to be "rather high kilted" for the kick. Then he went and collogued with some workmen who were making a low platform on which to build a house; then sauntered rather sadly through the settlement, thinking how long it would be before he came across such pleasant places and such kindly people again. Most of the folks knew that we were going, and came up to shake hands—men, women, and children—even the mothers held up their brown bambinos to say good-bye, at which most of them howled dismally, almost the only sign of bad taste we have found in the Society Islands. Why the deuce is it that we frighten the babies so? We may not be handsome enough to frighten a horse, but I don't think we are ugly enough to scare a baby.

Heigh, ho! this is the last day in Paradise. After to-morrow we shall see nothing but ugly copper-coloured savages, or dirty-black Fegeans; and then we shall return to sordid, practical, white people, black coals, shirt collars, actions for breach, and all that, growls the disconsolate P.

He went to say good-bye to Mr. Pierce, who was in great tribulation about a divorce case. (In the other islands the native rulers have taken the power of divorce into their own hands; here the missionary most unfairly has to untie his own knots.) And the case was this: two young people had fallen in love with each other, but as usual the parents would not allow them to marry. So they took a canoe, instead of a post-chaise and four, and paddled across to Raiatea, instead of to Gretna Green. King Tomatoa being found in a state which permitted him to understand what was said to him, married them as well as he could for the small sum of two dollars. And home paddled the young pair; but the parents still objected, possibly to the civil nature of the marriage, as thousands do in Europe, and went to the missionary for a divorce, which he very properly refused. Married is married however you are married, and I am of Audrey's opinion, "Faith, the priest was good enough, for all the old gentleman's saying."

The missionary said that he has sent away a quantity of people who came for divorces, and described the subject with an amount of liberality and common sense, which was highly creditable to him. P. tried to comfort him by showing that the frequency of demand for divorce was in itself a sign of improvement in the morality of the people, and that it proved

some idea of fixed affection, when one was demanded
after a slip.   He said, and what he said in Bora-bora
is of equal importance in England, that the first step
in improving the morality of these people must con-
sist in an alteration of the houses, dividing them into
separate apartments, instead of all sleeping together
in one common room as at present.   But he added
that he did not think they were worse than any others
under the circumstances, owing to the impossibility of
secrecy, and the fact of their being nearly all related
in some way or another.

Sept. 22.—Sailed with a light breeze and a heavy
heart, and after an interchange of dips with the royal
standard, stood out of the harbour.

Too much association with white folks has made the
pilot suspicious of evil beyond measure.   First of all
he refused to take any coins which had not the queen's
head on them ; and when this particular was conceded
he demanded to be paid entirely in half-crowns.   On
being presented with a pound of tobacco, he insisted
on opening the paper and counting the sticks.   He
was, however, passing honest, and returned the harbour fees, which by the king's orders had been remitted
in honour to the white ensign.

CHAPTER VI.

TUBAI TROPICAL BIRDS AND LABOUR QUESTION.

 HAT you want do next?" asked charming Queen Moé, of Raiatea. "One thing we want to do, madame, is to shoot boatswain-birds, the pretty white birds with long scarlet feathers, to show at home what lovely things there are out here." "Yes, yes, I know, but why shoot them? Why not catch them with your hands?" To this there was nothing to do but to murmur gently, and try and look as if we wished we could. "Yes," continued Queen Moé, seeing that there was a hitch somewhere; "don't shoot, go to Tubai, and catch them with your hands on the sand; I have often." This sounded strange, but Queen Moé was a person to be believed, and we asked about this island of Tubai, and heard that it was no very great distance from our next island—Bora-Bora.

So, on parting from Bora-Bora, we thought it but a chivalric duty to our beloved Queen Moé, to go in

search of the fairy island where one could pick up
Tropical birds with scarlet tails, as one gathers shells.
I hardly know why, but Queen Moé had made us believe so utterly in her, that had we never found the
island, or had all the birds flown away as soon as they
saw our top-mast-head above the horizon, we should
have believed in the picking-up business all the same.

From Bora-Bora we started with the lightest of airs,
and we had not sailed

> " A league, a league, a league, but barely three,"

when we saw coco-nut trees growing out of the blue
sea, just where Tubai ought to be.   But " looking is
one thing and kissing another," and it was four o'clock
in the afternoon before we reached the island ; we were
very much puzzled as we slided gently onwards by the
look of the sea ahead.   Long lines of apparent surf
showing here and there, which one could almost swear
were produced by coral reefs.   Even from the fore
yard it was very difficult to believe that they were
nothing but the glint of the sun between the clouds—
but it was so.   I suspect that many a " reported reef "
in the South Sea charts owes its existence to the same
cause.

The quantity of sea fowl, as we neared the island,
was immense. Hardly anywhere, either at Nepean
Island, near Norfolk Island, or at Handa in Suther-
landshire, have I seen a greater gathering than there
were here, fishing, fighting, or winging their way home-

wards with the family dinner. I wonder whether in
bad fishing weather the parent bird arrests its own
appetite, in order to save a morsel for the " wee yans "
at home? I should not wonder. I believe sea-fowl
to have very strong family affections, though they care
but little for nests. Their separate squattings, though
they be but on the bare rock, are jealously guarded,
and marked out as the new lands of a colony by the
government surveyor. On two stacks of rock, near
Stackpoole in Pembrokeshire, thousands of sea fowl
appear for two or three days in November, chattering
and screaming and evidently discussing some important question connected with the next year's
nesting time. This decided they all depart, and not a
bird is to be seen near the place till the next spring;
surely they are laying out the sections in time, so as
to prevent a row when the lady birds were housed and
impatient to lay their eggs. Rooks have also somewhat of the same habit. The Island of Tubai was
certainly inviting, though the invitation was rather of
a doubtful nature, being, as far as we could see, a belt
of coco-trees, guarded by a most ferocious surf; we
made an attempt to land, however, in that most hard-
working of boats, the " Fish Fag " or the " Bet of
Billingsgate," so called from her excellent fishing
qualities, and pulled round and round just outside the
break of the rollers, vainly endeavouring to find a passage through. Once or twice there were half propositions made to " ride a roller " and trust to Provi-

dence, but wiser counsels prevailed, and we gave up
the attempt for the night, and consoled ourselves by
getting specimens of the sea-fowl ; now a most painful
subject ; for every one of the rare, curious, and beautiful skins we obtained that night is at the bottom of
the sea.   Some of the birds were so tame that we
could knock them down with the boat's stretchers as
they hovered over us; others, like the grand fork-
tailed frigate bird, gave themselves the airs of falcons
and pursued the smaller terns; not to eat them, but to
eat what they had eaten.   The plaintive shrieks of the
tern when he is being chased, indicative of his agony
at the prospect of having to give up his own hard-
earned dinner, or the supper he is bearing to his
starving nestlings, are heart-rending.   He generally
has to do it, however.   One day I myself saw a curious
thing : a frigate bird was hard pressing a small tern,
and would soon have had possession of the result of
his day's fishing, when another larger bird, entirely of
a different species—interfered and drove off the pirate,
flying away afterwards on his own affairs with all the
consciousness of having done a good action.

I really believe that birds have some sense of right
and wrong.   I remember once on Exmoor seeing two
small cock chickens commencing a fight, which was
speedily stopped by an old matronly duck coming
between them and bringing them to order by tweak-
ing billsful of feathers out of each.   I avenged one
tern by slaying his persecutor, and was surprised to

find that he was a much smaller bird than he looked; the great breadth of the wing and the long swallow tail aiding the deception.

The brilliancy of the green of the trees on the white coral bank, and the purple and crimson of the evening sky are not to be described, at least by me. After a long and fruitless pull we returned to the schooner, and hove to for the night with six Society Islands in sight.

Friday, Sept. 23. Still bobbing about this tantalising ring of coco-nuts, but apparently as far off from picking up tropic birds, like shells, as ever. At last we descried a big white flag, and with the aid of the telescope, saw a group of men about it, who, by various motions and wavings, evidently desired to attract our attention. Pulling for the place, we found two groups of brown men placed on each side of a narrow crack in the reef, not much wider than the boat, and a big rock in the centre, up and over which the surf was boiling in a most unpleasant way. It looked a very nasty place; but as the men signalled to us to come, we backed a little till a big roller came in. "Give way, men, all!" and on his back we went, with a vengeance! steered deftly into the very eye of the crack. The boat was seized instantly on both sides by our brown friends, who lugged her into the shallow water before the next roller could break, and dragged her across the reef some two hundred yards, picking out the deeper spots amongst the coral till, her poor

L

old nose rested safely on the real beach of pure white sand. A jovial set our friends were. Brown savage islanders, who were civilized and nice, as all savage islanders are. I don't mean the savage island of the story books, but the savage island of the Admiralty chart; the island where they ran at Captain Cook "like wild boars." There was one Penguin Island woman amongst them, who owned to have eaten human flesh in the days of her youth and innocence. I believe this is rather a rare case, as "long pig" is generally "tapu" for the chiefs and warriors.

These savage islanders are a pleasant-looking and cheery people, not unlike Maltese, but not nearly so well grown or handsome as the Society Islanders. Their islands being over populated, they are willing to emigrate as workmen, and they are to be found wherever plantation labour is required in the Pacific. Here they are paid twenty-four dollars a year and found in everything. There is no doubt but that an immense amount of this labour can be procured, if the confidence of the people is once gained, a far more paying way in the end than by using fraud and brutality.

At their head we found Mr. Blackett, a Nova-Scotian, who rents the island from the King of Bora-Bora, for the purpose of making coco-nut oil. He received us with the greatest kindness, and led the way across the coco-studded belt of coral rock to his establishment, situated close to the edge of the inner

lagoon, for Tubai is a real "Atoll," a circular reef,
enclosing a lovely lake within it. I should think that
a walk of a quarter of a mile brought us to his place,
the principal building of which was a large and comfortable house, principally built of interwoven palm
leaves. Within it was roomy and airy, and contained
all sorts of luxuries, clean beds, good furniture, and a
fair stock of books; and moreover with many nice
brown women and girls hanging about, well mannered, clean, and well dressed—indeed remarkably
so—really *nice* people. Without there was a wealth
of animal life—gigantic pigs of the purest English or
Chinese breeds, too fat and warm to do more than
wink, dogs, cats, and fowls, all tame and kindly.
You could not make the most trivial remark to a
passing cat without her putting her tail erect into the
air, rubbing herself against your legs, and answering
with a kindly mew. I will not insult Mr. Blackett by
calling his establishment "patriarchal," that is, if the
present Arab be a type of the patriarchs, which is
more than likely. I will only say that it is what a
patriarchal establishment *ought* to have been.

The working stock consisted principally of a wee
steam-engine, which drove one or more iron heads,
studded with projections, to which were held the cleft
coco-nuts, grinding down the "meat" into pulp most
rapidly. This pulp, placed in long canoe-like troughs,
went through private processes of its own, and then
was squeezed into palm oil. At least, that is the best

description I can give. I do not feel justified in revealing trade secrets.

After inspecting the pigs, talking to the dogs, and colloguing with the cats, we went down to the lagoon, a nearly circular sheet of water, most beautifully blue or green, according to the depth, which is reported to have altered sensibly during the last few years. We embarked in the whale boat, pulled by the larky, laughing, savage islanders, who were as full of fun as they could hold, and even more, and after a row of some two miles, landed on a white spit of elevated coral sand, with a few coco-trees and scrubby bushes scattered about it. Through a depressed bit we could see the surf flashing and foaming over the very spot we had thought of landing on the night before, and very glad indeed we were that we changed our intention.

The savage islanders and the rest landed, and immediate skylarking began, in a manner which showed that the relationships between employer and employed were on a good and kindly footing. For our part, not believing in our Queen Moé as implicitly as we ought to have done, we began shooting the tropic birds as they flew over us; but we soon gave it up, for two reasons. First, that we found that if we got a rocketter, the chances were ten to one that we cut *the* scarlet feathers out of his tail; and secondly, because we discovered that by diligent peering under the bushes, we might pick up as many live uninjured specimens

as we liked. I never saw birds tamer or stupider,
which tameness or stupidity may be accounted for by
the extreme smallness of their brain, which is really
not larger than that of a sparrow. They sat and
croaked, and pecked, and bit, but never attempted to
fly away. All you had to do was to take them up,
pull the long red feather out of their sterns, and set
them adrift again. Queen Moé was right. On Tubai
you may pick up tropic birds as easily as a child picks
up storm-worn shells on the sea-shore.

It was really no small comfort to be able to get
specimens of this beautiful bird without betraying
their confidence by shooting them from the schooner.
Small-brained as they are, they are gifted with an
extraordinary amount of inquisitiveness, particularly
in the early morning. As we bowl along before the
flashing trade-wind we hear a few harsh screams, and
up come a pair of "Bosens" with their bright scarlet
tail feathers glowing in the morning sun. They make
two or three sweeps around us, evidently comparing
notes, and then away into the deep blue, on their own
private affairs. They fish generally like the tern, to
whom I suspect they are cousins germain; but they
have a way, sometimes, of hovering perpendicularly,
with the bill pressed against the breast, that I have
never observed but in one other bird, the black and
white kingfisher of the Nile. When the "Bosen" has
sighted his prey in this position he turns over in the
deftest manner, and goes down straight as a gannet,

up to his neck, no farther, and remounts for a fresh hover. I have never had the good fortune to see the white-tailed Phaeton fishing, often as I have looked for him. Indeed, I have rarely met him out at sea at all. The finest I have seen were hanging about the high cliffs of the Society Islands, and I do not exaggerate when I state that I have seen more than one with a glorious waving white tail feather, two good feet long though the bird itself was not much larger than a black-headed gull. What they do with their tails when they feed, passes my comprehension.

Not only did we find full grown tropic birds but we found their eggs and young. The former about the size of a hen's egg, prettily splashed with reddish brown, laid on the bare sand, under a bush. The latter really handsome creatures, about the size of a herring gull, beautifully marked with black and white (like a falcon). The bill at this stage of their existence is black, not red. When you find your young friend under a bush, he is ensconced in a small basin of coral dust, without any nest at all, and his surroundings show him to be a cleanly thing. When you come upon him suddenly he squalls and croaks, and wabbles about, and is as disconcerted as a warm city man when you try to drive a new idea into him, unconnected with money. But he sticks stoutly to his dusty cradle, and never attempts to escape, saying plainly enough, " My mother told me to stop here till she brought me my supper, and here I am going to stay."[1]

We gleaned a few specimens for stuffing and two to be tamed by pretty Miss Esther, who I fancy could tame most things; and collecting our savage island crew paddled back to the settlement, mightily contented at having solved a question which had troubled us for some time.

As we went back an opening in the reef was shown us through which a small vessel *might* enter; yes, she *might* but how could she get out again?

There is a small noisy parrot on the island, like those at Bora-Bora and Huahine, but we did not get a specimen. Mr. Blackett tells me of a small woodpecker who lives in holes in the trees, and kills his fowls, knocking them off their perches at night with his sharp bill. A theory was started that it was attracted by the glitter of the fowl's eye in her darkness. A pretty enough theory, but do not fowls shut their eyes when they go to sleep? And have I not heard something about their putting their heads under their wings?

I suspect this woodpecker to be a kingfisher.

---

[1] Though fairly enough deserving the name of tropical bird, the phaeton sometimes is found outside the tropics. We saw our first solitary flying to the W. in lat. 28·27, long. 150·15. Our last cape pigeon was in lat. 32·34, long. 151·02, and our last albatros, in lat. 35·48, long. 159·09.

There are. two glorious *real* Labrador dogs here,
very different from the clumsy cross-bred brute we
call a Newfoundland. "Bosen" and Tray, or as
pretty Miss Esther prettily pronounced it, Te-rai, are
up to any amount of lark, and have even invented one
for themselves; this is, fish-hunting in the shallow
water on the reef; one of them starting the game, and
the other pouncing on it as it shoots past him, turn
and turn about.

After an excellent and merry dinner, which I remember included more hard boiled eggs than had
ever been seen at once before, we wended "homewards" to the sea shore; on our way being shown a
stone as big as a cricket ball, firmly embedded in the
stem of a palm tree, a good three hundred yards from
where the surf is breaking at present, showing what
fearful rollers occasionally burst on the reef. After
swapping libraries to a certain extent, for Mr. Blackett
is "death on books," we parted with a hearty farewell, he to his house, and. we, away over the blue sea,
laden with pretty coco-nut cups, scraped as thin as
the finest china—eheu!

I object most strongly against making personal remarks, particularly anonymously, not being a weekly
reviewer; but for the life of me I cannot help saying
that we left on the island a gentleman who, from the
way he shut one eye and smiled, put me wonderfully
in mind of a very distinguished ex-colonial governor.
I mention this fact, so well-known in North America,

because I want to air a theory I have formed on the subject, and which has cost me much thought and reflection.

One of the best ways of discovering the use of an organ or custom, apparently useless amongst the higher animals, is to trace them back amongst the lower, till you come to the point where they are indispensable. And something in this way I attempted to solve the mystery of the shutting one eye, when you were particularly on your guard. After running through a world of curious theory, I came at last to the Skye-terrier, who, when he has a difficult matter on foot (connected with rats and such like), always tucks up one leg and goes on the other, thus reserving one fresh and sound for any unexpected contingency. And so it is with this eye-closing business. The crafty Yankee closes one eye, because he knows that the human eye becomes fatigued after a time, when it has been peered into to see what is going on in the brain.

Think of what a comfort and strength it must be to shut the wearied one, and open the other, brilliant and flashing, just as your adversary has tired both his or hers!

Some folks, lawyers and ladies especially, take to spectacles for much the same purpose, and get an unfair advantage over you, looking into your eyes without letting you look into theirs. I know a very distinguished man, who is so perfectly aware of this that he keeps his eyes fixed on the ceiling, in a rapt and devotional manner the whole time he is conversing with you.

Let me warn future travellers that this island must not be confounded with one of nearly the same name in the Austral-group, the island on which Fletcher Christian, of the " Bounty," intended to settle when he left Tahiti. We passed this Tubai, but landed not, as the " South Sea Directory " states that " the harbour inside is unsafe, and the anchorage outside insecure and rocky, with bad holding ground." A pleasant place !

By the way, the said Fletcher did good service in his way by landing here again with four hundred pigs and fifty goats and a native of Bora-Bora. However, his party could not agree with the Tubaiese, and left in 1789.

It has a high, broken, and peaky aspect, and doubt-less contains many a lovely gorge and glen for the enjoyment of the man who is contented to be left there. As it is marked as a French island, it might be worth the while to stop there to study the French mission-aries, who have the credit of performing infinitely more fantastic tricks than even our own, which is saying a good deal.

Wednesday, Sept. 28.—In the morning awoke by the singing of native songs, and going on deck found that we were close to a " labour " schooner, with 121 men, women, and children on board, from the Hervey and Cooke groups, bound for Tahiti.

Certainly, judging from appearances, nothing could be more happy and agreeable than their position; and if most general singing be a proof of ease and well-doing, they possessed both in a high degree.

I hear, however, that these people *always* sing, happen what may, after they have left their islands for a day or two, however rough the parting.

The worst of it is that they engage themselves to work—that is, such work as they have been accustomed to at home, an easy hour or two in the cool morning, and the rest of the day spent in the *dolce far niénte*. I am afraid that when they find they have to labour through the long hot day, they often wish themselves quit of their bargain.

Still I think that this shifting the inhabitants of these islands from one to another is a good thing if properly done, and is in fact the *only* way of civilising some of the more savage tribes. Moreover, they *must* emigrate from some of the islands, or starve.

It is, however, a great pity that there is not some strict supervision exercised over the " labour vessels " flying the British flag. There can be no doubt that there are great outrages committed by reckless ruffians, and revenged on the next arrival, innocent or guilty.

It was in consequence of his having landed at Eromango after an outrage of this sort, that stout hearted Williams was killed, and by far the greater number of massacres of whites in the South Sea are produced from this cause. And no wonder! I have had a vessel pointed out to me in Auckland harbour whose captain, I was assured, was in the habit of running down the canoes at sea, in order to pick up the natives and sell them. And this was considered rather an exceptional bit of humanity than otherwise.

A tenth part of the money spent in trying to prevent the Imaun of Muscat supplying himself with labour from Africa, which is no earthly business of ours, would keep up a smart little gunboat or two in these seas, which would be quite enough to prevent all the mischiefs of the labour trade as at present carried on. This really is our business, as the ships fly our flag and our fellow citizens employ the labour.

It is of no earthly use a big frigate popping in now and again into one or two of the largest harbours. We want a small, smart boat, able to go anywhere. There are really very few ruffians employed in the trade, and were these rooted out and a set of regulations laid down like those relating to emigrants, for instance; and, moreover, consuls appointed who understood the native languages, the trade might be made a very great blessing to all parties.

I should insist on the consuls being well up in native languages, for ignorance on that head makes him absolutely worse than useless when he has to certify freshly imported labour. There is no want of men in these seas perfectly capable of filling the office, though few so thoroughly up in the matter, as our consul at Samoa, who has, however, but little of this sort of thing to do.

I was told of a case in which the consul, with wild gestures, lugs the newly imported "labour" by the arm about the office as a means of rendering *à la muette de portici*, "Were you taken away by violence?" and asks the question, "Were you engaged for one year?" by holding up his forefinger interrogatively. As no native would ever dream of saying anything but "yes" to a white consul, he gets answers which perfectly satisfy him, if not the unfortunate devil who has gone to the risk and expense of importing the men.

And these planters really require some protection. Think of a case in which a vessel is seized by a British man-of-war for being overladen. The natives not sent home again, but handed over to the acting British consul, who distributes them amongst his friends, to work on their estates for nothing during the trial of the case at Sydney. The case is given against the captain of the man-of-war, who is promoted and returns home.

The men whom he took are now working on the estates of the consul's friends, and will be made to do so till their time is out. And the unfortunate importer, who gained his case and sold his schooner to defend it, is beggared without the possibility of redress; the brother of the late consul still brutally refusing to let him have even the last remains of the labour he has paid so dearly for.

I believe that I have understated the iniquity and

injustice of this affair. And remember that the victim here was no long-shore loafer, no square-gin-drinking "beach comber," but a man of birth and education; and who would, in all possibility, have made his fortune had he not had the luck to win a lawsuit against a philo-negro captain of the navy.

There would not be the slightest difficulty in obtaining labour were confidence re-established between the white man and the brown. They are often willing enough to come; I can say that in the course of our cruizing in the South Seas we might have picked up any number of men. In the Isle of Pines, I remember, that we had to force them out of the boat, so anxious were they to take a cruize with us.

I wish the thing could be done, but I fear there is some adverse influence at head-quarters which does not think that it is in its interest that affairs should be put on a good footing, or that the islands should be colonised. I think I know what it is, and why it acts, and recognise its wisdom—that is as far as its own interests are concerned. But I have no wish to poke my head into a hornet's nest—and *such* hornets! the real bilious black and yellow breed.

Chapter VII.

RARITONGA.

Friday, Sept. 30, 1870.

SIGHTED Raritonga, and knocked about all night.

Saturday, Oct. 1.—Beat up to Raritonga. A long ridge of beautiful mountain, wooded right up its precipitous side. The cliffs and pinnacles of black trap rock, sharply defined against the clear blue sky. The reef is fringing, not detached, at least on this side.

To our astonishment we made out a large ship, standing off and on under the lee of the land. As we drew nearer we hoisted our white ensign, which she did not seem to like, for she first made sail, and then shortened again, as if uncertain what to do. Then she hoisted a colour at the peak, which we could not well make out, but which looked American, and then, as if she had made up her mind what part to act, hauled it down again, and run the Peruvian flag to the mast-head. As we neared her we saw that her decks were swarming with infinite yellow faces of the most decidedly Chinese type, which increased our be-wonderment. But it was no business of ours, though she evidently thought it was. We hove to and went on shore, where we were greeted with the greatest kindness and hospitality by the missionary and his wife; also with equal warmth by every man, woman, and child we met: evidently the Raritongians are a fine and genial race.

Sunday, Oct. 2. After many deliberations and doubts, we were persuaded by the jolly old pilot to trust the yacht to the keeping of the harbour of Raritonga. "Safest harbour in the world." It may be so; but still I wonder how those suspicious-looking ship's bones came to be scattered so thickly on the coral just at the entrance? It is a curious place, and I fancy few would take it for a harbour at all, were they not assured of the fact by the proper authorities. Unlike most of the island harbours, you do not enter by a deep and narrow break in the reef, into a snug and secure lagoon, but into a mere saucer-like depression in the reef itself, which really looks infinitely more dangerous than the open sea. We calculated that it was about twenty to one that you were wrecked going in, fifty to one that you were wrecked going out, and even chances that you were utterly cast away inside. However, inside we got—(where could not the captain take the "Albatross?" wet grass is enough for her!)—and divers performed the most marvellous submarine feats, their brown bodies wriggling and kicking far down below in the clear water as they tied knots and passed hawsers through the rings of the mooring anchors. Of these we had plenty; in fact, when we were made fast, the poor old dear looked like an astonished spider placed in the centre of some one else's web. We had the pleasure of knowing that every wavelet that seethed in over the reef chafed one or other of our warps against the sharp coral edges; a process by no means conducive to strength or security. One really felt like a nesting coot in a flood. However, there we were; and if we were wrecked we were not likely to be drowned, so we accepted the situation and began our prowls on shore.

As in the north world so in the south world; civilisation and manners tend from east to west. As we drop down from island to island in the ever fresh trade wind to the westward, we become sensible of an ever-increasing want of finish, a provincialism, in fact, amongst the islanders. They are still very charming, but their mouths and noses are altering. The face generally is growing coarser, and one begins to sniff the negro taint from far-distant Papua.

The Raritongian would, however, most indignantly deny the sniff; and indeed it is but a faint one. Nor would he for a moment admit the lessened civilisation. For not only has Raritonga a newspaper printed in pure Raritongese, and therefore highly available to the general reader, but she has a real stone church—a church as the churches of Britain ! Oh, that church ! that church ! that vile black and white stone abomination, paralysing one of the most beautiful bits of scenery in the world ! Truly, indeed, may it be said, with horrible sarcasm, to be like too many of the churches at home. For sheer blank unmitigated discomfort and ugliness, I will back it against the most civilised nonconformist ranting-box in England, Scotland, or even Wales. Upon my word, I feel inclined to say that this most intolerable and pretentious building is the only really and truly hideous thing I saw in the South Seas. Did I think that there was the slightest chance of those who agreed to and subscribed for its erection ever reading this, I would launch out into still more truculent abuse. The thing is an abomination, and the man who designed it ought to be grated slowly to pulp against its black and doleful walls. It has even glass windows ! Glass windows in this climate ! Surely there was a glazier brother in the connection and the thing was a job—a job more iniquitous than the employment of Raphael for the decoration of the Vatican ! Galleries, too ! Good Lord, as if they had not half the island to build on were they so minded. No ! there were galleries in their own little narrow sphere at home, and so there must be galleries here. What makes the matter worse is, that the native churches in the South Sea Islands are generally perfect in their way. Large and cool, low-eaved, with a wall nearly all window, for the crisp sea-wind to whisper in and help the congregation to sleep.

Not only is this church hideous, but the very church-yard is utterly detestable in every respect. I do not like to say too much on the subject, but surely those horrible tombs were not built without some reason; they must have cost the early converts something somewhere. Pah! it makes me hot to think on't.

If the same man who built the church built the mission-house and laid out the grounds around it, hanging would be infinitely too good for him, for the latter are as remarkable for beauty and arrangement as the former is for their absence. One glimpse of that most lovely mission-house would make the Duke of Devonshire let Chiswick fall into instant ruin from mere hopelessness of competing with it.

We visited the church, or rather attended afternoon service, in company with the king, a well-dressed and particularly gentlemanlike man, who was kind enough to come on board with his prime minister, to invite us to seats in the "Pew Royal." The congregation we thought more attentive than any one we had seen in these seas, but it was really painful to see both men and women dressed according to the lowest style of European "go-to-meeting." Instead of those long, delicate, graceful "saques," of which we have become so fond, and head-dresses of fresh flower wreaths or neat arrowroot crowns, the women wore detestable waisted European garments, with vulgar and tawdry

hats and feathers, which utterly destroyed all their
native ease and grace. Where on earth did the earlier
missionaries pick up that curious idea of the necessary
identity of piety and ugliness ?

In front of us sat a grave and reverent elder, with
the most broad church cut of black coat and white tie,
and a mighty pair of spectacles, looking exactly like a
very bilious Scotch precentor.   He kept his eyes
steadily fixed on his hymn-book during the singing,
and bore his "burden" by keeping up that prolonged
humming drone, so popular as an accompaniment in
these seas : a harmless paganicity, for which I suspect
he would have been "cut off from the connection" in
some of the neighbouring islands, or at least have been
mulcted in hard dollars.   This "hum" is by no means
unlike the drone of a bagpipe, and I suppose answers
the same purpose, whatever that may be.   I have an
indistinct recollection of attending a cottage dance,
somewhere in the Highlands, long, long ago ; when,
for want of better music, one man played the Jew's
(or jaw's ?) harp, and two or three others kept up a
prolonged monotonous nasal drone, very like that of
my friend in the front benches. It is here by no means
an unpleasant noise, as they manage to give it a metallic resonancy which no "Pakeha" or "Papelangi"
organs could ever imitate.   It is something like the
drum of the emu, or the answering note of the wekka,
indefinitely prolonged.

After service, having shaken hands with a good half

of the congregation as they filed before us, we sauntered up to the mission-house; past a mighty sacred
tree, overthrown by the hurricane, lying like a prostrate idol, and concerning which there is many a
strange legend; past a cricket-ground in course of
preparation, in which, if the natives take to the game,
there will in time be formed an eleven hard to beat;
and so—through lovely and well-kept grounds, on the
edges of which the bushes were blossoming with pretty
brown faces peeping at the strangers—up to the cool
verandah.

One does not wish, Yankee-like, to gossip about
the private affairs of those who kindly admit the
stranger within their gates. Let us merely state that
the warm-hearted sensible Highland lady and gentleman who represent the mission at Raritonga are very
different people from the typical missionaries of the
South Pacific.

By no means believing that they can wash the
black-a-moor (or rather brown-a-moor) white by a
sudden application of Calvinistic white-wash, they try
to make him as good a brown-a-moor as they can, and
their labour has certainly not been in vain. How
easily this white-wash cracks and peels off may be
seen or heard by any one who keeps his eyes or ears
open. One fact which we heard from a "high personage" rather tickled us. A short time ago a native
drum was brought to Raritonga from one of the neighbouring islands, and the very moment the first finger

taps were heard, all the girls, down to the wee chits
ten or eleven years old, began to wriggle and squirm
like so many galvanized frogs; showing plainly that
the old dancing blood still ran in their veins, and that
even its peculiar forms of expression had not been
forgotten. In fact, the newer missionaries are quite
wise enough to see that the natives do not care to
"let them know everything;" and the quiet, decently-
behaved visitor may see a good many things which
the others wisely blink.

The older missionaries reported (and possibly still
report) that Christianity has utterly stamped out all
these pleasant paganisms. The newer ones and *we*
know perfectly well that it has done nothing of the
sort, nor will it do so for a very long time to come.
The Gawazee of Egypt and the Gitana of Spain have
kept to their old dances, in spite of priest or mollah,
for many an age, and so it will be here. If any real
improvement is to take place, I should propose that
each ball should be attended by the missionary and
his wife. I will warrant that under these auspices
any evil element will soon be eliminated, and the
native dance be rendered as decorous as the quadrille.
What right has an English or French missionary to
say to a whole race, "You shall not dance, you shall
not sing, you shall not smoke, under the possible
penalty of eternal damnation in the next world, or the
certain loss of dollars in this? He dares not preach
the same doctrine in Europe, or even if he does he

cannot help feeling that all he gains is the ridicule of
the sensible and the applause of fools. As I said
before, let the missionary and his wife encourage
decent dancing by their presence, and the lower form
of that healthy and natural amusement will soon be
unknown.

Seated in the pleasant verandah, enjoying the cool
green of the English grass lawn, the only one worth
the name in the islands, and possibly smoking a cigar,
we were joined by two native gentlemen, dressed in
the most correct black coat and white choker (literally *choker* in this climate), a vile taste and a ridiculous, which I hope may soon give way to something
better. I suppose that in the older times the converts, when thus dressed, supposed that they were
approaching the image of their demi-god, the missionary. I think that I have observed in these
regions that the farther from " the establishment " the
more clerical the rig. The attire in which I believe
one noble true-hearted man—a real bishop—sometimes addresses his good words to the savage heathen
of Melanesia would scandalize all Dissenterdom;
though 'tis for the most part a time-honoured garment,
and, moreover, in his case, a comely and well-fitting
one. Of course the newer and more rational missionaries dress as suits the climate and, I think, their
profession. Why a minister of light and purity
should dress in garments more suited in colour to the
worship of the devil himself I could never make out.

One of our visitors was an honest soul, and on our host producing some grated kava in a bottle, he immediately recognized it, and so we experimented on him at once by giving him a tablespoonful and a half in a tumbler of water. He said that it was just enough to make him comfortable, though as far as I saw it had no appreciable effect on him,—not more, certainly, than a glass of beer or sherry would have on one of us. He might have fallen asleep, however, at afternoon service for anything I know to the contrary. Our other friend, though outwardly white-bearded and venerable, was, I fear, a humbug. On being shown the kava, he gazed upon it with lack-lustre eye, as a thing unknown and void of all interest, and listlessly demanded its name. On being pressed, he confessed to have heard of such a thing amongst the unregenerate in his hot youth, but for *his* part—oh, dear no!

As both we and his friend were rather piqued at this assumption of superior purity, we shifted the subject to the cheerful one of cannibalism, and demanded of him, categorically, whether, at a former period of his existence, he had, or had not, with his own hands, cooked a fellow-sinner? He confessed that he had, but denied that he had ever tasted his own cookery. A likely tale, quotha!

Had it not been for the introduction of pigs and other animals, it is possible that cannibalism might have existed here to this day. The pigeons are being rapidly thinned out by the rats, who are far better

tree-climbers, even in England, than is generally supposed. The dogs, which I believe they had before
the arrival of the Europeans, and which Dr. Gräfe
tells me are specifically distinct from those of Europe,
were mere dainties for the chiefs, and flesh must be
had. By the bye, it is whispered that even in
civilised Raritonga bow-wow is to this day by no
means an unpopular dish, but it is not polite to talk
about it. As in Spain, you eat what is given you,
and ask no questions, though the claws in your plate
may put you in mind of Ponto or grimalkin, as the
case may be.

Amongst other civilisations, the missionaries have
introduced photography, to the no small marvel of the
natives. My white-bearded friend laughed loud and
long when he was told that his beard would return to
its pristine blackness on being dipped into that
shallow dish of clear transparent fluid. He tried it,
however, and the missionary was exalted into the
seventh heaven of conjurordom. The case of a young
lady, however, ended not so happily. She dipped
her pretty finger-tips into the innocent-looking fluid
in the " yellow room," thinking no evil. But on
emerging into the blazing sunlight, her fingers began
to develope into blackness still deeper and deeper, till
she burst into a flood of tears, fully persuaded that she
was going to the devil in some new fashion, for which
she had not been prepared.

Gossiping thus in the verandah, we looked out into

the blue offing, and saw the mysterious barque still hanging about, some fourteen hundred tons burden, and reported to be laden with Cochin Chinese. Rather an odd cargo, and looking as if the French had been bustling up in those regions.

The captain gives one account of her antecedents, and the mate another, which most clearly proves that the captain is a liar; but the captain has got the best of the argument, by simply clapping his mate into irons till he agrees with him, a straightforward course, and one highly likely to produce unity. The Peruvian (heaven or the other place only knows why) wants to shoot his semi-celestial rubbish on to the island, and to sail away with a clear ship. As there are several hundred Cochinese, and Raritonga is none too large for its present population, the chiefs do not see it in the same light, and if the Peruvian persists, there will be a fight. He is reported to have tried to wreck his ship three times on the reef, in order to settle the question easily. People do free and easy things in these seas; and piracy, kidnapping, and murder, are not utterly unknown. Hence grave doubts as to the captaincy and ownership of the good barque " Dolores Urgarto."

Since the above was written, news has reached England of the burning of the doubtful Peruvian barque " Dolores Urgarto," with five hundred coolies, during a voyage between Macao and Peru. *Captain and crew* (with one exception) *saved of course.*

That we went on board the yacht this evening was entirely our own fault, for the missionary put his whole establishment at our disposal with the most generous and unfeigned hospitality. But when one has been seeing things all day, one likes to think them over in the evening at home; and a home our kaurie-lined, green leather cushioned cabin has become to us, both from lapse of time and old associations.

A young English gentleman staying on the island sauntered with us down from the mission-house to the schooner, piloting us through a network of narrow paths cut through a dense thicket of bananas, guavas, cocos, and coffee-bushes, which seems to have been laid out expressly for a flirting ground. There was always a new path up which to turn if any one, or rather two, saw you coming, which, indeed, this evening seemed to indicate the existence of a perfect maze or labyrinth of paths. The pretty native huts were closely sheltered in the bushes, and numbers of women emerged from them and greeted us kindly. One gushing young thing, after squeezing —'s fingers, kissed them tenderly, and then *fugit ad salices*, which a beach man would translate, "cut into the coffee-bush." She fled alone!

The question of the queer Peruvian is settled. He is to have water and vegetables, and then to depart to his own place, wherever that may be. So there will be old floating of tubs of fresh water to him over the bar to-morrow.

In the evening, about eight o'clock, we heard a noise, as of one beating with a stick an unfortunate kettle, to which he bore a personal grudge. We supposed it to be a species of curfew bell; and deciding that Sunday was over, we caught some beautifully marked file fish, and another species, a "perfect love," with regular creamy white stripes on a brilliant scarlet ground.

The people on shore struck us as a shade darker than the Society Islanders, and some of the women have a slightly Chinese oblique-eyed expression about them. Spanish, as talked by our Peruvian friend, they do not like. "Like oui-oui (Frenchmen), talkee plenty too much with fingers." They consider Raritongese to be the first of languages, and after that— some way—the English. They are evidently full of fun, though possibly of a different kind to ours; but then, who can translate humour.

"Well, good night, old fellow!"

Monday, Oct. 3. About twelve o'clock, a pleasant English-speaking chief came on board, to conduct us to the king, who we supposed was going to present us with the usual complimentary present of bananas and coco-nuts. We sauntered along the beach towards his house, taking and giving kindly salutations and hand-shakings at each step, till we reached our destination, a long, low, one-storied whitewashed building, with a cool and roomy verandah running along its whole front. It was raised, some two or three feet from the ground, on a substantial stone basement, and was embosomed in all kinds of beautiful shrubs, and overshadowed in front by tall coco-palms. A straight white coral sand path led from the door down to the garden gate, which opened on to the sea beach. When we arrived, instead of being greeted by enthusiastic crowds, we found the place bare, except of some of the looser sort, who were evidently mere spectators. However, our chief gave us a chair apiece, on each side of the door, and then went his way, leaving us, like a pair of idols, guarding the sacred threshold. Now and then a stray native came up and shily worshipped us, retiring immediately to squat in the shade, but still gazing reverently, but that was all. And if real idols do not have a livelier time of it than we had, I do not care much for the profession. Still we waited patiently, as beseemed us, not knowing what might happen should we descend from our pride of place.

After a time, there approached us from the right hand path a marvellous old woman, with hair as white as snow, and leaning on a long staff, bowing low and reverently at every step. P— descended to greet her, on which she, snatching her straw hat from her white locks, seized his hand, and actually "mumbled" it with delight. I never saw a more darling old lady! She is a woman with a great history, being no less than the very one who placed the first (native) teachers under the historical tree, now to be seen in the mission garden, and mounted guard over them the livelong night. Even now, wreck as she is, she has a grand granite look about her which makes it easy to believe the tale of her early heroism. After embracing P— she wagged her head at the younger folk, gave a series of orders which no one regarded, and subsided majestically at the foot of a palm tree.

There was inflicted on us a sharp, clever, conceited prig of a man (for there are brown prigs as well as white ones, and even *better*) who had spent five years in England, and who was married to a half-caste Corsican, a jovial soul, who had evidently had a glorious figure once, but now fallen into that crummy state so much deplored by Mr. Bailey. Verily, there be strange mixtures in these seas !

To while away the time we peeped into the house, and found that it consisted of two fair-sized rooms, separated by a passage, opening straight through into the field beyond. The rooms were principally furnished with beautiful mats, and seemed rather reception than living rooms, having but few signs of domesticity about them. Indeed we fancied that this building plays the part of St. James's to the real Buckingham Palace.

Another thing which helped the time to pass away was the contemplation of a young girl who, mounting on the boss formed by the aerial roots of a coco-palm, had fitted her lithe back and limbs into the curve of the stem in the most graceful manner. We agreed

that we had never seen a more lovely study for a
sculptor.

After a time appeared a small procession formed by
our missionary friends and the king, who was dressed
carefully in black; he was attended by his ministers,
and there were warm and kindly greetings on all
sides.

Gradually the open space under the trees began to
fill with natives; the women, to our great comfort
were dressed in pretty white sacques instead of those
vile waisted gowns which they sported yesterday.
Gradually, also, the verandah began to fill with the
aristocracy of the place; amongst whom were admitted
the doubtful Peruvian skipper, a small, sharp, intelligent man, speaking excellent English, and by no
means looking the piratical and sea-roverish person he
is supposed to be. What he would look like if he were
not particularly well pleased I do not know, but I
fancy that it would not take much to put a knife-edge
on him; as some one observed, "his Peruvian bite
might turn out even less wholesome than his Peruvian bark."

As we sat exchanging greetings we became aware
of the "rub-tub-tubbing" of marvellously slack drums,
and being placed in the post of honour, the meeting
was declared open. The gate at the end of the walk
being removed from its hinges, there swarmed through
its portals a succession of sights stranger than we ever
saw before or can ever expect to see again. Had we

been short-hand writers, writing the shortest possible hand, we must have left an infinity of quaint and curious things untold. First poured in a mass of men who, though habited reasonably enough after the manner of the "reach-me-downs," chose for some private reason to assume a gorgeous head-dress, compounded apparently of a mixture of the popular idea of the hat of the late Guido Fawks, the grenadier's cap of the early Georges, with a slight suspicion of the tiara of the Pope of Rome. There seemed to be no masquerade about it, and it might possibly have been the recollection of some native gala-dress of the pre-missiona ristic time.

Yelling yells, which would have passed for very tolerable "View Hallohs!" in the shires, they advanced up the path, some bearing beautiful mats, and others waving very much less beautiful flags.

In front of them, dressed principally in a white shirt, with a native cloak of many colours, barefooted, and bearing a weapon half spear and half paddle, with great goggle mother-o'-pearl eyes, which he manœuvred like some sort of ante-diluvian spontoon, advanced the spokesman of the deputation. Advanced? advanced is too mild a term; for he frisked, and bounded, and gambadoed, like a very David before the ark—ay, in more ways than one!

Arrived within good "View Halloh!" distance, the presents of the chiefs were *thrown* down, not leisurely parted with, as with regret, but honestly thrown at

you, as if the owners were only too eager to show you
honour; and the spokesman, dressed in the old coloured cloak of antiquity, began to speak, or rather to
bellow like the most Bashantic of bulls. Indeed, some
of his utterances really put us in mind of the strange
alternate rumblings and squealings of an excited bull.
He roared and gasped at P— furiously and convul-
sively, gambadoing and cutting strange *entre-châts* all
the time, terminating every three words or so with a
shrieking yell that went through one like a knife.

"Here are bananas! Yow! yow! yoicks!"

"Here are coco-nuts! Yoicks! yow! yow!"

Pigs! (as before); mats! (rare and valuable); an
awful ankle-twisting gambado! and a yell that made
us tremble for his blood-vessels; and so on, till we
became accustomed to these terrible civilities. When
familiarity brought not contempt but tranquillity, we
began to have the dawning of an idea that we had seen
our paganesque friend somewhere before; and to our
no small astonishment we found that we were gradually constructing out of the features of this hospitable
but savage howler the grave and spectacled ones of
the douce elder who had done the bass at service but
yesterday,—the elder, who had actually held forth to
the saints from the platform of Exeter Hall! Ay, and
why not? thought we to ourselves. Why not encourage this harmless effervescence and exuberant good
will as far as possible? Is it worse in any respect
than whisky and water and fires, Kentish or otherwise?

N

All honour to you, Monsieur le Missionnaire, for your solid good sense.

Somewhere about this time natives brought a glorious mat, and spread it over the steps. Also let us remark that the king had at the very beginning of the fantazia removed from the verandah, and posted himself under a tree a little distance off; the proof, we thought, of rare good taste and delicacy. He evidently wished it to be supposed that all the homage was offered to P—, and that his presence had nothing to do with the feeling of the people.

Soon afterwards the chief of one of the districts and his queen advanced, and shook hands with P—, and immediately the verandah was literally stormed by his whole tribe, men and women and children. Such laughing, and swaying, and squeezing ("I like being squeezed, sir!" said the old lady to the lord chamberlain) was never seen, even at Her Majesty's drawing-room! Every finger was invested instantly, and P— solved the difficult question of how to shake hands with ten women at once. What made the confusion worse confounded, was the fact that each individual, from the weeist piccaninny to the oldest granny, had brought a present, which they deposited on the mat at the entrance before shaking hands. Some brought a mat, some pretty baskets, a tiny bag of coffee, a shell, a feather, an ancient stone weapon, or an unfortunate fowl, the latter of which added their discordant "squawks" to the general din, as they were trampled on by "the bare feet of laughing (or larking ?) girls," struggling in the press. The mass became more and more condensed, till finally, with a convulsive struggle which shook the house, they burst through the narrow passage into the field beyond, and we heard them, chuckling, panting, and clicking over the grand lark they had just had.

Then in the distance more "rum-tum-tititum" of approaching drums announced another procession from another district. As they came on in a dense cloud, stepping short, and almost marking time, we saw two men dancing and gesticulating in the wildest manner, apparently on the very shoulders of the crowd. As the mass opened out a little, we saw that they were on a rude platform, which formed the dancing floor. The dance itself was a most weird and strange one, one of the old pagan dances, which were supposed to be extinct thirty years ago. There were certainly some reasons why it should be extinct as it was danced before us, but with a little judicious pruning it might be rendered quite as proper as a polka or a valse. It is certainly infinitely more grace-ful than either, and the waving motions of the arms were really beautiful. As they advanced, the bearers raised and lowered the platform at intervals, rhythmi-cally, as one might say, accompanying the movement with deep "hughs !" like those of a pavier at work, though infinitely deeper and louder. Now and again the bearers introduced an impromptu performance,

which was neither contemplated nor enjoyed by the
dancers, as it threatened to cast them down violently
from their pride of place, amongst the feet of the mob.
So they objurgated, and the crowd around roared and
yelled louder than ever. This strange myriad-legged
beetle, for it resembled that more than anything else,
struggling up the path was a thing to remember.
Strange also it was to see how rapidly the old tarantula
poison spread amongst the people, and how the young
ladies, starting up from beneath the coco-trees, betook
themselves to the dance in the most *prononcé* fashion.
Indeed there was no knowing the lengths to which they
might have proceeded had not our venerable friend,
Precentor David (who had not been a whit the better
himself twenty minutes before), brought the broad end
of his goggle-eyed paddle to bear on the stern of the
liveliest young lady with a force which produced a
very distinct and decided " smack ! " a smack which
required such an amount of energy to be expended in
rubbing as to leave none for dancing.

At last the platform approached the steps, and we
saw that, besides the dancers above, it was laden with
an infinity of pigs, taro, bananas, &c., suspended from
its rafters. At a given signal the whole affair was let
go by the run, pigs, dancers, and all, to their extreme
discomfort and the increased merriment of the mob.
Then another storm of hand-shaking and kissing and
present-making, till we stood knee-deep in coffee-
berries and shrieking chickens.

The next procession was preceded by a company of handsome young fellows, dressed in dark green uniforms, and armed with wooden muskets, with a slight sprinkling of rusty fowling-pieces here and there. The colonel, who would have passed anywhere as an Italian officer, and a monstrous good-looking one, too, was very well got up indeed. The only drawback was that he had rather spoilt the general effect by attaching a big, unmistakable butcher's steel to the belt where his sword ought to have hung. His second in command, despising pretension, carried a good honest wooden sword, and was not ashamed of it. Any feeling of absurdity which might have been produced by their dress or accoutrements was entirely obviated by the intense expression of gravity and reality which pervaded their countenances. They had no idea of any " make-believe," but had honestly and painfully done their best to please us, showing how they appreciated civilised manners, and wished to imitate them.

Their drill was perfectly wonderful. They formed in single file on each side of the path, smartly enough, and went through the manual and platoon, in a strange manner, which showed most clearly that the greater part of them had been taught the motions without the slightest idea of their meaning. One pretty but not particularly useful manœuvre consisted in the whole party whirling their muskets round their heads, till the line looked like a double row of catherine-wheels.

When the speechifying was over, and P— had shaken hands with the army, the king's present was brought, a—gorgeous piece of seamless tappa over thirty yards long,—the one end borne by the talking man on his shoulders, and the other by the proud woman who had wrought it. This kind of tappa is reserved for chiefs, and when they wrap themselves up in it, they look like ancient Romans in their togas. This having been presented and rolled up, the king's body guard, dressed in red shirts and looking rather like marines, formed on each side of the path with the other troops, forming a lane up which the king and the rest of the royal family walked with great grace and dignity; somehow putting us in mind of an old print in which good old King George and his family are doing much the same thing. This was the first time the king and his guests had been together since the commencement of the ceremonies, and with many hand-shakings and " Yer hannahs " we waited for the last scene.

The darling old lady, who had mounted guard over the proto-missionaries, was evidently a " grande dame de par le monde," as Brantome would say, for she and she only was permitted to bring her present after the royal one. It was another piece of tappa, quite as long and fine, if not longer and finer than the king's, and was presented much in the same manner, the dear old lady, mother of missionaries, hobbling before on her long staff, chaunting strange canticles in her sweet quavering old voice. One end of the tappa was wound round P —'s neck and the doorpost at the same time, whilst the other end was held up by natives afar off,— a pretty way of symbolising the intimate relationship existing between himself, the house of the king, and the general people.

Then we had a general review of the troops. The chief justice made a pivot-man of himself, and the entire army did some mysterious manœuvres, with him for a centre, which were far too profound for our crude volunteer experience.

The country districts having had their turn, the people of the home settlements began, and the fun grew fast and furious. What happened in the wild confusion I hardly know. A storm of women, infinitely wilder than any that had yet appeared, rushed upon P—, and for a moment I thought that he was going to suffer the fate of Orpheus. They embraced him wherever they could · get hold of him; they crowned him with riva-riva crowns; they girded him with strange belts, and clothed him with wild-coloured mattings, till he looked like a cross between a Roman Catholic priest in full canonicals and the youthful Bacchus. They beat against him as the waves of the Atlantic against the Eddystone, and it was quite a comfort to see him emerge unscathed, now and again, from the *brown* sea foam. Had he been shorter, I believe they would have kissed the face off him: as it was—

" She who could not kiss his lips
　Was fain to kiss his clothes ! "

After the storm was over, and something like calm
produced, the Life Guards were, by particular desire,
put through their evolutions, and such a drill, I fancy,
was never drilled before. No part of it had the
slightest reference to any military necessity, but was
a mere *ballet d'action.* If the fellows had to fight in
reality, they would strip and take a spear. One
manœuvre consisted in porting arms, and nothing
else, with a regularity and pertinacity worthy of a
better cause. Another still prettier, and equally useful, consisted in their casting away their arms of iron
(or wood) altogether, and betaking themselves to their
arms of flesh. Counter-marching in double lines, they
waved them to and fro, and in and out, with the most
marvellous grace and precision, giving the regiment,
when seen end on, somewhat the appearance of a
gigantic red caterpillar, trying to walk with its legs
uppermost, or twisting in mortal agony on its back.

One is heart-broken to think how miserably mean
is this description of a most rare and curious scene.
Even the white residents had never seen anything like
it. It was a sudden outburst of the old Pagan hospitality, so nearly destroyed by modern civilisation.

Thoroughly knocked up with the noise and excitement, we went on board the yacht, the queen promising to forward the " tons " of presents ; and to
follow with her family, in the course of an hour or so.

Soon after luncheon troops of natives, principally women, began to flock on board, and decks were soon covered and cabins filled. Such nice, kind, cheery souls! There were *acres* of smiles on board. On a portrait of P——'s mother being shown to one she "clicked" with pleasure, pressed it to her lips, and then put it reverently back again; all done so prettily and gracefully as to be a positive delight. On some compliment being paid, "Yes," quoth the young lady, "I kees it!" All the English she knew, and about the first they learn, I fancy, in these "Paphian bowers."

Then they proposed singing. "They want to sing; they so glad to see the sheep," explained one. And so about twenty of them settled themselves down wherever they could—a perfect bunch of brown tulips bedded in snow—and gave us several pretty melodies in the native fashion; amongst which we could trace the beloved old "Home, sweet home!" strangely altered, but by no means spoilt.

Soon after arrived the king, queen, and royal suite. Her majesty was got down the narrow companion with extreme difficulty, on account of her enormous size and weight; which also gave us the most extreme uneasiness as to how she was to be got on deck again whole.

The spirit of impropriety having entered P——'s soul, and the missionary being safe on shore, he proposed to have some real native dancing and singing. The merry old king was by no means averse to a lark, and some twenty girls shook themselves down and began.

At first they were, or pretended to be, mighty shy and modest, probably afraid of the authorities ; but the king and the chief-justice egging them on with many a queer crip and crank, they gradually became so excited that P— began to think that he had lighted a fire which it would take some trouble to put out. A song in his honour produced a perfect *furore,* and such a cloud of waving handkerchiefs never was seen, certainly not in the cabin of the " staid Albatross." Warmer and warmer they grew. Three of the handsomest girls separated themselves from the mass, and danced before P——, waving their handkerchiefs in his face, until at last the very handsomest of them all so far lost her head, or her heart, as to declare her deep and unalterable affection in terms more pointed than proper.

Alas for her young loves ! The queen, seeing that P. looked a little confused at this public declaration, was seized with an attack of the most intense virtue, and rating the unfortunate victim of the tender passion soundly and sharply, ordered her to sit down, which she did in evident astonishment and confusion. Poor dear ! the missionaries had not taught her Latin, or she would have known that—

" Est *modus* in rebus."

The fire was, however, by no means put out by the

extinction of her particular flame, and they performed a really pretty dance. Two girls dancing opposite each other, and at certain times crossing each other quickly and kissing as they passed. Then things got more lively than ever, and the young ladies, finding the cabin warm and their garments cumbersome, evinced a strong inclination to assume a garb which Lord Sydney would not have tolerated for a single moment, even at the Alhambra. This was all very well in its way, but *under the circumstances* would hardly do; and so, with deep regret, the extinguisher was reluctantly but firmly put on.

To the philosophical mind this presence and prominence of the handkerchief in these amatory saltations is very curious. In Japan, it is true, where I am given to understand that the art of love-making is carried to the highest perfection, it does not obtain, as the Japanese have not, in the strict sense of the word, any pocket-handkerchiefs to use. But every nation possessing pocket-handkerchiefs bring them into play somehow or another. Does not the sultan—not the soldan of Babeloun but the sultan of the opera—does he not, like a conceited brute as he is, throw his handkerchief at his favourite sultana? Did not I myself, at the "Baïle Nacional," up a flight of wooden steps, right hand side, Calle something or other, in the good town of Seville? did not I see Donna Maria Dolores, after a most brilliant fandango, cast her handkerchief into the lap of the staid and astonished governor of

Gibraltar? I am told by experts that the handkerchief plays a very prominent part in those abstruse
amusements—"kiss in the ring," and, beloved of
white New Zealanders, the "French-tig." I never
played at them myself, though their names sound
pleasantly, particularly the first; but I have a hazy
recollection of seeing a good deal of business done with
more or less white pocket-handkerchiefs at country
fairs, long ago, in some of the dances. Indeed the old
paganesque use of the pocket-handkerchief seems to
have been introduced even into religion:—why do
maid-servants always wrap up their prayer-books?
But stop, the subject is expanding too rapidly; let us
rejoin the ladies.

The hint to retire being given, our lady friends
packed themselves in the boats as tight as they could
sit, leaving hardly room for the delighted sailors to pull a
stroke, though I don't think they tried very hard. On
the boats grounding in the shallow water, with screams
and squalls they tucked up their garments quite as
high as necessary, and squatterd on shore like a skein
of white wild ducks. Some of them, however, preferred the dignity of being carried, and it was a sight
to see Loui, a most diminutive Norseman, strongly
suspected of being that sailor's terror, a "Russian
Fin," staggering to the shore with a skirling damsel,
thrice as big as himself, perched on his shoulders.
Whilst he was performing this act of gallantry the
boat, frightened by the row, I suppose, drifted into

the deeper water with half a dozen girls in her, who
kept the little man trotting about in the water, just
paddling out of his reach with their hands, and laughing at him. As he always had a very big lump of tobacco in his very small cheek, he could not laugh in
return, but one saw his lips strained to cracking.

Then with extreme difficulty the queen was got up
the cabin companion, really, I believe, like a wire, the
longer for the process, so tight was the fit, and placed
in the stern-sheets of our biggest boat, the nose of
which immediately cocked out of the water as if astonished at what had happened. It is rude to talk about
ladies' weight or lightness, but I really believe that
her majesty weighed twenty-five good "stun !" The
Princess Royal, the queen of Atia, her niece, was
weight for age,—well worthy of her, and would have
turned the scale at fifteen stone easily. She it was
who formed the heaviest billow which had surged
against P— in the morning, leaving her spray on the
top of his head in the form of a glorious crown of riva-
riva. She was as great a mass of solid good-nature
as ever was seen, but within that monstrous bulk were
"feelings." When P— gave her his portrait, she
kissed it again and again with the most sentimental
devotion, and pressed it (within a couple of feet) to
her beating heart. An elephant in love was nothing
to it.

During our stay at Raritonga a smart Yankee
whaler arrived, on her way to her southern winter

fishing grounds. Her skipper, a charming little fellow, bright and full of strange experiences, which he told in a most enviable style, came on board once or twice for doctoring and gossip. Amongst other things, he propounded the strange doctrine that whaling is a safer employment than carpentering, taking into consideration the barking of shins with adzes, the chopping of toes with axes, and the mutilation of fingers with gouges and chisels.

As my friend looks now he is just the sort of man I should like to ship with for a cruize, but does he always look as he does now? Few things are more curious than the difference one often sees between a skipper on shore on his good behaviour and on board possessed of almost absolute power; more particularly when the first mate is in irons for smashing the second mate's skull with a marlinespike; for half-murdering the black cook with a " knuckle-duster ; " for throwing a bucket of sludge over the cabin-boy, for shaving the ship's cat's tail! As he is, however, he is very nice, and discourses pleasantly. Whaling seems to be a tremendous science. Sperms, right-whales, hump-backs, sulphur-bottoms, and so on, all being attacked in a different fashion, suited to their different habits and the angle at which the eye is set. If you attack a sulphur-bottom at the angle which would suit a sperm, you would very speedily find yourself in a place where sulphur was a mere drug. The skipper expressed this last sentence much

more tersely, but I think that that is what he meant.
He tells us that his Fejeeans are very brave and good
harpooners ; he brought two or three of them on board,
and they looked and spoke as if they and he were on
good terms. Again—whaling is quite safe ; all you
have to do is to keep cool, and mind the whale's eye :
that is all ! Whales signal danger to each other by
turning up one of their " flukes, " as natives do their
paddles ; and each whale passes on the signal to
another, and descends into the abyss. When you
find your boat resting across the flukes of a whale, you
are in a tight place, and had better get out of it. The
best thing to do is to jump overboard, and dive as far as
you can, and then come up again, and be picked up by
the second boat. It is hardly worth while looking for
your own, unless you wanted a tooth-pick. But there
is no real danger—Oh, dear no ! so it seems !

When you go to sea you must either believe *all* the
yarns you hear without unravelling them, or none at
all. I prefer the former course myself. Surely there
is no great harm in simply believing what may not be
strictly true, as long as you do not actually practise on
it to your own injury or that of society ?

I remember once, in a dead calm, some distance
from land, I embarked in the ship's dingy, accompanied by one of the most honest truth-telling seamen
I have ever met with, and, moreover, a man of intellect, and, for his position, considerable cultivation.
Our object was to disport ourselves with the shooting

of sea-fowl, which we did right joyously, getting fine
steady " pots " against the sides of the great rollers,
or nipping them neatly as they showed over the tops.
Moreover we enjoyed the sight, at one moment, of the
entire of our little schooner, as she showed herself,
copper and all, at the top of a water-mountain two or
three yards off, and then wished her good bye ; as all
disappeared but a yard and a half of her top-masts,
with their little gilded trucks shining in the sun, as
she sunk into the valley on the other side.   The
freckle of the coming breeze on the leaden-silver sea
warned us on board.   On exposing our spoil, there
was a slight murmur amongst the men :—" Why,
them's Mother Carey's chickens ! "   " Tut ! " quoth
my friend, " don't you see that these have got two
webbed feet, and is it not a known fact that the real
Mother Carey has one foot like a cock and the other
like a duck ? "   " 'Tis so, no fear ! " responded the
growler, and peace was restored.

I like the feeling amongst sailors which prompts
them to resent the wanton shooting of sea-fowl from
the deck.   In a long sea-voyage the smallest Cape
pigeon becomes a companion, and gives a sense of
life and companionship to the " waste of waters."
(" Waste of water," growls an old salt, " it aint a
waste of water ! what would navigation do without
it ? ")   No one has any right to shoot a sea-bird except
for scientific uses or food.   They are far too easily
killed to give any real *sport*.   *Fishing* for albatrosses

and Cape pigeons is quite fair; though in the case
of the albatross, what is it for a man to set his wit
against so foolish a bird? This fishing, though the
expression may be slightly Hibernian, is a strictly
legitimate sport. You set your intelligence against
theirs, and if they lose the game, they have no right
to grumble at paying the stakes. Even if you win your
game, you can throw it overboard again, not much
damaged, and even have a fresh deal. I have seen an
albatross, caught, thrown overboard, and caught again,
in a very few minutes. But shooting the poor brutes is
quite another affair; more particularly when, as is generally the case, you have no chance of picking them up.
I wonder, by the way, whether they hove to to pick up
the albatross the ancient mariner shot, or whether it
fell on the deck? I suspect the former. His crime
was not honestly fishing for his bird; and the rest of
the crew got tangled up in it by heaving-to and lowering
a boat to pick it up, wishing to make pipe-stems out
of its wing-bones, and 'bacco-pouches out of its feet.

Cape pigeon catching is to albatross fishing what
trouting is to salmon fishing. The sharp little
spotted beauties are cautious, and require fine tackle
and delicate handling. Small gut roach hooks, baited
with an infinitesimal morsel of fat, is the best *moyen
de parvenir*. Top-baiting with shreds of fat or crumbs
of bread is very useful. The albatross cares nothing
for the coarseness of the line; but there are rules to
be observed even with him, not from his sharpness,

O

but from his clumsiness and stupidity. The common
idea of his pouncing on his prey, and even splitting
open the head of the man overboard are, as far as I
have observed, mere moonshine. I know no bird
with less picking up or striking power when on the
wing. I never yet saw an albatross which did not
sit down, soberly and calmly, to his dinner, and even
then he was as likely to miss it as to get it. Bits of
fat, small, and floating from the passing ship, or the
fragments of squid from the whale's jaw, are what he
seems to be in quest of, and very hard work he seems
to have to find them. When an eligible morsel
appears, there is no lack of convives—pecking, caw-
ing, and barking, whilst the sharp little Cape pigeon
deftly conveys the morsel from under their enormous
bills. The life of an ocean-bird in stormy weather
must be a hard and poor one. I suppose when in
luck they get a great gorge at once, and that lasts
them a long time. The albatross rests much more on
the water than is generally supposed, and when he
alights he is as careful of wetting the soft under
feathers of his wings as a lady is of protecting the hem
of her petticoat against the mud of the kennel. To
finish this albatrossian screed, let me record that an
albatross in a *dead* calm is one of the meanest birds on
the wing I have ever seen.

October 4th. Still with our brains a whirling mass
of white muslin, black eyes, glancing teeth, smiles,
drills, and dancings, as if we had spent a fortnight, *all*

night, in the Mahometan paradise. For want of something better to do we overhauled our presents, and here is the account, as made out by Mr. Stevedore Mitchell.

To Presents received.

1. Two rolls of tappa (chiefs' peculiar), each ninety feet by eight.
2. Thirty native mats (choice).
3. Sixteen worked baskets (mixed).
4. Three old native dresses complete, with sea-weed trimmings and riva-riva crowns (very valuable).
5. An ancient sacred staff (the owner having retired from the pagan business and entered the ministry). Unique, alas!
6. Shells (principally of the cowriaginous class). Coco-nut cups (as per invoice).
7. Several old stone axe heads (irreplaceable; very like Danish celts).
8. A sack and a half of raw coffee berries, about one hundred pounds (and they are also at the bottom of the sea, every berry of them!

" Deep in the ocean *berried.*")

9. Three pigs, one turkey, nine fowls, one bull, or bullet, or little bull.
10. Coco-nuts, bananas, yams, &c. &c., *ad libitum*; which being interpreted means, as much as we can carry.

The schooner was flooded with natives, almost from day-break. Several chiefs came off, either to bid us good bye, or to invite us to their houses on the other side of the island. One brought a boat-load of fruit and fowls, as a special present to our gallant skipper. It really seems as if these people could not help giving.

Our bull arrived, and after some trouble was hoisted on to the deck, about which he skated in the most unpleasant manner, doing occasionally four inside edges at once, which produced a perfectly new figure of the "spread eagle" pattern, out of which he had to be hoisted by main force. He was, however, a kindly bull of the true Raritongian temper, and ate bananas instantly out of our hands, in whatever position he found himself. All day long the natives had the full run of the ship—the cabin full of women, perfectly free and unwatched; and yet not a thing was taken or even asked for, nor did they ever for a moment become rude or intrusive. These people are most certainly, most nice, gentle, generous, civil, and easy to please. We showed them maps, pointing out England, or "Britane," and Raritonga, which pleased them mightily, evidently proud of being in the map at all. Then P— shewed them Leech's sketches in the "Comic History of England," and they appreciated them immensely, crowding round with their strange "Um, um, um! click, click, click!" which is their mode of expressing delight and wonder combined.

When the last batch of visitors had departed, John, the jolly old pilot, appeared with his native crew, and we prepared to get under weigh, with some anxiety, as it was blowing a fresh breeze right abeam. The only way to get out was to make sail, point her head straight for the opening, with a couple of strong warps from the stem and stern out to windward, and, letting go, shoot straight through the opening, that is, if she chose to do so. At last all was ready, and ten seconds would decide her fate. "Let go the head warp!" A native, who had been watching this signal, threw up his heels and, diving like a seal, pulled the slip knot with which we were made fast to the anchor. "Let go astern!" yelled the pilot, but the skipper would not be hurried, and let her swing off well at first. "Luff! luff!" screamed the pilot. "Mind them braces, or you will be all aback!" "All right!" quoth the skipper, "don't flurry yourself! keep her off now!" Coral and breakers within ten yards on either side of us. "Luff again! Keep her off! Now! All clear!" And we drew the deep breath of satisfaction.

I don't think that you will catch us in *that* "harbour" again, Master John, though it be the " safest in the world !"

Chapter VIII.

SAMOA.

HAT a quantity of *old* things there are on this world of ours! Things so old that one reads of them in old, old books, which speak of them as old, even in their time. So old that possibly there is no phase of thought or action which our race has passed through, in its onward progress, which is not represented in some hole or corner of the existing earth. Even in hackneyed old Europe the man who is wise or strong enough to wander on foot, comes continually across bits of human life which carry him back into ages long past away. We are too apt to talk about "antiquities" as connected with dead stone and timber, while, in fact, there are under our very noses live antiquities,—men, women, and children, hundreds of years old; thinking the same thoughts, wearing the same garments, and playing at the same games that their "forbears" did in the misty distance of ages. When one reads an old Coventry "miracle-play," for instance, how infinitely far off the time seems, when such a form of amusement was not only popular but pious ! And yet if you go—not to the Ammergan affair, which is a new periodical excitement—a " curio," but to Segovia for instance, you will find the real old thing played night after night, producing full houses and intense interest in the minds of people whose habits of thought are those of the fifteenth century. As for " dress antiquities,"—shoe-buckles, knee-breeches, and things of that sort,—they may be found in many an out-of-the-way German Dorf. Nay, do not the coachmen even of our own " upper ten" still retain a shadow of the wig which was the glory of the great grandfathers of their masters ? Do not the farmers' wives in Wales still wear the tall hat of the women of England in the seventeenth century, under the insane idea that it is a " national" costume, and the correct " Cymraig ?" And again, do not the Highlanders of Scotland, under a still more insane idea, retain the " Sula " of the South Sea islander, calling it a " kilt ;" though it is no more like the kilt of '45, than a Sunday-coat is like a coatamundi ? Do you not find there other antiquities in the shape of broadswords and bagpipes, and haggis's, which were kicked out of South Britain as useless and intolerable two hundred good years ago ? Antiquities indeed ! Look at South Britain herself, with her innumerable old paganisms which cunning priests have taught her to look upon as pieties, and then "muse," whatever that may be, on the strange way in which some manners and customs are drawn out through the ages, like the threads from which some insects cannot detach themselves. I have seen human beings in South Western Australia who were older than Adam himself, at least their dresses were, for they had not even arrived at the art of sewing their wild-beast skins together, which he was taught in Paradise; being arrayed in a mere dangling mass of foul peltry, without either stitch or pocket, except possibly that of the original kangaroo owner. This sort of thing is *real* antiquity, though possibly it ought to be called novelty, as the newest thing on the face of the earth, we civilised folk being the real ancients by right of age. A bothering question! For we know not how long the Australian has been on the earth; we know not whether he may not be the last exercise of the creative power, which formed the earliest races of man, still expanded into our time, or whether *his* ancestors were the first men placed on the earth millions upon millions of years ago.

We are beginning to see that there is a history of our race to be puzzled out on the surface of the globe. We are beginning also to see that there is an antiquity far beyond the antiquity of civilisation, or what is ordinarily called history; an antiquity which brings us dangerously near Darwin and Wallace, and which whispers darkly that man, after all, may be but an imperfectly developed animal: rising higher and higher, as the ages roll on, with more perfectly developed organs permitting the freer action of a nobler soul, but still, as far as this world is concerned, an animal—an integral part of that creation which, as far as our finite organs can see, had no beginning and can never have an ending.

New or old, it is worth while to look at the coloured races of mankind as an instructive collection of fossils, which may be studied by the ethnologist as the others are by the geologist. There are some very old fossils of this sort to be found, like the habit of crouching, not sitting, for instance, which to me always savours rather of the remembrance of tails; or the apey toes, useful as hands, to pick up trifles or to hold the wood to be ignited or drilled; the sharkey grin, no real smile, lighting up the face from within, but the mere removal of the lips from the hideously large and regular teeth; or the brown opaque eye, bloodshotten like that of a vicious horse, reminding one of a plover's egg with a boiled prune for a yolk, infinitely inferior in expression to that of a well educated dog. These are the sort of things I should call human fossils, and let us hope that they will be well studied before they disappear, for the destruction of Egyptian monuments and literature by the early Christians of Alexandria is as nothing compared with the effacement of the early records of humanity by South Sea whalers, Yankee riflemen, and missionaries, who seem to act as so many pieces of moral india-rubber in effacing the old marks and lines of our species. Not that it is of any use complaining. This rubbing out seems to be a part of the great scheme of the world. Who rubbed out the history of Stonehenge? Who smeared out the tale of the American tumuli? *Quien sabe?* Is it that our world is such a small slate that it has to be wiped clean, ever and again, in order that new generations may cipher the better on it, not being puzzled by the records of their predecessors' mistakes?

There are fossils and fossils, as there are antiquities and antiquities; some coarse and repulsive, some graceful and pleasing; some mere flint chippings, others the very perfection of artistic beauty. It is the same with our human fossils. Think of the difference between the "black-fellow" of Australia, and the Kanaka of the Society Islands!

The pleasantest forms of the human fossil we have ever met with have been in the South Seas. India and the East are doubtless highly fossiliferous, and pleasantly so; but the great mass of specimens have been terribly worn, and have lost their real old edging and sharpness by civilisation. In the South Seas, spite of the missionary, pure unpolished specimens may still be found.

The missionary has, however, succeeded in very nearly destroying one fossil, only to cause the introduction of an infinitely more mischievous novelty in its place. He has, wherever he could, destroyed kava, and in consequence has caused the introduction of orange rum.

The problem of how to get drunk on a piece of dry wood, or rather root,—for though kava *en bloc* looks like the former, it is the latter,—seems at first sight rather difficult to solve, but the kanaka has solved it satisfactorily, at least as far as he himself is concerned. How the occult properties of such a very untempting vegetable ever came to be discovered one knows as little as in the case of jesuit's bark, or in fact of any wild plant; and what makes the case of the kava more curious than usual, is the fact, that not only is the root most untempting in aspect, but it requires a peculiar preparation in order to develope its qualities.

How the Kanaka has solved his problem, I will tell you by-and-by; what the kava is, I will tell you now. It is the root of a plant carefully cultivated by the natives, to whom it serves the purpose of tea, maté, alcohol, coffee, betel, and all that class of stimulants, or "arresters of the decomposition of tissue." The plant itself is, I believe, what the man who names the plants in Kensington Gardens would call, a "piperaceous shrub." When nibbled, it tastes like a chemist's shop in general, but has, withal, a certain peppery pungency about it by no means unpleasant.

When I say that the kanaka has solved the great question of how to get drunk on a piece of dry wood, do not understand me to mean that he necessarily gets drunk every time he drinks kava, far from it! And even if he does exceed, the intoxication produced is very different from the riotous, dangerous drunkenness

of beer or spirits. It was from not understanding this
that the ignorant and self-conceited men, who were
taken from the grocer's counter or the cobbler's stall,
to preach their wretched idea of gospel truth, fell
into so grave and mischievous a mistake. Kava was
utterly tabooed, as pertaining to the fiend, and the
consequence was, that the natives invented in its stead
the poisonous and maddening orange rum, which is
never drunk without producing an indescribable orgy.
Kava, in moderation, is quite as harmless and wholesome as tea or tobacco, and I really believe was
tabooed more from that arrogant fondness for forbidding, which was the characteristic of the elder missionaries, and which still lingers in some of the more
out-of-the-way islands, than from any real belief in its
mischievous qualities. It is hard to believe, but we
were told by a missionary, that tobacco-smoking is
absolutely prohibited in one of the Cook's group at
this present writing, and that under heavy penalties.
And these same penalties are not to be trifled with.
The chiefs have found that immorality may be made a
profitable source of revenue, and so wish for sin to
abound, in order that dollars may still more abound—
in their own pockets. In fact, as far as I can see, so
far from eradicating the old vices of the islanders,
these good people have introduced a new one, which
was certainly not there before their time; a vice which
they possibly brought with them in their clothes or
faces—that sneaking, slant-eyed rascal, *Hypocrisy*.

I beg to observe, if you have not already perceived it, that kava is only a thought peg, and I shall hang as many thoughts upon it as I like. What right have you to drink " kava " after a journey measured by the inches of these pages when I had to go thousands of miles for it ?

What was I going to say ? Oh ! about the abuse of kava—not that anybody abuses it in the proper sense of the word, except the aforesaid missionaries, but the excess of kava. What happens if, in the language of Mr. Richard Swiveller, you "pass the rosy" too often ? There is the charm of kava—nothing whatever happens ! It is a negative, not a positive intoxication. I never took too much kava myself, not having had an opportunity of doing so ; but I have heard from those weaker or more tempted vessels who have, that it produces a quiet and transient state of " nirwana," a simple annihilation. Like the farmer in church, you "simply put up your legs and thinks o'nothing." Should your convives, in the transition stage, be larkily inclined, they will not cork your face or grease your boots, but they will stick pins, fish-spears, stingaree-stings, wood splinters, any handy thing with a point, into you, and you will blandly smile on them, unconscious of pain, till you fall asleep. It seems, from all accounts, to be a most marvellous anæsthetic, but then to be anæstheticised you would require a regiment of the strongest jawed—but this is too precipitate.

You sleep, say, for twelve hours; and then the right thing to do on awakening is to eat a little roasted faës, or wild plantain—the " soda-water tree," in fact, of these regions—and then go to sleep again for any number of hours you like. I am told that you are none the worse when you wake up finally. The brain does not seem to be exhausted, as from the excitement of alcohol or opium; and, in the vernacular, you rise as " fresh as paint." I am also informed that if you persist in drinking too much kava your nose gets red, but as the European nose in these regions is invariably like the claw of a boiled lobster in colour, that does not much matter.

It is doubtless wrong and naughty to waste so much time in doing nothing, but then even if you were not drinking kava you would be equally doing nothing, there being nothing to do; and if you are asleep for twenty-four hours you may at least be pretty certain of being out of mischief for that period. Still be it remembered that kava-drinking to this extent is a very exceptionable affair, and that ordinarily it is a mere matter of a cup of tea.

It was at lovely Samoa that I first got initiated into the art and mystery of kava-drinking; an island that would be called the loveliest in the world were there not scores of others equally lovely, gemming that glorious South Pacific Ocean. We were anchored in the Bay of Apia, which forms almost, if not quite, a semicircle, barred from the sea by a coral reef, stretch-

ing from point to point like the string of a bow. And
how exquisitely delicious is the curl and flash of the
never-ceasing surf on the edge of that same reef.
Great rollers, that come straight up to the coral without a break, and then, making a startled leap in the
air, fall with a heavy, crashing thump, which subsides
into a cooling hiss and swish as it runs up amongst the
bright-hued branching coral. Apia would not be
habitable were it not for the idea of snow and coolness
the foam of the breaking water gives one in the
blazing, shimmering heat.

This same reef is rather remarkable as one of the
few stations in the world where the polulu fishing, or
rather worming, is carried on. These singular creatures—long black and green annelides, from two inches
to two feet long and as thick as a crow-quill—pullulate
quite suddenly on the reef, where the water is a foot
or two deep, twice a-year, and always at a time so
certain, that the natives turn out with almost unerring
accuracy for the fishing. This year the crafty polulu
chose Sunday for their first appearance, and, as the
greatest rascal on the island told me—" Sunday is a
great day in religion," they escaped a whole day.
The swarm only lasts two days, and only then for an
hour or two before sunrise. Polulu fishing is one of
the great larks of Apia. You turn out in an out-
rigger canoe at four in the morning, and find yourself
in the dark amongst a crowd of others, filled with men,
women, and children—laughing, squalling, skirling,

and flirting, the noise almost overcoming the incantations of some of the old women, who sing either to
the sea or some sea-goddess to " pullulate polulus
plentifully and prodigiously," all waiting for the first
tinge of light to guide them to their prey. Your
fishing apparatus consists of anything you can get,
from a bit of matting up to a magnificent net made
out of a piece of window-curtain stretched on a bent
stick, like a battledore.

As the light increases you become aware of the
fact that the water is alive with myriads of wriggling
worms : you have but to dip and you bring up lumps
of writhing stuff, which puts one in mind of the confused mass of brittle-stars' legs which you bring up
sometimes in the dredge. This you empty into your
bucket or calabash, and dip again. There is no law
on the water on these occasions. If you see Moé in a
good place, you are perfectly justified in twisting her
canoe round by the out-rigger and taking it yourself.
If Toé is flirting instead of attending to her polulu,
you have a perfect right to reach over and empty her
bucket into yours ; and if she splashes you with her
paddle you splash her with yours, you won't spoil her
clothes—and so the fun goes on. The dawn gradually
gets clearer and clearer, bringing out the splendid
statuesque figures fishing for big fish, on the outer edge
of the reef, with long bamboos, in the most artistic
manner, casting their bait of squid into the very surf
itself; until at last—

"Nor dim, nor red, like God's own head,
    The glorious sun uprist!"

and sends his level rays gleaming through the blue
water walls of the surf.   Then instantly all the sport
ceased.   The polulu vanished, not to re-appear for six
months more ; and sky-larking, racing and splashing,
we all sped homewards.   On examining my share of
the spoil, I found that I had got a quart or more of the
aforesaid worms ; and certainly anything which looked
more hopelessly uneatable I never saw.   I had got my
white elephant, but what to do with him I knew not.
But instructed by the charming Coé— (I put an accent
on the e to prevent scandal)—I learned that they
should be wrapped in a piece of banana leaf and baked.
Moreover, that they would keep for a long time if they
were occasionally rebaked, so as to keep them dry.
When cooked I found that I had by no means a disagreeable mess before me, more like a lump of dark
spinage than anything else.   In taste it was like a
mixture of spinage, laver, and crab ; and with oil,
vinegar, and cayenne, was by no means to be despised.
On toast, like caviare, it was also very good.   Almost
the only objection to it was a slight suspicion of that
very disagreeable coral smell, which always puts me in
mind of phosphorus.

To show how accurate are the calculations of the
natives, let me mention that we all turned out the
next morning (Tuesday), and did not collect a tablespoonful of polulu amongst the whole fleet.   The

P

crafty brutes had taken advantage of the sabbatari-
anism of the natives and swarmed on Sunday.

If I remember right, it was on this day that I first
tasted that suave and delectable liquor "Mononjahela
whisky;" but what liquor would not have been am-
brosial, presented by the rosy-brown finger-tips of Coé
herself, as a consolation for our disappointment!

To say that Apia is in the South Seas, is almost to
say that the shore is fringed with a noble belt of coco-
palms (I spell it coco, but I am by no means sure that
it should not be "koker"). Around the feet of these
are masses of hybiscus bushes, all ablaze with crimson
and yellow flowers; other plants there are which we
cannot distinguish by the eye, but every light waft of
air from the land bears with it Sabean odours, which
fully realize one's old fancies about the spice islands:
indeed, lovely Apia, to the best of my recollection, is
the only place where the sweet scent of land flowers is
distinctly perceptible at sea. Scattered about beneath
the trees are the bright white houses of the European
settlers; and kindly, pleasant, and hospitable houses
they are. English, American, and German, vying with
each other to make the stranger at home in a strange
land. Beside them nestle more modestly the brown
huts of the natives, built generally of cunningly interwoven palm leaves, a real brown hamlet. This native
town is just now in a somewhat dilapidated condition,
in consequence of a prolonged "war of succession,"
caused by the too evenly-balanced state of the different

parties. There is a truce for the moment patched up,
I think mistakenly, by the missionaries; it will prove
but a hollow one if all I hear is true.*

Behind the coco-fringe, the land sweeps up into
lovely wooded hills some four thousand feet high, not
so abruptly picturesque, perhaps, as the general tone
of the Society Islands, but marked with beautiful
curves and long graceful sweeps of vivid green. Here
and there, valleys permit one to see far away up into
the mysterious heart of the hills, where many a strange
and weird thing may be enacting at this moment in
the gloom of the forest. Far away is the gleam and
glitter of an enormous waterfall, marking the green
with a silver bar, which it takes a whole long day's
walking to reach. The timber, generally, is finer than
that of the Society Islands, and the varied richness of
the colouring infinitely superior. Much of the beauty
of the Society Islands has been injured by the guava
shrub, which has overrun large tracts, and gives an
unpleasant monotone to the landscape.

The land generally has an older look than the islands
to the N.E. Every thing is rounder and less abrupt;
there are fewer buttresses of trap, standing out like
black ruined castles from the green hill sides; and the
lines seemed washed down to their present angle by the
gentle hand of time, instead of being decided by the

---

¹ This has since proved to be correct. If they had been
allowed to fight it out at once it would have been much better.

mad dice-throw of the volcano. When we penetrate
into the interior, indeed, we find ravines, sharp and
abrupt enough to be highly picturesque in the true
sense of the word, though even there the grimmest of
crags has almost invariably decked his bald pate with
the loveliest greenery. Oh! the heat of those breath-
less ravines! the black rocks seem to pulsate and
throb under its intensity,—heat too great, even, for
the native birds, who sit silent and gasping on the
branches, longing for evening,—a dead silence, broken only by the occasional solemn boom of a pigeon
dreaming of love in his doze. One odd thing connected with these ravines is the fact that the higher
you go the more water you find. You toil up over
gigantic lava boulders, polished as glass, and slip off
them up to your ankles into dry and dusty volcanic
sand, till your soul is parched within you, and a
ghastly terror takes possession of you, that as there is
no water where there is generally most there will be
none where there is generally least. It is not so,
however. Unlike the Thames, which begins, I believe, in half a mile of dusty lane, and expands in its
brimming breadth as it approaches the sea; a Samoan
stream begins in bubbling plenty and ends in utter
drought a mile or two from the salt water. Gradually
as you ascend you become more and more hopeful;
moist patches of sand appear here and there, then tiny
pools that a fallen leaf might cover, then larger ones
with little thread-like runs of water between them;

larger and larger, till at last you reach some hard
ledge of trap, over which a glorious stream gurgles
and splashes into a pool ample enough for the bath of
an elephant, and you cast yourself down and plunge
in your face to the ears. There are fishes in these
pools,—brisk, bright little fellows, shaped exactly like
small dace with bright yellow tails and fins, cruising
about in wee shoals, and rising at the tiny flies in the
most sporting manner. Wait a little quietly, and from
under the stones will come a purple and red cray-fish,
of no small size, who will winkle and twinkle at you
with that strange expression of mystery and concealed
wisdom, which is after his kind. Here in the cooler
part of the ravine come the birds to drink towards the
afternoon; splashing and dipping within a yard of
you, and looking up ever and anon, as if to ask you to
appreciate their enjoyment. Lovely little black and
crimson honey-birds, and jolly little impudent " ripi-
duras " (pardon the word; if you do not like it I must
give you a still harder Maori one), who flirt, and chir-
rup, and coquette with you within reach of your hand :
singing, I heard none—but the boom of the pigeon is
wondrous pleasant and drowsyfying, and suiteth well
with tobacco.

Before the ruthless missionary came there was a
pleasantly idyllic sort of sport in these valleys—now,
I fear, vanished for ever. The sport in itself was
utterly harmless, but was tabooed (horrid word!) as
leading to possible harm. It was a species of pigeon-

fancying. The great delight of the natives was to
build a bower of branches green, just large enough to
cover them securely, and then, placing a tame pigeon
outside, to ensconce themselves within, waiting until
his or her blandishments tempted down a wild bird to
indulge in a little flirting; then slowly and cautiously
emerged the brown paw of the concealed Samoan, and
the wild bird was wild no more. This was not for the
base purpose of eating the beauty, but merely that the
coco-leaf hut should have a pet the more.

> "I have found out a gift for my love,
> I have found where the wood-pigeons breed"—

sort of business. How could harm spring from this?
But it did, or was supposed to do so; which to the
nose of your true "smell-fungus" is the same thing.
It happened in this wise:—it was not absolutely
necessary to go alone to the mountain to enjoy the
sport; indeed, on the contrary, the long hours of waiting, day or night, rather made a companion desirable,
and so they went in pairs, and, as Pistol would have
said,

> "Conclusions past their careires."

"Smell-fungus" not being inclined to superintend
the pigeon-fancying portion of his flock personally,
an act which would necessitate some active physical
exertion, put a stop to the whole affair, and so there
is no more Strephon and Chloe-ing on the ridges of
Samoa. Is it not strange that on both sides of the

equator those innocent little birds, the pigeons, should, as Rob the Grinder pathetically complains, lead to so much mischief?

Dr. Gräfe, a naturalist working this glorious island, told me that one day he was as nearly as possible committing Samoacide in one of these valleys. Seeing a pigeon fluttering about in a curious way, he stalked it, and was just on the point of firing when a grey pate and brown face popped up through a hole in a heap of leaves and demanded quarter.

By the way, these islands are rather famous for their pigeons, though I saw nothing to equal the lovely little green, mauve, and yellow gems we used to get in the Isle of Pines and New Caledonia. One of the most remarkable here is a reddish brown bird, rejoicing, I believe, in the euphonious name of didunculus, which is confined to these islands. Even in Samoa it is so rare as to have been supposed to be nearly extinct, until the present war drove skirmishing parties into out-of-the-way places, where they discovered rookeries (all breeding places of birds or seals are rookeries in the South Seas), and we were fortunate enough to procure a pair. Its great peculiarity is that it seems to be doing its best to grow into a parrot, its bill being thickened and notched in a most un-pigeonesque fashion—a fact dear to Darwinians. May I state, as one of the few Europeans who have ever tasted it, that its flesh is brown and delicious! There is another pigeon, much petted,

which is called, in Samoan, Tu Eimeo, or something
like it; which, being interpreted, means "the pigeon
which is sulky with its food," which seems a great
deal to be contained in so small a word. It seems
that the natives after eating have a custom of washing
their mouths and hands, and casting the water outside, leaving a moist splash at the entrance of the hut.
The tame pigeon, coming to share the family meal,
feels hurt at his friends not having waited dinner for
him, and flies away to a tree to sulk with injured
dignity. Knowing this peculiarity of temper, evil
boys splash the ground outside the hut before dinner
has commenced, with the certainty of hurting the
feelings of the fowl.

These Samoans are wonderful bird-tamers, which
I think arises from their slow and gentle movements;
nothing abrupt, brusque, or startling—all calm and
quiet. He who wishes to make a friend of a cat must
follow their example.

Coming down from our ravine we pass through a
wilderness of imported plants and shrubs, flourishing
in wild luxuriancy. That red and brown flower,
which makes such pretty wreaths for the girls' heads,
and the down from whose pods is so dangerous to
the eyes, is an importation, Heaven knows how, from
America; and not only is it an importation, but it has
imported its own butterfly with it, that splendid yellow
and brown fellow who looks as if he had got half his
colour from his natal flower. Here we push through

a bush of indigo, then through one of bright glittering
green coffee, through which shoots the green pillar of
the quaint, prim, but pretty papaw,—here used only
for feeding fowls, the natives being ignorant of its
tenderising effect on beef-steaks, had they any beef-
steaks to tenderise. Even nutmeg trees are here, but
I am given to understand that they are not the real
Banda species.

As we pass along we hear a skirling and a splashing, and come plump upon a bevy of island beauties,
disporting themselves in a pool of muddy water, having first filled their calabashes, which stand in order
on the bank. The water is so muddy as fully to act
the part of garments, more particularly as it is much
the colour of their skins, and they joyously splash and
shriek, and ask for tobacco. Asking for tobacco seems
here to mean little more than a form of kindly greeting.
They begin to beg a little here ; from Tahiti to Samoa
we were never asked for a single thing; and even
here the begging is of the very mildest possible form,
particularly to those hardened by the perpetual
" Backsheesh " of the east. Indeed, amongst many
of these people, not only is begging or asking for a
thing unknown, but they have no word to express
thanks or gratitude. If they want a thing (amongst
themselves) they take it, expecting their neighbours
to do the same by them. There are no thanks, because
it is a right, not an obligation, and there is nothing to
be thankful for : to a certain extent the Sam Wellerian

form of philosophy, "If I wanted a thing I took it, for fear I might be led to do something wrong for want of it."

As we emerge from the thicket on to the bright white beach of coral sand the sun's rays are beginning to slant, and the natives to wake up from their siesta. As we pass along, however, we may still see some of them enjoying their nap, sheeted from head to foot in white tappa, and the back of the neck reposing on a bamboo rest, to save the treasured head-dress; they have rather a ghastly look, and a stranger might easily mistake them for "streekit corpses."

The cause of this wrapping up is those most infernal flies. Apia is certainly the very head-quarters of Beelzebub, where " each man walks with his head in a cloud of poisonous flies " by day, and where by night

"Most *un*delightful is the ceaseless hum"

of that most hateful of created beings, the mosquito. There is no sound in nature expressive of such venomous, acrid spite as the "ping" of a mosquito; and though they rarely bite me, the mere wickedness of the expression keeps me awake many a hot and weary hour. The only sound I know at all to be compared with it, is a peculiar way women have of saying "my dear" to each other.

This superabundance of winged life has been the origin of one characteristic of Samoa—the flyflap, which every one with the slightest pretension to respectability carries as invariably as we do an umbrella. These flyflaps are made of delicately plaited coco-nut fibres, attached to a prettily carved handle about a foot long, and when not in use are carried gracefully over the right shoulder. When in council, the sages, leaning on a long staff, whisk it solemnly to and fro, and seem to consult it as a Japanese does his fan, or a Levantine his string of amber beads.

As we saunter along we find our course impeded by a broad, bubbling brook, and we pause for a moment to decide whether we will pull off our shoes and stockings, or walk through with them on; a problem I always, somehow or another, find difficult to solve. Indeed, it is not as easy as it looks. If you walk through with them on, you are bored to death by that abominable squelching which proceeds from shoes full of water; and if without them, you are perfectly certain to tread on some infernal thing or another, which sends you hopping and "cussing" for half an hour after. I know few things more difficult to do than taking a splinter out of the sole of your foot whilst standing on one leg, particularly in a strongish stream.

We, however, are saved the trouble of deciding, by half a dozen strapping young fellows offering their backs, with every sign of good nature and civility. If you want to get the tone of our bearers without going round the world, remember Velasquez's Borracios at Madrid; they are wonderfully South-Sea.

The opposite side of the stream brings us face to face with the horrors of war ;—desolated Taro patches, ashes of burnt huts, and the stumps of charred coco-trees. Was it not the French in Egypt who conceived the brilliant idea of injuring the enemy by killing the male palms ? See what science can do in the way of labour-saving ! Here the savage burns down all his enemies' palms indiscriminately.

Soon we reach the settlement, built since the peace, and showing by the flimsiness of the workmanship of the huts, that there is no very strong belief in its continuance. They are generally simple, low-eaved affairs, —some not more than four or five feet high ; some six or seven, oval, and from ten to twenty and even thirty feet long,—a mere ridge-roof of interwoven palm-leaves supported by posts. The low eaves make them dark and cool inside, and they are always clean and neat ; the bright matting which covers the floor making the most perfect of carpets for a hot climate.

What small cooking they require is generally done outside, but I have not unfrequently seen a small square fireplace inside the huts, more for lighting cigars, I fancy, than for roasting bread-fruit or plantains.

Bending low, we enter the hut of the chief, at an undignified angle of forty-five degrees, which produces a sense of shyness. It is not pleasant to present yourself to a society of grave and reverend signiors in the attitude of a telescope, and one slinks

shily to the place pointed out to one. There is
etiquette here; you must sit cross-legged, or at least
with one leg doubled under you; to sit with both legs
extended is an unpardonable impropriety. It is bad
to lean against the wall of the hut, as the chances are
that it gives way unexpectedly, and leaves you on the
broad of your back gazing upwards into the faces of
the astonished outsiders. Put your back against one
of the supporting posts, where, if not comfortable,
you are safe. The great drawback to this position is
the fact that these posts serve as "arm-racks," and
around them are arranged the chief's stock of "fire-
irons," from the old brass-bound Tower musket to the
smart new match-Enfield, with its platinum-lined back-
sight. Round the hut are seated the principal chiefs,
glimmering with palm oil, and dressed for the most
part in the simple "tappa" "sulu" or kilt. By the
way is this word "tappa" derived from the rap-tap-
tapping noise produced in its manufacture?

The chiefs and great men who sit around us are
all men of mark, though there is but little to distinguish them from the profane vulgar, as far as dress
goes. Amongst the most remarkable among them is
a fine young fellow, who has lately fought his way to
high eminence, by storming, almost single-handed,
one of the enemy's fortifications; and not content
with that, using it, Nelson-like, as a bridge to storm
others: and be it remembered that these fortifications
are something serious—good wall and ditch work.

The sulu in which the men were dressed permitted us to see their glorious forms in full perfection, and there are few finer races in the world than these Samoans,—a little heavy and provincial perhaps, and wanting somewhat of the delicate grace of their cousins to the south-east, but still magnificent men. We fancied that they had more decided and aquiline noses than the Society Islanders. Time was when I used to think that no sculptor of the "nude" could ever be worth his salt, unless he had spent a year or two in Africa. Now, I should most certainly send him to the Society Islands, where he will see his fellow-men as they ought to be,—not cramped from infancy by strange ligatures and straps and shoes, but with every life-bearing artery and vein unconfined, permitting the perfect development of every part. No sacrifice of one to the other as with us, but a true harmonious balance of the whole. We are apt to boast, and not without some reason, that we are not as other nations are, as regards the early physical education of the more fortunate of our children, but we are as far behind these islanders, in some of the mysteries of early infant training, as we are before the flat-headed Indians.

My brown friend on my left is not a 'flat-headed Indian, though his head looks as if it had gone through some queer squeezing process early in life, which makes him look very different from the rest of the society. So odd was his look, that I could not help

studying him, and he seemed flattered with my attention. His forehead ran up to a peak, not a Shake-
sperian peak, but a sharp point, something in the
style the profane used to draw poor old Louis Philippe,
in the days of the great pear joke. There the re-
semblance ended, for instead of the heavy masses of
skin which hung over the eyes, and the heavy jowl of
" Le Roi Poire," the eyes are as clear set as a diamond
au jour, and the lips and jaw sharp and cleanly cut;
the lips thin, not as to the inverted part, but from
without inwards—so thin, as to make one fancy that
one could see the markings of the teeth through them
—mobile and in constant action, as if the very muscles
thought, or at least, answered every thought; and so
the muscles of the mouth do till weaned out of the
practice by civilisation and society. I will wager
that Touchstone had many such a queer buccal twist—
not a grin, but rather a bottling in, as it were, of
the half-developed whimsicalities. This sort of mouth
is by no means rare in Italy. There was something
in my neighbour's eye, too, which struck me,—an eye
which did not like to be found out; not from conscious
rascality, but from the perception of some hidden absurdity which would not do for the general public, —
an eye capable of giving very quiet and solemn winks
to itself—a Touchstone eye again.

How it fell out I know not; whether we winked at
each other, and found a similarity of souls in that
simple action, or that the mysterious ether of Tom-

fooldom, emanating from each of us, intermingling, caused a mutual recognition, must for ever remain a question. But the fact is that the recognition took place. Neglecting the great ones of the earth— chiefs, consuls, and earls, he attached himself to me alone, and taking the palm-leaf fly-flap from my hand, he fanned me with an expression of the most intense interest and affection. He was the court fool.

Being late we found that our friends were weary of waiting, and had already prepared their five o'clock kava, which was being strained by an ordinary native woman, by means of a handful of vegetable fibre. This was evidently a nice operation; I don't mean what Prescott Hewett would call "a nice operation," but one requiring considerable care. A general clapping of hands indicated, either that they were glad they were going to have their kava, or were impatient of further delay—I rather believe the former ; and a pleasant-looking slip of a lad presenting half a coco-nut shell to the woman, she squeezed about half a tumbler-full of the gruelly fluid into it. Then the talking-man of the chief chanted out the name of the man to whom it was to be delivered, adding a string of compliments, a sort of Samoan, "for he's a jolly good fellow" business. The proper thing is, to clap your hands gently when you hear your name mentioned, to show that you appreciate the compliment but are not proud. You should also look a little the other way in a deprecating manner, as though to say

—" Oh dear! you're very kind, *but*—." You take
the bowl, drain it, and cast it with a graceful skim on
to the mat-covered floor. A slight grunt, something
like the throat-clearing " Hum'm " of the old Puritans,
thrown in here, does well, and indicates a genteel
satisfaction. The first drink is given to the greatest
chief, the next to the highest talking man, then
another chief, then another talking man, and so on.
I thought this a very graceful recognition of the
nobility of intellect, amongst a race so aristocratically
inclined, as to have two distinct dialects, a court and
a plebeian one. I was most glad to see that my friend
Touchstone was by no means the last man to have his
drink served out to him. I would have given a deal
to know what he said, for he is looked upon as the
sayer of infinite good things, but who could translate
his winks, let alone his words.

About this time a performance took place which dis-
turbed the local colour, and somehow put me in mind of
Baker Street—a place I hate. The chief's wife, a good
and genial soul, with her hair cut short to her poll, and
a sore hand, but such a pretty one! had a tray of tumblers before her—vile glass grog tumblers, filled with
coco-nut water (it is *not* milk, or anything like it), spe-
cially prepared for us slaves of civilisation. I would none
of it, as disturbing to the proper kava frame of mind.

After the bowl of kava was finished there was a
pause—a pause of contentment and satisfaction, and
looking out of the corner of my eye into the glorious

golden sunshine, I saw that something great was in preparation outside. What I saw I cannot describe in words. Titian might have sketched it in a happy moment, or Velasquez have made a painted poem of it; but my poor pen and ink are utterly unable to produce the slightest outline worthy the original. Let me merely hint that it was as though brown angels were undressing and dressing themselves, or rather *vice versa*, for when I think on't, they put on a great deal less than they took off. The "tiring-room" was a small hut of coco-leaves, and branches of small bush —the stumps of the bushes which had furnished their quota standing thickly about it, to the no small danger of the bare toes of the rank and fashion assembled around, evidently brim full of expectation. They were utterly without rudeness, and infinitely better mannered and behaved than the surging mass of snobbism which thrusts its snub nose into the carriages of ladies going to a drawing-room at home.

At last, from under the eaves of the tiring room appeared a figure of strange loveliness, which fairly took my breath away. Shimmering in the golden setting sun-light, like a gun-metal (not bronze) statue, stood a live princess—*the* princess, the greatest beauty and richest match in all Samoa. A really beautiful creature, in all her half-developed early girlhood. Self-possessed, gentle and modest, every movement and gesture showed the true lady. Her face was a face one could dream of as that of the reigning beauty

of the court of an early Tothmes. Her only dress was
a most beautiful mat, soft and lissom as the most on-
doyant satin, wound round her hips with exquisite
grace, the fringe below hardly hiding her dainty little
feet, that—No ! I won't quote Suckling this time. I
wonder how many of those who do ever read the original ballad ?) Her charming head was—it pains me
to say so—shaved, but still so shaved as by no means
to detract from the general effect ; on the contrary, to
an eye accustomed to the weird head-dressings of European women, it was rather pretty than otherwise. The
forehead alone was shaved, and down her pretty shoulders hung a long and ample lock of straight brown
hair. Whatever unartistic there might have been
about this was relieved by a glorious wreath of intensely crimson hybiscus flowers, which would have
utterly "put out" any European face, but which
lighted her's up like—well ! like r—ge. Round her
neck she wore a double row of crimson berries, as
large as small walnuts, and altogether a daintier darling, or a more graceful, eyes have seldom seen. With
her was another girl, stout and handsome and more
fully developed, but far inferior to her in grace and
delicacy. This was her maid of honour. She was
dressed in a kilt of white tappa, particularly high
kilted ; also, she wore a wreath of hybiscus flowers,
but as showing the necessity of her inferior beauty
being heightened by adventitious ornament, or as a
hint of her wealth rather than her breeding, she wore

diamonds, that is, the representatives of diamonds in these parts—a necklace of sperm-whales' teeth scraped down so fine as to look like the claws of some gigantic tiger—a necklace of utterly incalculable value!

The two girls seated themselves gracefully on beautiful mats spread in the sunshine outside, and the great kava-bowl was placed before them with mighty care and reverence. It was hewn out of a single block of dark wood, oval in shape, some two or three feet long, by half as much broad; very shallow, and supported on elephantine legs. I am told that your kava-bowl should be old; it is not good to put new kava into new bowls, something in the sap of the wood, I suppose, acts on the kava at first; the test of excellence is, that the interior and lips are of a fine golden bronzy tint, like that on good old Japan ware.

The princess *looked* to her maid of honour "Am I all right?" and the maid of honour looked back "Love-ly!"—and so they sat and were admired of all.

Then the point of interest changed to the interior of the hut in which we were sitting. A great officer handed a lump of kava-root, about the size of half a cottage loaf (the bigger the root the better the kava) to the great chief, who, casting it gracefully at P——'s feet, said, "Let this be a sign of friendship between us." Upon which P——, being properly instructed, cast it gracefully back again to him, and answered, "Let it be prepared for our mutual gratification."

(*Mem.*—I am not responsible for these translations;
I suspect the last word ought to be "jollification.")
The lump of dried root was then handed to the high
official, who, bearing it to where the girls were sitting,
chopped small thin slices off it with a wild looking bill-
hook, and laid them before them. After carefully
rinsing their mouths with a coco-nutful of fresh water,
each beauty took a bit and commenced the process of—
chewing ? Pah !—Mastication·? Bah ! let us say
rumination ; steadily, quietly, and nicely, as the
daintiest Alderney in her grace's fancy dairy. This
may sound strange, and possibly even disagreeable to
some, but I declare that there was a grace and dainty
delicacy about the whole thing, even to the way they
picked up the chips of kava with their slender finger-
tips—that had its charm. I should as soon have
thought of quarrelling with a " Cordon-bleu " for
dipping his forefinger into the sauce to test its
quality, as feeling offended by any part of the process.
The young ladies did not ruminate entirely alone ;
near them sat a stalwart young fellow, who, turning
half away from them and us, quietly took up a piece,
and, judging from the action of his jaws, ruminated
too. This is the thing to do,—the delicate thing,—
the nice thing !—the real quiet unobtrusive way of
showing your nascent affection ! You help *her* to
ruminate kava. I am not, I trust, more than properly
envious of other men's good parts, or social accomplishments ; but I confess that I should have liked to

ruminate for her better than he did! But after all it
might have been that he ruminated only for the maid
of honour. I thought I saw the faintest twinkle of a
wink hover for a moment in the corner of her eye—if
so, well! If not, may he come a cropper the next time
he carries the missionary over the boulder-encumbered
stream—and then, my word!

After about ten minutes or a quarter of an hour,
three balls of vegetable matter, each the size of a
largish walnut, were placed in the bowl. The young
ladies then filled it with fair water, stirred all up
slightly, and then entered the hut in which we were
sitting, seating themselves at the end opposite to us.
The bowl was then brought in and placed before them,
and the second act of the mystery began. Taking a
large handful of the white inner-bark fibres of the
hybiscus, the princess dipped it into the bowl, and
then, with many a graceful twist and twirl of her
dainty hands, wrung out the fluid part of the mess;
repeating this again and again, the gruelly fluid became clearer and clearer, the fibres of the bark retain-
ing the vegetable debris of the kava root within its
interstices. This was really a pretty business from
the great grace and delicacy with which H. R. H.
managed her hands and arms. Sir Joshua would
have made a glorious picture of her as "La belle
Blanchesseuse," portrait of her grace the Duchess of
Washington washing her own lace; "But lord!" as
Pepys would say, " to see the care her maid of honour

had of her, though brown, and how she guarded her mat against the drippings."

A shy coquettish smile told the company that the kava was ready, and we clapped our hands as grace- fully as we could : taking a carefully shredded hand- ful of hybiscus fibres in her dainty fingers, she dipped it into the bowl, and squeezed it into the coco-nut, which went merrily round till all was done.

I was really surprised to find how utterly free from all unpleasant associations the process was; that is, if you did not look *too* closely, and I drained my first bowl of kava without hesitation, whatever my secret fears of the consequences might have been. It struck me as tasting like thin gruel, into which the slightest suspicion of white pepper and rhubarb had been cast; and though possibly not particularly pleasant, it left a warm stimulating flavour on the palate, which I can well believe might become, through use, exceedingly refreshing and agreeable in this exhausting climate. I waited patiently for all sorts of effects, mental and physical, but none came ; I might as well have drunk half a bottle of flat ginger beer, for that matter.

When we had finished the bowl, the young ladies giggled and flirted amongst themselves for a time, either making personal remarks upon us, or remark- ing the effect their own personalities had upon us. Then entered men bearing mighty baked fishes in woven baskets, which they laid at our feet. One of them was an enormous filo fish, eight or ten pounds

weight, with his great jagged dorsal spine sticking out
of his back like a boat's mast. We needed no warning
to eat none of him, his own recommendation preceded
him from afar, and a morsel for politeness' sake was
enough; he was, however, borne solemnly to the
yacht, from whence he was, on our arrival on board,
most promptly returned to his native element.

A little smoking and a little conversation served as
a screen to the proceedings of our young lady friends
at the other end of the hut, who were evidently in a
state of preparation for something or another, having
been joined by two others apparently of like mind to
themselves. As for their hair-dressing, they were
much like the princess and her maid of honour; but
as to their ornaments they were different: instead of
flowers they wore coronals, made of the last pearly
whorl of the nautilus shell, sewn on a bandeau of some
material, a really pretty head-dress. Let me remark,
whilst these preparations are going on, that these hair-
dressings and head-dressings are serious things amongst
the young ladies of Samoa—that is to say, amongst the
unregenerate. When a young lady joins the church
or forms a connection, matrimonial or otherwise, with
a white man, she lets her hair grow, and all the
mystery and poetry of the thing is gone. Amongst
the unconverted, however, there are certain capillary
signals understood by the initiated. For example, the
lock or tail of hair worn by my princess is a sign of
great goodness, like the old Scottish snood, rather a

rare article now-a-days. If the whole head is shaven
it is a bad sign, and betokens fastness, not to say
looseness, and many such delicate devices. Again, if
a girl should have, as sometimes happens, a head of
golden-brown hair it is "tapued" by some great
chief, and not a hair of it must be cut till it is in its
full harvest of gold. Then comes the great chief,
bringing with him rare and soft mats instead of money
(no jokes about matrimony!) and casts them down at
the feet of the bearer of the golden fleece, which he
shears off to weave into his own elaborate wig. If
this sort of thing did not happen every day in Europe,
particularly amongst the golden-haired girls of Brittany, what savages we should think these Samoans!

It is wondrous strange that hair fashions should
just at present be the same at London and Samoa. The
blonde fashion at the latter place reigns supreme, and,
oddly enough, is served on both sides of the equator
by much the same means. The taste for reddish hair
in good Queen Bess's time found means of expression
by the use of a ley of woodashes; in good Queen
Victoria's time it is managed by much the same thing
—strong alkaline washes; your Samoan uses coral
lime for the same purpose, but he or she has the
decency to say that it is done more for the destruction
of animalcules than from any feeling of personal
vanity. At any rate the custom has an odd effect as
far as the men are concerned. Imagine a brown London footman seized with raving madness just at the

moment he has finished powdering his hair, tearing off his garments and swaggering up Pall Mall with nothing on but a dinner-napkin, and you have a good idea of a Samoan swell. In full fighting fig, a Samoan is magnificent in a gigantic bush of hair standing out two or three feet from his head like the nimbus of a saint. The care required to keep this glory intact produces, as in the case of the full-bottomed periwig, a stately and gorgeous gait, which was never sketched properly except by Thackeray, who has caught the careful pose of the advanced leg marvellously. I really think there is something fine in the fashion, I know the wearers do. A brother of one of the chiefs sits for hours in the cabin merely to be looked at; indeed, I rather suspect that his brother brings him as a show, which has to be paid for in handfuls of broken biscuit, and really he is worth it. His beard and moustachios are also always very carefully trimmed, and though his entire garment may be only a fathom or two of tappa wound round his loins, the Samoan gives one the idea of a dressy man, who takes considerable interest in his personal appearance. By the way, any theologian who wants to understand the real meaning of Solomon's "oil which maketh man to be of a cheerful countenance," should come out here. I know not why, but certainly a good rub of coco-nut oil over a brown face lights it up like a smile.

The young ladies having completed their arrangements favoured us with a little singing and dancing.

The songs were very strange and wild. The very quick time to which they were sung, the slapping of the hands on the thighs, and the drumming of their knees against the ground had a wonderfully exciting effect. It would hardly do to describe the dancing very particularly; it was certainly pretty in its way, and of that style which I think Mr. Murray mentions in his "Handbook for Spain," as having obtained amongst the "improba Gaditana," which I suppose may be translated "the improper Cadiziennes." It is the same dance all over the world; from the gipsies of Grenada to the gawazee of Egypt; from the gawazee of Egypt to the nautch girls of India; from the nautch girls of India, all musk and patchouli, and silk, and gems, to the dirty little gin, of Western Australia, with her stinking bundle of possum-skins, it is all the same; nay, even in the jig of Ireland and the almost pious reel of Scotland, Smell-fungus can detect the lingering relics of pagan impropriety.

In this case however the young ladies danced neatly and properly, and the most severe guard municipal would not have interfered. One little *ballet d'action* was prettier to see than to describe, and had a *mignon* grace about it that delighted me and made one think of Theocritus. The kid (the Princess) has lost her mother, and gently and fondly bleating, she advances in little jumps, first in one direction and then in another, pausing between each, with her head coquettishly on one side, and her eyes fixed intently to listen

for the response.   The chorus answer her with a
gradually increasing bleat, till at last she finds her
mother, in this case represented by P— whose paternity
she acknowledged by a pretty tap on the chin with her
fore-finger, and then fled back to her fellow-maidens
covered with brown blushes as with a garment.
Another pretty dance they have which is called the
" Pigeon " dance.   The girls whilst dancing keep up
a soft and inviting "*r-r-r-r!* " like the call of the
female pigeon, which is answered at regular intervals
by the sturdy "*boom!*" of the admiring circles of
males, really a graceful and pretty thing.

Oh ! why did I not leave well alone !   Why did I
not depart from Samoa with my heart aglowing with
the soft and timid purity of my princess !   What devil
was it tempted me to wander along the white coral
strand under the feathery cocos, in the soft moonlight,
and be induced by the rascally chief who had the
brother, to get up a fantasia by the light of blazing
coco-leaf baskets ?   There was my princess with five
others, each infinitely worse than any one of them,
frisking and gambadoing in the most *fearful* manner !
dressed in a garment which would not have been
tolerated at Highbury Barn, dancing dances that ought
never to have been danced, singing songs which would
blench the cheek of Terese, winking winks that ought
never to have been wunk, even in dreams ! making
the very coco-trees above our heads bristle with horror !
Oh, you naughty, naughty girl !

Chapter IX.

SHIPWRECK.

HERE are three great classes of fools in this world; first, the wise fool, who knows he is an ass, but considers the fact a secret to be kept between himself and his Maker. Secondly, the happy fool who considers himself rather a genius than otherwise. Thirdly, the fool of fools, who consciously and defiantly proclaims his asininity to the world in general.

I belong to the latter class, the consequence of which is that I am now sitting down to compile the history of our shipwreck. It is copied nearly verbatim from the log that I kept all the time, and is truer to life in nothing more than in its malignant dulness. If, when this is published, any respectable person could come to me and conscientiously state that the perusal of the account had bored him as much as the real shipwreck had bored me, I should rest happily, feeling that my work had been a success.

It is not tragical; it is not humourous. How can

one do any fine writing, sitting on a brandy case, with
the rain coming down in long perpendicular rods, not
drops, which break on one's head and trickle down
one's nose on to the paper ; stopping every fifteen
seconds to take a revenge on a dozen or so of mosquitoes that are grazing coolly on one's hands ; whereby
one spills the ink, drops the book, and loses the pen,
which is discovered some time after planted two inches
deep in the mud like a young tree : one can't even
grumble fluently under such circumstances.

Most people who have written shipwreck and Robinson Crusoe stories have invented them out of their
fertile brains, and those who have actually described
what they have seen and been through in that time,
have put their adventures on paper, after they had
been sifted in their memories till little more than the
tragic or romantic sides of them remain.   Or, if their
accounts have been actually committed to paper at
the time, they have been polished afterwards, and little
dabs of romance sentiment or tragedy stuck in to
please the gushing and sensation-loving public.

This is the fault of such stories, and partly out of
obstinacy, and still more out of laziness, I intend to
avoid it.

Besides this, I consider originality is a thing to be
striven after, especially when it is to be acquired at the
cheap price of relating bare facts.

Robinson Crusoe is a delusion and a snare ; even in
the credulous days of infancy I was always slightly

sceptical on the subject of the " Swiss Family Robinson ;" their inventions were so wonderfully ingenious,
and nature seemed to fit in with their wishes and wants
with a readiness that seemed scarcely real.   I never
pinned my faith on " Foul Play " for the same reason.
Did the heroes or heroines of those books happen to
want a hip-bath, a balloon, an umbrella, a pet animal,
or any such small thing necessary to a person living
on a desolate island, the ingenious author would
immediately provide materials and the way to use
them.   A hip bath ?   One of those large water gourds
cut in half, scooped out, and stuck upon legs, and the
thing was done — (here would follow a long and learned
dissertation from the well informed member of the
ship-wrecked party—there always is an abominable
prig of this sort to act as chorus in such books—on
the subject of the large water-gourds of the South Sea
Islands, cribbed out of an Encyclopædia or some book
of travels).   A balloon !   Of course there were india-
rubber trees on the island—I don't know exactly how
they would set to work, but give the author of such
stories the trees, some flat stones, a fire, some scientific
treatise on the action of heat, and perhaps an old fry-
ing-pan, saved from the wreck, and he would rig them
out a balloon in no time.

An umbrella ? the plaited leaves of the pandanus
or screw-palm was just the thing !

A pet animal ?   A seal will do capitally ; there
ain't any in that part of the world, but that don't

matter. And so on *ad libitum;* indeed, I really don't know why a man with plenty of books to refer to and a ready imagination should be shy of building a cathedral on a coral-reef.

" Masterman Ready," that most delightful of books, has got the stamp of reality about it, but the romance of the life is kept uppermost, while its unutterable boredom and countless petty miseries show too faintly.

I suppose I say this because I am not a hero.

I don't like being turned out of my warm bed at night into the cold and wet of a fierce gale to be shipwrecked and perhaps drowned.

I don't like being chucked from one side of the cabin to the other like a sack of potatoes, barking my shins and nearly breaking my ribs.

I don't like being banged and crashed on a coral reef all night, expecting instant death by the sea or future extinction by cannibalism.

I don't like landing on a beastly little island without water, except pouring rain, and living there.

I don't like sleeping night after night with the rain trickling into my ears, with a swelled face and a toothache.

I don't like starting up in my sleep at every little noise, expecting to be tomahawked.

I don't like wearing wet clothes for a fortnight on end.

I don't like being cramped up for thirty hours in

a little overladen open boat, in an unknown and dangerous sea, alternately soused with salt-water and burnt by a tropical sun.

Heroes like such things, I believe ; I don't, though I can put up with them if necessary, without much grumbling. And though the greater part of our shipwrecked company were as brave as men could be, they weren't a bit like the heroes one finds in some books. When the spray was flying over the doomed vessel, and the pitiless coral was crushing her groaning sides, &c., &c., they were *not* filled with a joyous exultation in defying the raging elements—not a bit. They thought the wet and the danger and fatigue confoundedly disagreeable, and were as cool and prompt and cheerful as they could be under the circumstances.

I believe those ideal heroes who delight in everything uncomfortable, exist chiefly in novels and lunatic asylums : I hope so, I am sure, for I shouldn't like to have to live with one.

We had had a most charming three months' cruise, from Tahiti to the Samoas, visiting all the Society Islands and Raritonga on the way. Everywhere we had been treated like princes, and our cabin was lumbered with all kinds of curious presents—besides a large collection of birdskins, some very rare and valuable.

We left Samoa the morning of October 18, 1870, intending to look in at Levuka, the chief port of the Figi Islands, and thence to sail to New Zealand. On

R

leaving Apia, the chief port of the Island of Upolo, we coasted along, and ran between it and Savai the largest island of the group.

At the south end of Sawaii is an immense bed or rather tract of lava, which has been poured out at a very low angle. The sea has worked long tunnels into it, which form " meres " like those in Pembrokeshire, (the existence of the finest of which, Bocheston Mere, I saw flatly denied in a pseudo scientific book not five years ago !) The heavy ocean rollers entering the tunnels, are driven out through the small opening at the far end in most glorious clouds and columns of spray; some merely like the blowing of a whale, others like the bursting of a shell, whilst others spout up in snowy white columns 150 feet high. The spouting is cease-less, and sometimes several will be seen at once. The beauty of the thing is infinitely enhanced by the dead blackness out of which the snowy puffs spring, and the vivid green of the background.

Oct. 19.—Light fair wind.

Oct. 20.—Cloudy murky weather. Passed Proby's Island (known by half-a-dozen other names), lately the scene of a terrible eruption. In the evening it came on to blow.

Oct. 21.—At about half-past three this morning I was aroused by a crash overhead that woke us all up, and we scampered on deck, thinking the fore-top-mast had gone ; but it was only the old fish-fag (one of the boats) that had got into trouble. A sea just slapping her underneath had neatly unhooked the tackle of the fore davit, the boom to which she was lashed had snapped with the sudden weight, and she was hanging by the stern with her bows dragging through the water. They seized her in the main rigging, and by means of the throat halyards and another tackle from the foretop got her on board again not much damaged.

It blew fresh all day, while the weather grew thicker and darker, which made us rather anxious and uncomfortable, as we were approaching the dangerous and intricate Fiji Archipelago. After several false alarms we made land ahead, which we concluded to be Explorer's Island, to the south of the Nanuku passage, by which we intended entering the group. The wind was now about E. by S. and blowing a gale, so we wore and reached out under what canvass we could carry, as it would have been madness to have run in among the numerous reefs and islands in the dark with such weather ; the vessel headed about N.E., and though we could not make much headway in such a sea, we were confident of weathering all the groups to the north of the passage, according to the chart about forty miles dead to leeward of·us.

The wind grew stronger and stronger all the evening, bursting down in fierce rainy squalls, and the sea very heavy. It was as dark as pitch, but thinking ourselves to windward of all dangers, and being confident in the sea-going qualities of the " Albatross," we cared nothing for it all. At about nine o'clock the lifeboat was got on board, and being rather drowsy I turned in.

At about ten o'clock, as I was dozing off, I felt a sudden shock, a terrible lurch, and long trembling grind. The doctor shouted to me that we had struck, but it needed not that nor the cries on deck to tell me what had happened. I rushed out of my cabin to get on deck, when a heavier lurch and crash sent me slithering right across the saloon under the table. I scrambled up again and made for the companion, Mitchell appearing from his cabin with a hurried " What's the matter ?"

" You may say your prayers now," replied I, with a ghastly grin, " for the game's up with us." We climbed on deck and found ourselves in about as awe-inspiring a position as could well be imagined : the vessel lying almost on her beam-ends, the foam flying over her in a white cloud, every sea lifting her up and bringing her down again with a sickening crash, that made the cabin-floor heave like an earthquake, and her whole frame tremble, the scream of the wind sounding even above the roar of the surf, and all these horrors magnified by an intense darkness. The doctor and I said " Good-bye ;" indeed at that moment I don't think anybody but the skipper expected to live ten minutes.

Nor should we if the vessel had been deep laden, in which case she would have been crushed against the edge of the reef and sunk in deep water. As it was, every sea drove us further and further on to the coral.

The courage and steadiness shown by all hands was very striking. Braund (the master) behaved as he always does in times of danger, his cheery voice ringing out above the infernal din, and his honest face lit up by a quiet smile whenever it became visible in the glare of the skylight. Jim Bougard (the mate) backed him up in a cool smart way, and the men did all that men could do. There was no confusion or unnecessary shouting; the boats were all got over to the leeside and made ready to be cut away at a moment's notice, a work of no small difficulty when the angle of the slippery decks and the perpetual jerks and plunges of the vessel are considered.

As far as my own feelings were concerned, I could not help being amused by noting that with all the awe of death, and wonder about what was to come was mixed a kind of sulky irritation at being turned out of my warm bed into the cold water, and a feeling of unutterable disgust at the destruction of all my knickknacks and curiosities.

And when I succeeded in realizing the end that I thought was coming so soon, a host of old familiar faces from all parts of the world flitted swiftly before my mind, never so vividly remembered, and never perhaps better loved than at that moment, striking me with a sharp pang of sadness.

The skipper came up to us, and kindly and gently

advised us to go below and get dry clothes while there
was yet time.   So down we went and sat talking at
the foot of the companion, cheerfully enough all things
considered, M—— and Warden (the steward) bustling
about to the imminent danger of their bones to
collect a few provisions and necessaries before every
thing was spoilt by the water that was fast filling the
vessel.

Then an alarm came that we were being driven over
the reef, and should sink on the other side, so we went
on deck again, and waited, ready to take to the boats.
Soon it was discovered that the water was quite shallow to leeward, so there was no fear of that particular
danger. We went below again, it being determined
to stick to the vessel till daylight if possible, and felt
quite cheery at the reprieve. It is wonderful how soon
men *get accustomed* to being in danger, whether it is
unconscious fatalism, or merely the natural carelessness
of human nature I don't know. The saloon was now
getting full of water, so we were obliged to cram ourselves into Mitchell's little cabin up to windward,
where we passed rather a terrible night, though we
laughed and joked as much as we could to keep our
spirits up.

Our prospects certainly were not pleasant; the ship
could not hold together long, and we might have to
go many miles in the strength of the gale in open
boats before we could reach an island; and if we did
happen to hit upon an inhabited one we should be

nearly certain to be killed and eaten by the inhabitants.[1]

It was a sad thing to hear the crashing and straining
of the old ship, and the mournful toll of her bell overhead, and to see the decks opening and the bulkheads
breaking up inside her, with the chairs, books, clothes,
mats, and a hundred odds and ends floating about the
cabin. But everything pathetic or tragical has a co-
mical side to it, and I could not help laughing to see
the steward scrambling about collecting various articles for preservation, and continually slipping up
when a heavy jar came, and almost disappearing in
the dirty water to leeward. To make it better he had
my watches and their appurtenances, and my pipes
and tobacco in his pockets; their appearance when
produced was rather "mixed."

Occasionally the skipper came down to report the
state of affairs, or advise what should be provided, and
though I know he was terribly cut up, he talked coolly
and cheerily, and was very gentle and considerate.

He told us that he was on deck when she struck,
looking out amidships. Louey was doing the same

---

[1] We found afterwards that our apprehensions on the score
of cannibalism were needlessly great; but I have decided to
give them as they were felt and written down at the time.
Our sole informant and authority on the subject was the
"South Pacific Directory," which described the Fijians, and
the Ringgold islanders particularly, as the most ferocious
cannibals.

forward, and old Nelson (the second mate), was on the quarter deck, but it was so dark that none saw the breakers until she struck the coral and was dashed upon it broadside on. The night seemed to pass away slowly; about every ten seconds came an awful jar and crash that woke me whenever I began to doze, and made us wonder how long she would hold together. Collecting provisions and necessaries, and longing for light, the weary hours passed away.

Oct. 22.—At last the day broke, gloomy, wild, and wet, and we went on deck to find out our situation. About a mile to leeward of us on the same reef appeared a small island, and about half a mile from that a rather larger one; the vessel was lying about fifty yards inside the first break of the reef in about three feet of water.

The very heaviness of the sea had been our salvation hurling us right up on to the coral ledge into comparative safety.

Then one by one the boats were sent off, laden with compasses, quadrants, guns, ammunition, provisions, blankets, &c. Joining company again clear of the breakers we made for the little island, thirteen men in all, and all ready to fight if necessary.

It was a little coral-sandy place about one hundred and fifty yards long, by one hundred wide, with a steep beach, and a second step or terrace about thirty yards back, as if there had been a recent elevation.

We landed, and emptied the boats of their soddened

and sloppy contents, and then by way of making things
more thoroughly miserable, the rain came down in a
black, hopeless, tropical torrent.

Depressed and exhausted as we were, it was certainly most wretched; we made a kind of shed out of
the sail of the life-boat, and at last succeeded by
means of a dead log and some tarred twine in making
a fire, which improved matters a little; then every
one except the doctor, Warden, Little Taff (cook's
mate), and I, went off to the wreck to fetch the live
stock, and save what they could. Meanwhile the
doctor went exploring for water, which he didn't find,
while I amused myself by trying to dry the blankets
and clothes as they came ashore, rather a futile occupation. Taff got us some bacon and tea, which we eat
ravenously.

As I lay down I seemed to feel the ground shaking
and heaving under me. I thought it was an earthquake at first, so did the doctor, but we found it was
nothing but imagination, produced by the continued
jarring and shaking we had had all night.

I could also hear the voices of the men shouting
above the roar of the surf, and several times the illusion was so strong that I went down to the beach,
fancying the boats had come back from the wreck.
At last they all returned, very tired, having brought
ashore the live stock, sails, preserved meats, pots and
pans, mattresses, meats, &c. After they had had some
food, they rigged up two capital tents, a big one with

the vessel's squaresail, and a smaller one for the doctor and me, out of the topsail.

Louey, an ingenious little Norseman, chopped himself some sticks, and made a splendacious bedstead to sling his mat to.

I have succeeded in saving my manuscripts, though they are rather damaged. "Whatever anybody may say of your poems, none can call them *dry*," remarked the doctor, with a grin.

Close to our camp is an old native "Marai," or place of sacrifice, formed of big flat coral-stones. A kind of rough line, about three feet wide, runs down the middle of it towards the sea, terminating in a *cul de sac*. The height of the charred posts on each side of it tells very plainly what has been hung to cook there. A most villanous looking hole! And a nice place for a lot of shipwrecked mariners to have within twenty yards of their camp; something like the skulls and bones that the old hermits used to keep about them, to remind them of their end.

We can make out two islands in a west by south direction; one a low clump of trees, like the one we are on, and the other a high mountain, some thirty miles off.

Though we do not know yet exactly where we are, as no place in the chart answers exactly to the bearing of this island, there is no doubt that we are somewhere in the Ringgold islands, the most cannibalistic part of the Pacific. So we may think ourselves very lucky to have hit on an uninhabited place.

Great reefs stretch away in several directions as far as we can see; more dangerous waters for navigation cannot be imagined.

It came on to pour again, but the skipper and his men rigged mats and boatsails round the bottom of our tent, and made us pretty snug. Nothing could be kinder and nicer than they all have been, and we are more grateful than we can say.

Made a capital dinner on chicken-soup, and soon turned in. Rained hard all night.

Oct. 23. Every one discovered this morning that they were very much bruised and knocked about, a fact that they were quite unconscious of yesterday.

At low water most of the party went off again to the wreck, and brought off more things.

The skipper tried to get an observation, but was put out at the critical moment by a bird settling on his head. The only reef resembling this on the chart is a place called Nukumbasanga, in the extreme north-east of the Ringgold islands.

The poor old ship is breaking up, her lee side being raised two feet or more, and all the butts open enough to put your hand between.

Our plan at present is to wait for fine weather, determine our position, and run right away in the boats for Levuka, some one hundred and fifty miles; for if we are compelled to stop anywhere, we shall have to fight to avoid being eaten. We have got five guns, two axes, two revolvers, and five tomahawks, and I think all of us intend to take "utu," as the Maories call it, for ourselves before knocking under.

The life-boat will tow the dingey, and by means of lights the Fish-fag will be able to keep close to us.

It is rather provoking to think that we are within sixty miles of islands flowing with milk and honey, and yet daren't go near them. If we had been lucky enough to get wrecked in the Society's, Cook's Islands, or Samoas, we should have been half-killed with kindness, and made little gods of; whereas now we pray fervently that no one may see the wreck and find us out.

I don't approve of this kind of thing. If ever I am shipwrecked again I prefer doing it in the regular magazine-story style—a dismasted vessel—a lee shore —half an hour's agony—life or death—a rocket—a life-boat—a gallant preserver—a lovely female (with or without a sweet infant, according to the taste of the author)—and then a watery grave, or warm dry blankets and hot brandy and water! Warm dry blankets! I can hardly bear to think of such luxuries.

There are a few coco-nut trees on this island, but the chief vegetation consists of small india-rubber trees, with big broad leaves, on which certain curious crabs perch, and run about like birds. There is another kind of crab here that runs so fast, that one mistakes it at first glance for a small bird skimming along the shore, the more so as he takes occasionally the most extraordinary flying leaps.

There are quantities of pretty little terns, their breeding-place being close to our camp; the eggs are just laid on the sand, and the young ones hidden under the large black stones.

By the way, these black rocks that cover the beach on one side of the island are very curious; they are quite hard and solid, but they have been boiled in such a hurry as to have great shells imbedded in them.

There are also man-of-war birds, curlews, rats, pigeons, mosquitoes, flying foxes and lizards. Any amount of beautiful shells are scattered about the beach.

After a good dinner we went and sat under the life-boat sail by the cooking fire, and had some pleasant talk about past adventures. Every one hopeful and cheery, though this weather would give Joe Miller the blues.

Rained hard in the night, and my bedding getting drenched I had rather an unpleasant time of it. Besides this I had a fearful night-mare; dreamt that we were attacked by savages, and woke finding that I had got hold of the doctor, who had stumbled over me trying to get out of the tent.

Oct. 24. It cleared a little in the morning, and the camp soon presented the appearance of a great washing establishment, every wettable article being hung out to dry. I went to get a dip in the sea when I met old Nelson, rushing violently through the bush in pursuit of an imaginary turkey (we have turned all our live stock loose on the island). Mitchell afterwards went out on the same quest, armed with a gun, wounded the turkey, and a pig in the nose, who disappeared squeaking, whereon Mitchell came back disgusted.

His appearance is rather wild; he has been working like a brick for the last three days, and has worn his knees sore with the friction of his wet breeches. So he sports a pair of " pajamas " which he tucks up above his knees, and which, combined with a flannel shirt and a pair of Davy's boots unlaced, and about three sizes too large, gave him an appearance of a cross between Robinson Crusoe and a brigand in a play.

Jim went off in the dingey and saved some more miscellaneous articles.

The captain got an observation to-day that makes him pretty sure we are on the Nukumbasanga reef, though it is quite misplaced on the chart.

Most of the company are rigged in my socks, which I should think would want tying up at the toes to make them fit.

In the afternoon a regular hunt after live stock, the skipper managing to shoot a pig. Killing the fowls for dinner is great fun: we go after them through the bush with long sticks, driving them towards each other, and making long sweeps at them whenever we get a chance, but the trees generally get in the way of the stick and the fowl scuttles away into the bush triumphantly, till at last some one makes a lucky shot and bowls him over.

At four o'clock it came on to pour heavily again.
This is miserable weather.

After dinner we went down to the big tent and had
a talk. It would have made a splendid sketch in the
flickering candlelight—the two long rows of men on
each side, lying on their mats or bedding in every
kind of position; some dozing, some smoking, talking,
or reading old scraps of newspapers that had been
saved by some chance, while in the centre were heaped
up cases, guns, clothes, and all kinds of odds and
ends.

There we turned in for the night; the skipper, who
could not take more care of us if we were his own
children, looking in to see that we were all right.

Oct. 25. Went out of the tent with bare feet and
trod in an ant's nest. I understand now why the slug-
gard is to go to the ant. It will make him lively if anything will.

No change in the weather, except that it is blowing
harder—very depressing. The dingey went off again
to the wreck: no amount of knocking about seems to
injure that little boat, whereas both the others have
suffered a good deal.

Mitchell has painted a placard, and nailed it to a
tree : "Albatross—wrecked. Oct. 27th, 1870. Start
for Levuka the first fine day."

All pretty cheerful in spite of the weather. Old
Nelson trots about the sea-shore like a schoolboy pur-
suing crabs, and studying natural history generally.

He is afflicted with cramps, and dreams of savages at night, that cause him to awake with unmelodious yells, and clasp his neighbours by the throat, much to their disgust.

The doctor goes fishing daily, but seldom seems to catch anything definite, except wet clothes. As he says himself, "If he was being ferried over the Styx he would stop Charon to let him have half-an-hour's fishing." Mitchell, the skipper, the doctor, and I played cards in the evening.

Oct. 26. I find that sleeping on the top of an aneroid, two revolvers, a pair of boots, and a cigar-box, is not the most comfortable way of passing the night. The fact is, my bed got so swampy that I was obliged to turn off the mattress.

Gloomy and wet as ever. The captain went off to the wreck and got us some books, a great godsend. The vessel has been driven in nearly another length, and is slewed head on to the shore.

"D — the rain," said I heartily. "Damming's just what it wants," replied the doctor, "but unfortunately there is no way of doing it." However, to-day the sun shone for nearly ten minutes and quite dazzled us.

The doctor caught some fish for dinner, after which we went and played cards in the big tent.

Oct. 27. I woke before daybreak, drenched with rain, with a toothache, a slight cold, and half a stiff neck.

Rained hard half the day, and then drizzled. All hands employed in rigging bedsteads to keep them out of the wet as much as possible. Jim and Mitchell made us two splendid four-posters. If it had not been for the porous nature of the coralline soil, we should have been all knocked up before this.

Harry (the cook) tried to catch a pig to kill it; whereupon a certain old sow ran at him, and made hostile demonstrations till he was obliged to let go. The captain caught a big crawfish.

We should sleep better if it were not for the perpetual alarms of savages. Last night, as I was rolling about on my mattress, I heard the doctor cry, "Qui vive?" My hand was on my revolver in a moment. "What's up?" I whispered. "Something has been moving between me and the mouth of the tent for the last minute. Why it's your head!" At which we both laughed, and went to sleep again.

Jim told me that for the first two nights he could scarcely sleep at all, and even now the slightest noise wakes him. And the skipper told me that he woke the other night all of a tremble, fancying that he heard the doctor crying for help.

Half an hour's clear weather would enable the savages in the neighbouring islands to see the wreck, and bring them down on us *en masse*.

A pleasant position truly for a lot of harmless innocents like us.

No change in the weather. Some of the party

visited the other island, where they found some wonderful eels (murena), shells, and "curios" generally. This would be a wonderful place for a naturalist, but unfortunately our sojourn here is a miniature type of life :—we can carry nothing away with us,—so it's no use collecting.

I cannot help groaning occasionally over the tremendous loss of utterly irreplaceable things, all pleasant to look upon, for the sake of the generous people who gave them.

"Oh, Moé! where are the mats you gave me, and the pretty little arrowroot hats, and the reva-reva prepared by your own little brown fingers? Oh, Tampoa Wahine! where are the native dresses you sent to your most obedient? Oh, maidens of the Society Islands! where are the crowns you worked with such care, and threw down before my unworthy feet! Oh, Te Mitiki, commonly called Mitchell! where are those sixty precious bird-skins you prepared with such care? Oh, chiefs and chieftainesses of Raritonga! where is your tapa? where are your mats? where your sacred staffs? where the precious garments with which you decorated me?" Oh, bother! that's flat. This is the lament of Te Pemeruki, Rangatira of the Kaibuke Albatross. Oh, that I might eat the man who surveyed these islands!

However, the mats and live stock have proved invaluable in our adversity.

This is an awful place for sores; the slightest cut

or scratch refuses to heal. Every one is longing ardently for clear weather and a start. Rained in the night.

Oct. 29. " Look what I've found ! " said the skipper, as I came out of our tent in the morning; " a cross between a crab and a turtle." It certainly looked very like it, being a great white crab, like an inverted saucer, the legs and claws fitting in underneath it when drawn up, giving the idea of some ingenious portable invention. Weather a little finer, but the sky not yet washed and painted blue.

Harry killed one of the pigs, Tim and Taff warding off the attack of the old sow with a stick. I don't much believe in that old sow. She is a philanthropist —I mean a " philporcist," a regular Mrs. Jellyby of a sow. She neglects her own children in the most careless manner; but if any one touches one of the other pigs that are no connection of hers, and, indeed, come from a different island, she manages to work herself up into a state of most vicious (she would say generous) excitement. If ever her soul transmigrates into a human body, it will either get up a flannel waistcoat and moral pocket-handkerchief society for infant blacks, and make virulent speeches at Exeter Hall, or else it will go in for the opposition business, become a " religious," desert its family, and fuss up and down in a blue dress, with a great starched napkin on its head, and a large quantity of rope and rosary dangling about it.

They got an observation to-day, and decided we were on Nukumbasanga, which is considerably mis-placed on the chart. How we ever got so far to the westward is a problem. There must have been some extraordinary current springing up with the gale, for we were swept thirty miles nearly dead to leeward in less than five hours.

The noise of the rollers on the reef when we were wrecked was very like the falling of great trees. Often since, when I have been in a brown study, and the men have been chopping down trees for fire-wood, the crash of the falling branches has made me start, and half expect to feel the shock of the sea.

The doctor, the skipper, and Mitchell went off to the wreck, which is gradually breaking up.

I feel as if I had been months in this place, and, strange to say, am getting quite contented with the life. I get up at day-break, and bathe; then, if it is not raining hard, pick up shells and so on till break-fast. After that smoke pipes, read Shelley, write up my log, help to hang up the clothes to dry, and take them in again drenched half an hour after; then lun-cheon; then more pipes, and a stroll round the beach to study the habits of terns, or throw stones at them; then dinner, and cards or a chat in the big tent. When I want exercise I go and chop down a tree. But where's the romance of this kind of thing? unless you call it romantic to hear the terns screaming on the other side of the island in the middle of a dark wet night, and to creep through the bush towards the place where they are crying, expecting to find a canoe full of hungry, murderous savages, just landed, with the head chief serving out sherry and bitters to give them an appetite for supper.

Well, there is a certain grim pleasure, certainly, on such occasions, in grasping a tomahawk or a revolver, and thinking of the life you will take as payment before you give up your own. But that is a selfish, avaricious feeling, not worthy of the name of romance.

It strikes me more and more forcibly every day, how strangely cool and fearless men get when they have been placed for a little while in a desperate situation. We all of us know, I suppose, what we have got to go through in making our escape— fatigue, exposure, misery and danger, for thirty or forty hours on end at the shortest, and an indefinite time if the wind comes ahead, besides the prospect of certain death if it comes on to blow hard. And yet no one seems funky, and we are all longing to make the attempt. The main reason for this is the almost superstitious confidence we have got in the courage and resources of the skipper, who is one of those men created especially to lead others. We all feel that he will bring us safe through if it is possible, and if not, we can but die once.

This morning we found the tracks of a turtle on the sand, that had visited the island in the night; but it had laid no eggs. Probably she had been suddenly

confronted by an inquisitive pig, and gone away in a
sulk.

Polished up the guns and revolvers to-day. The
camp is beginning to stink of decaying animal matter.
If we are not off soon we shall have dysentery.

Oct. 30. Hurrah ! fine weather ! or rather, the best
imitation of it they can get up in this blessed island.
The skipper at once determined to start to-morrow;
so the sheep were hunted down and slain, the fowls
had their necks broken, after being knocked down
with sticks, and Harry set to work to cook everything
he could lay hands on. Now we *must* go, or we shall
be starved. Our fleet consisted of a small lifeboat,
by White of Cowes, eighteen feet long, sharp at both
ends; the "fish-fag," a rough, serviceable boat, about
the same size and shape, but much less deep; the
dingey, a wonderful little craft, fifteen feet long, like a
whale-boat with ten feet taken out amidships. They
were all more or less damaged by the bumping they
got at the time of the shipwreck, but were good sea-
boats, and fair sailers.

The doctor, the captain, Harry, the cook, big Taff
and I, man the lifeboat; old Nelson, little Taff, and
Louey, the dingey; Jim, Mitchell, Warden, Tom, and
Davy, the "fish-fag;" which consequently will have
the strongest crew, as is necessary. If the dingey
turns out too slow, she will be towed by one of the
others.

We shall be forty-eight hours at least, I should

think; and with calms or head-winds any time. Unpleasant, but can't be helped. If it comes on to blow, with our deep-laden boats, God help us!

I believe the proper platitude to use on such occasions is "trust in Providence;" but it seems to me that people who do so are as likely as not to be disappointed. I mean no irreverence, and am quite ready to trust in Providence, in the wider sense of the expression, but I don't believe He changes the wind and weather, or anything else in this world, for the benefit of particular individuals. The men on whom the tower of Siloam fell were no worse than any one else in the town. Two sparrows do not fall to the ground without God knowing it, *but the sparrows fall all the same.* We shall either be providentially drowned or providentially saved.

11 A. M. We have changed our plan, and start as soon as the meat is cooked, as every hour of calm weather is of vital importance. Now for the pinch!

There are two kinds of mosquitoes here, a small black one, and a big spotted one. Both bite only in the daytime.

By three o'clock the boats were all loaded and ready for a start. The men very naturally wanted to save all their things; the consequence of which was that the fish-fag and lifeboat were filled with lumber even above the thwarts, and, with their crew of five men each, were almost down to the water's edge at every little lurch, by no means a proper trim to go one hundred and fifty miles through open sea, tide rips and perhaps breakers.

However, we didn't like to throw away anything till it was absolutely necessary; so as soon as the dingey, that had been used to bring off the cargoes of the other boats from the shore, was ready, the sails were set, anchors weighed, and with the lifeboat as commodore leading the way, we crossed the reef and bid farewell to Nukumbasanga.

We had three courses open to us: either to run to leeward of all the Ringgold Islands and then haul up for the Somo Somo passage; or to keep to windward, and try and weather all the reefs and islands till we got into the Nanuku Channel, some twenty miles distant; or else, if we could not succeed in weathering them, to lay on our oars for the night and run between them next morning. We determined to take one of the two last, and stood away closehauled about south by east, the lifeboat taking the dingey in tow.

But our troubles began early; though the weather was fine and there was no great sea, the boats were so deep and dead that they made very little way; and the fish-fag and lifeboat could only pull one oar with any effect under sail on account of the lumber. We kept at it as hard as we could till sundown, but there were still no signs of the Nanuku reef, which we judged to be right a-head or on the weather bow, while the long chain of smaller reefs were somewhere close to leeward of us.

Just before dark we perceived the crew of the fish-fag, that had dropped astern and to leeward of the other boats, making signals to us, and we bore down to them to see what was the matter.

We found them in a very uncomfortable state of mind. She was as dead as a log, they said, and they could scarcely keep her free by baling : if she wasn't lightened she would sink under them. We could not help them by taking any of their load, being in much the same predicament ourselves, the water slopping in on all sides; but we shifted Warden into the dingey (which was much more buoyant than either of the others), and told them to chuck the things overboard if necessary, as we should have to do in our boat.

The fish-fag's painter was then made fast to the dingey, and the three boats went on their course attached to each other. But in the dark our position became far more exciting than pleasant ; we knew we were close on to the reefs, and every breaking sea was the cause of an alarm.

" There it is to windward ! " " I see it to leeward ! " " Breakers right ahead ! " Very trying to the nerves of me, the steerer, being the only one who could not look out a-head.

After about half-an-hour of this work, the skipper decided to down sail and lay on the oars till day break. We were disappointed, but there was no help for it, as we should have been amongst the breakers before we had time to turn in the dark. The order was passed to the other boats, the painters were cast off, and the masts were unshipped. At this critical moment, when the boat was lying helpless in the trough of the sea, " big Taff," who was unrigging the boat, looked over his shoulder and yelled out—"There it is, sir; close on the leebow!" and leaving go the mast made a snatch at an oar, and nearly tumbled overboard. The skipper promptly got a paddle over the stern and slewed the boat round, but it turned out to be another false alarm.

Then the boats closed up and were kept head on to the sea. Sometimes as one of them forged up alongside, emerging out of the darkness like a white ghost, a small attempt at chaff or a joke would be made, but it died a natural death; everyone was too tired and wretched.

An awful night it was! hour after hour pulling and baling in a rough broken sea, wet to the skin and tired to death. Listening nervously for the roar of the surf, watching the black masses of water as they charged our bows and shut out the dim horizon, and gazing up anxiously at each cloud as it rose and hid the stars.

" What a precious scrape we are in!" I kept thinking. "I wonder if we shall be living still two days hence? I always used to complain that I never met with any adventures in my travels, but this business will set me up in that line for some time if I get out of it alive." And then again a ghostly procession of old faces and places passed before me, with an intense vividness and reality in their perfect love and happiness, that seemed like some bitter devilish mockery.

A feeling of want of sympathy is the mainspring of human misery. In joy and in sorrow the stars twinkle, the wind blows, and the sea moans alike. And then from the depths of a man's soul rises the cry that has been the origin of so many great religions:—" Oh, God ! give me a sign that I may know that I am not utterly lonely and forsaken."

Few men *trust God enough* to be rationalists. Few men have humility, faith, and courage to say :—"There is a great Power that made the illimitable universe, and all that is in it : I know not why it was made, nor the purpose of all the pain and misery that I see round me ; I know nothing except that I am placed here with certain instincts of right and wrong ; God is omniscient and my understanding is limited ; I must learn what I can of His laws, and fearlessly trust the rest to Him that made me."

For most minds this is not sufficient ; there is a natural longing for something tangible and sympathetic to cling to. There is something so terribly dreary, lonely, and forsaken in that confession—that the misery of life, and the purpose of the universe can never be known or explained by man.

Who can look up at the stars without some such feelings ? Where is the end of that dark, mysterious space overhead ? What is happening in those countless worlds that we are gazing on ? Perhaps souls higher than we can conceive, and natures to which ours is as a rough sketch by the side of a finished master-piece, are doing their work there to some great end. How many millions lie beyond our view ? Perhaps the universe is illimitable ! Who shall say ? It is as easy to comprehend that, as the past eternity which must have been. Where was the beginning ? where will be the end ? and what is the purpose of it all ? Go mad, man ! Go mad ! for the wisest sanity is but infinite ignorance.

You cannot tell me why that moth that has just flown into the candle was made to suffer those agonies. Pious people say it is because Eve eat apples, but that seems precious hard lines on the moth. Go mad, I tell you ! But you won't, you man ; you are but an animal yourself—you eat, drink, sleep, die, marry, and are sold in marriage, and are only superior to the other animals in that you can wonder occasionally what it all means.

I remember when I was a little child the awe with which these things used to fill me. They used to seize me like some magic spell as I lay awake at night. I could not escape from them ; but would try hour after hour to realise in my baby mind the idea of past time without a beginning (that was always more awful and strange to me than the endless eternity), until I was half-mad with terror and bewilderment, and with a gasp, like a drowning man rising to the surface of the water, would struggle back to my animal life again.

I don't think these terrors of childhood are things to be laughed at and depised; they are the first dawnings of the infinite mysteries of creation and life on the young soul.

As men grow older the vividness of their wondrous reality grows faint by their constant presence, but to the child they are new and terrible in their sublime immensity.

Everything is so strange and vast that nothing seems tangible or comprehensible. Well I remember the awful agonies of prayer and despair that used to seize me,—the desperate onging for some absolute and comforting revelation to believe and trust in implicitly.

Bang! Splash! and a bucketful or so of cold salt water souses me all over, and completely puts an end to my prosing reverie.

At last the day began to break, and as soon as it was light we got the other boats alongside, and served out their biscuits, brandy, and water. Such a pale woe-begone set of wretches as we looked in the morning light I never saw. Fashionable young ladies after a heavy ball at the end of the season were nothing to it. I believe we would all have sold our birthrights for a cup of hot tea.

We found that we were literally on the reefs, the water being quite shallow, but it did not break anywhere as far as we could see : this accounted for the nasty short sea we had noticed all night.

Budd's Island lay about W. by N. of us, close to that were Holmes and Maury Island, while to the S.W. we could dimly see the peaks of Lauthala and Kamia, for which we steered as soon as the sails were set. There was a fine fresh breeze aft of the beam, but finding that we were rather dropping the dingey, we waited for her and helped her by a tow line ; when the Fish-fag took the lead.

The little boat made capital weather of it, and the Fish-fag did pretty well ; but the lifeboat was so heavily loaded that she could scarcely rise to the sea, and took it first over the weather quarter and then over the lee gunwale, in a most unpleasant style.

The doctor, who had had his spell at the oar, went fast asleep, in spite of the continual sluices of cold water, which were scarcely enough to keep me awake, as I was steering, though I had done no pulling in the night.

We passed right over the long chain of reefs, there being no actual break on them that we could see, but soon after got into a very nasty tide-rip that we were very glad to get out of again, with the boats in such a trim.

In about five hours we had run pretty close to Kamia, and then, being assured of our position, we made all sail before the wind for the north point of Taviuni, whose great heavy-clouded mountains began to grow distinct. There we managed to get something to eat and drink, and though the chicken was strongly-flavoured by the various articles it was jammed against in the locker, and the biscuits were steamy and inhabited by cockroaches, we felt much more lively after it.

It was a pretty sight to see the three little boats bowling along together before the crisp fresh breeze under their mainsails and squaresails.

No one but the steerer appeared to be awake in the Fish-fag, and we were much in the same condition.

On reaching Taviuni we ran close along the shore, and to our surprise saw unmistakeable traces of white inhabitants, but we determined, if possible, to get to Goat's Island before night, and didn't land.

The shore here was covered with splendid trees right up the steep slopes and gorges, with great masses of pendant creepers rising to and hanging from the very tops of them—a grand bit of hill side.

In one of the bays was a small schooner standing off and on the shore, and, running towards her, we tried to speak with her ; but apparently she did not like the white ensign that the lifeboat carried, and made all sail away for the Somo Somo Straits.

On this the lifeboat ran in shore towards a house that had a missionaryish look about it, while the other boats kept their course. But seeing nothing human fairer than mahogany, we stood out again in the track of our companions.

At last we rounded a point and were fairly in the Strait. The wind here died quite away. Tired and "played out" as we were, we could not help being struck with the strange beauty of the scene. On one side the beautiful Taviuni, the garden of the Fijis, as it is well called, with its splendid vegetation stretching from the shore up the sides of its precipitous mountains and wild dark gorges, mysteriously half-hidden in dense masses of cloud; before us a glassy sheet of water, calm and smooth, yet gloomy and dreary, only broken by the wooded rocks of the Little Goat Island, that seemed like a bubble on its surface; while on the other side the peaks of Vanua Levu rose one above the other till they were lost in the dim distance.

Soon we observed the other boats stop and wait for us, and on coming up they cried to us that they thought they saw a ship lying at anchor in the distance.

We looked, but were not certain, as it was a long way off, so we determined to pull for Goat's Island, try fairly with a telescope, and then make for the ship, if ship it was.

The masts and sails were stowed, a modest go of liquor served out to put a little life into us, and away we went.

The lifeboat had forged some way a-head of the others, when it occurred to us to ask questions of our suspicious friend the schooner, that was lying becalmed not far off. As we drew up to her we perceived a lot of natives on board, but only one white man. We

pulled under her stern, and asked, " What vessel is that
lying at anchor ?"

" ' The Duke of Edinburgh,' bound for Levuka to-
morrow ;"—(spontaneous relief, joy and excitement
in all our countenances)—" Do you belong to a man-
of-war ?" said he.

" No ; a yacht, wrecked in the Ringgold Islands.
Are you an Englishman ?"

" No ; I'm a Swede."

Whereon the doctor became inspired and spoke to
him in German. What a weight seemed taken off our
minds.

When the dingey came up we gave them the welcome news, and then the weary Fish-fags.

Another sip of brandy to give us a "gallop for the
lawn," for our troubles were nearly over. And then
away we went, and a precious pull we had : the tide
was against us strong, and the deep laden boats seemed
as heavy as lead to our weary muscles. When, at last,
we got alongside, and found ourselves on the deck of
the vessel, I could scarcely stand from cramp and
fatigue. The passengers looked curiously over the
bulwarks at the strange boat procession, each laden
with such an extraordinary cargo of notions. And
well they might stare, for we certainly were not pretty
to look at.

Our clothes had been dirty and drenched with salt
and fresh water for nine days on end : our arms and
faces were of the colour of a boiled lobster, with the skin

T

peeling off them—my nose, in particular, being litc-
rally raw; — our eyes fearfully bloodshot, our lips
cracked and bleeding—altogether, an imaginative man
might have taken us for a gang of over-worked fire-
men, from the infernal regions, coming up to get fresh
air. However, they were all very obliging and kind,
one old gentleman in particular, who provided us with
blankets, &c. to sleep on.

The sun was just setting as we reached the vessel,
and we soon sat down to a capital tea, with butter
and real bread! My word! — as they say in the
colonies. Oh, the pleasure I experienced that night
in hearing the pouring rain, and knowing it could not
get at me.

And so this unpleasant adventure came to a happy
conclusion. It is nice to look back upon now, and if
I were to re-write this article I could make quite a
romantic story of it, without much alteration or exaggeration. But I vowed a vow to use no rouge or
pencils, and with the exception of that dreary reverie
in the boats, only admitted on the strength of its extreme prosiness, I have kept my oath.

I had another small turn at the shipwreck business
about a month afterwards. The steamer bound for
Levuka to Auckland running into a coral reef in Suva
harbour. But it was a very kid-glovey kind of shipwreck, the vessel being got off in twenty-four hours
without the smallest damage ; indeed, its only re-
deeming feature was the extreme terror of a selfish,

cantankerous old parson, who was so concerned for
the safety of his soul, or, perhaps, its vile earthly tene-
ment, that B——— had to be sent for to soothe and
comfort him. He had been making himself ob-
noxious to many of us, and we gloated over his
misery. I was even wicked enough to say, mysteriously and solemnly to a friend in his hearing, " If
we don't get off this tide, and a breeze should spring
up, the vessel will break her back and sink suddenly,
to a moral certainty." It was brutal, but I have no
mercy on a cowardly parson ; a selfish fear of death
being a direct contradiction, in practice, to all his
preaching.

I hate cowards, but since I have learnt what danger
and discomfort really are, the ideal story-book hero
has become my pet detestation.

It used to puzzle me why so many people, represented as villains of the deepest dye, were always
trying vainly to knock him on the head, shoot him,
stab him, poison him, or get rid of him somehow. I
understand it now, and sympathise deeply with those
villains ; the fact is he was simply unbearable to
ordinary mortals,—we were a good-natured, tolerant,
peaceloving set of Christians on the whole ; yet, I am
certain that if we had had one of these danger-and-
discomfort-loving heroes amongst our shipwrecked
party we could not have borne him for more than three
days. His perverse lunacy would by that time have
become intolerable, and after a solemn meeting and

deliberation we should have attempted to cut his
throat. I say attempted because we should never have
succeeded in doing it ; he would have made his escape
on the back of an alligator, or something of that kind ;
or else after successfully sticking him, and suffering
agonies of remorse for five years, he would turn up
again, and we would discover that we had not murdered him but some one else, who was our long-lost
brother, second cousin twice removed ; or, better still,
the chief instigator of the dire attempt. You can't
kill these people until they have married some equally
uncomfortable heroine, when, I suppose, the spell becomes broken, and they finally die a natural death, surrounded by a rising generation of young idiots, like
themselves. If it wasn't for this law the breed could
never be kept up.

If it should ever be the destiny of any reader of
this work to be shipwrecked, let me advise them to do
it in a dry climate, at a fine season of the year : wet
weather adds to the misery of the thing a thousand
fold. Rain is a detestable invention, and it really
makes me quite sad to think that since the creation
no better way of fertilising the earth has been found
out and adopted. In the innocent days of childhood
I used to fancy that it came from some tap in the sky
which was turned on whenever the sun parched up the
earth too much ; this might seem an awkward and imperfect method, but it was at least comprehensible as

regards its utility. But as I grew older I was obliged to discard my poetical ideas of angels with big watering-pots, being informed that rain came not originally from the sky but from the earth itself. Why on earth they can't leave the water where it is, instead of first sucking it up and then sluicing it all down again, it is difficult to conceive. Perhaps they use it to wash the cherubs with, or clean their teeth : they have got teeth according to the pictures, though what they want them for I don't know, as they can't eat any thing with only a head and wings ; but this is getting too glaring a copy of the style of St. Thomas Aquinas, who used to calculate the exact number of angels that could dance at once on the point of a needle, and debate seriously as to whether certain things existed and were used in heaven that are not ordinarily mentioned in the gilded saloons of duchesses. He was a saint and an early father, and so might write what he pleased ; I am not a saint, nor even an early father, so I musn't.

Metaphysical theology is to me much as Charles the First was to poor Mr. Dick in his memorial. If I had to write an article on ladies' chignons, clockmaking, the Court of Chancery, or any thing you please, I am quite sure I should find myself analysing the theory of the fall of man, or the foundation of belief in miracles, before I had got half through my paper.

I wrote my chapter on Missionaries first, in the hope of working off this tendency for the time, but I find that my case is hopeless: I feel the fit coming on me strong at this moment, and lest I convict myself irretrievably I shall bring this story to a close.

CHAPTER X.

MISSIONARIES.

S Christianity the only true and useful religion in the world, without which none can be saved?

Is religion an end, and not merely a means to an end?

The majority of Christians would, I believe, answer these questions with a dogmatic, and rather indignant affirmative; but there seems to be a small but steadily increasing body of educated men, who, if they do not at once deny such propositions, at least hesitate before giving their unqualified assent to them?

Is it not a bold thing to state that the religious belief of one portion only of humanity is a direct revelation of truths from God, while those of the rest of mankind are mere inventions of man, or of that humanly invented Bogy the Devil?

As I pass from one race or religion to another, from the Christian to the Moslem, from the Moslem to the Buddist, and from the Buddist to the Hindû, and see each faith, contradictory or imperfect as it may be, doing more or less good to the morals or mental development of the people who hold it, I had almost said, I cannot help feeling a conviction—that each is a step in the Almighty's great plan of improvement leading to some great end, which as yet we can scarcely guess at; and that every religious system in the world is a ray of light more or less indistinct and imperfect from the same great luminary.

Such a doctrine might seem at first sight to tend to a dangerous quietism, checking or sneering down that enthusiasm of belief which has caused the most extended creeds of the world to spring up and spread with such marvellous quickness and vitality. But this is not the case if it is more profoundly examined, for it teaches us how, step by step, God has allowed His laws and ways to become revealed, however slowly, to the different human races; and it teaches, above all things, a belief in the continual progress, however gradual, of the mind of man. A religion or a nation comes forward, does its work, and dies of old age and inability to keep up with the onward march—a higher development of race being possibly necessary to appreciate a higher religion, another steps into its place, and the universe moves steadily on to that destination, known only to its great Leader and Creator. This kind of belief naturally inclines me to judge of a tree solely by the fruit it produces. If I was a believer in the doctrine that there was no salvation out of the pale

of my own particular creed, I should be the first to
worship, help, and encourage the man, who, humanly
speaking, wastes his life, talents, energies, his own
and other people's money, for the sake of making a
few very doubtful Christians out of the same number
of tolerably respectable Mahommedans or Hindus.
But, looking at the case from such a mental position
as the one I have just sketched, I am naturally inclined to say that it is a pity and a mistake, much as I
may admire the individual who gives up anything for
what he believes right.

Wherever I see old and evil customs, such as cannibalism, human sacrifice (though the idea of the latter
lingers in the most respectable religion), or any such
little weaknesses of ultra-savage life, suppressed by the
incoming of a higher religion, I hold that it has done
good (though there is good reason to believe that the
mere intercourse with higher races would have abo-
lished them without the necessity of any distinct *religious* teaching); but when, on the other hand, I see
the general customs, morals, and character of the
people very little if at all altered for the better by their
change of faith, I am inclined to look on it as a sheer
waste of time, talent and money, squandered on an attempt to teach people a religion that is utterly unsuited
to their temperament and understanding ; a tithe of
which, expended at home, would have produced results
of incalculable value.   Some such idea as this seems
to have been used by the Hindus, to the slight bothe-

ration of the Baptists in India. One of the brethren complained piteously that the Hindus do not think it right to " win souls." " According to their system all religions are right, all are but so many different ways to one blissful end. Provided every one has faith in the religion of his own peculiar country and nation, he will be saved at last. Religion is a *national* thing all the world over ; and for an Englishman to disown Christ, or for a Mahommedan to disown Mahommed, is, in either case, the most grievous sin a soul can commit." [1] The brother does not give his answer to this argument, which puts one in mind of the old rhyme :

> " Many a one,
> Owes to his country his religion,
> And in another would as strongly grow,
> Had but his nurse or mother taught him so."

My personal acquaintance with individual Missionaries is perhaps not very extensive, but the species is such a large and prominent feature in South Sea society, that it is impossible to help hearing a good deal about them, whether from their fellow-workers, traders, white residents, or natives. In a very short time one seems to know half the reverend gentlemen of the South Pacific by name, and to have a general sketch of each one's character and method of working.

The Missionary, especially on the smaller and less frequented islands, is a public character, or great chief,

---

[1] Seventy-eighth Report, Bapt. Mission, p. 51.

on whose character and policy depends, to a great degree, the success of the trader, be he Beachman [1] or merchant skipper.

It is a disputed point whether the Roman Catholic or the Protestant missionary is the most powerful, not to say tyrannous over his dusky flock. It depends very much on the form and strength of the native government. If that be central and strong I should think the Protestant would have the advantage if he made himself useful to the reigning chief: in the other case I should think the Papist would have what in these seas would be called the "pull." Their men are more. highly educated and cultivated than the greater part of those sent out by the various Dissenting bodies. They are also more successful in keeping other religions at a distance, and by no means particular as to the means they use to gain their end, and which they carry out in bland opposition to all human rights as at present understood. Not that I have any reason to believe that the Wesleyans are much better at heart on that point, they only want the power, not the will. This, for want of that iniquitous and horrible power the priests gain over their flock through the confes-

---

[1] Beach-man, or "Beach-coomer," is a slang name for the white men who have settled down among the natives. They are generally ex-whalers, men-of-war's men, or merchant sailors who have "run" their ships and not unfrequently are to be found "gentlemen," who think it unadvisable to revisit civilised communities.

sional, they cannot get. Though I believe that some sort of monthly catechising and ticket system, answers somewhat the same purpose.

Whatever good the Wesleyans may do " spiritually " the mischief they work " commercially," whenever they have a chance, is beyond counting, and the common name of their missionary schooner, " The Palm Oil Trader," is, according to their own account, well deserved. If the Wesleyan Society had not published the facts themselves I should have hesitated to state them. Can it be believed that out of the kindly credulous Tonga Islanders, just struggling into civilisation, and whose every dollar, hardly earned, should and would be spent on the improvement of their country, were it not for these canting sharks, they get " the noble and astonishing sum of £4,489 16s. 2d., which with £1,550 received as *class* and *oil* money, makes a total of £6,000, being £3,500 above the current expenses of the Mission for the year, to assist in sending the glorious Gospel of Christ to regions beyond."[1] Beyond where? To those who know the generous excitable natures of the South Sea Islanders, this must be looked upon as sheer pillage.

However, as I don't want to be impertinent or to hurt any one's feelings, as Daniel O'Connell said when he called the Speaker an idiotic old fool, I must carefully distinguish mere hearsay information from that which I

---

[1] Wesleyan Methodist Missionary Report, April, 1870.

know from personal experience or have learned from
the missionaries themselves.

I will begin by a bit, not of hearsay, but of printed
and published information, which bears on my state-
ment anent the Roman Catholics and the Wesleyans,
and I am the more induced to do so as the authority
is of the highest though the publication is not easily
attainable.

Dr. Gräfe, an eminent naturalist, who thoroughly
knows the Kanakas and their ways, tells us that the
inhabitants of the beautiful island of Uvea have already
had severe combats with the Tongans in order to
maintain their independence. The last took place in
1832, when an army of Tongans, with their chief,
sailed from Keppel's Island for Uvea, on board a
whaler, under the pretence of spreading the Christian
religion amongst the then heathen Uveans. This they
proceeded to do somewhat after the good old fashion
of " Olave the *Saint.*" They descended on the little
island of Nukatea, which did not belong to them, and
founded what they called a Christian colony, from
which they were to extend their " privilege " to their
neighbours. Not finding the *suaviter in modo* do
much good, they tried the *fortiter in re,* by threaten-
ing an influential man called " Sohni " with destruction in this world if he declined any longer to insure
himself from worse in the next, at their office. He,
however, resisted, and his people rose against the
religious invaders. These had come provided with

plenty of arguments in the shape of muskets and ammunition, and when the Uveans attacked them many were killed; this slaughter, however, only nerved the heathens to greater efforts, and with nothing but spears and slings, they won the Block-house on Nukatea, and put to death all they found there. So far so bad. Now comes the second part of the story. About twenty years ago the Uveans were " converted" by the French Catholic Marists, and thereupon conceived a vast dislike to the Protestant or Wesleyan religion, on account of the old attempt to convert them, and they expelled all the Protestant converts and the missionaries. King George of Tonga, upon whose island these suffering ones landed, was naturally anxious to get rid of them, not only for their sakes, but his own, and determined that they should be sent back, even with force of arms if necessary.

" How far the Wesleyan missionaries in Tonga spirited up the King to this action is unknown; but it is worth observing, that it is stated that the captain of an English man-of-war, 'The Brisk,' which visited Uvea in 1867 (?), insisted on landing Wesleyan missionaries on a Roman Catholic island, and, to stop all remonstrance, pointed to the guns of H.M.S. as a part of his argument, which there was no gainsaying. If this be true, (and it is published in Dr. Gräfe's " Reisen nach verschiedenen Inseln der Sud-See, 23 and 24 of 'Ausland,' 1868,"—*Gotta of Augsberg*) it is only another proof of the astounding liberties

taken by sentimento-religious captains of men-of-war.
Whims are always dangerous, be they religious or
laical; but when a man backs his opinions with Queen
Victoria's powder and shot, the thing becomes very
serious. But it is of no use appealing to common or
any other sense on this subject. Those who do these
things are so encased in a rhinoceros hide of self-
conceit and self-laudation — believing that they and
they only are doing the " work of the Lord," that the
ruin and misery they inflict pass them by as things
of no import, and if at any moment some twinge of
conscience hints to them that all is not quite right,
half-an-hour on the sacred platform of Exeter Hall
acts as an effectual anodyne, and soon stills the re-
membrances of the men they have ruined, and the
nations they have insulted, to say nothing of the flag
they have dragged in the mud in the prosecution of
their own miserable little narrow-minded " beliefs."
Of all the reckless mischief-makers in the world, com-
mend me to a captain of a man-of-war attached to a
" strong religious persuasion !" Would they were all
knocked on the head like that worthy who received
his quietus "introducing the gospel," with " the
sword in one hand and the Bible in the other," as if
Her Majesty's navy was instituted for the propagation
of " Dissenterdom."

In order to prevent any confusion arising from the
vague terms " Kanaka," or South Sea Islander, which
may be construed to mean either a hideous little squat

Solomon Island negro, or a great, perfectly-formed, yellow Marquesan, I will lay down a set of definitions which may serve to prevent mistakes, however erroneous they may be from a scientific standpoint:—

1. Polynesians, inhabiting the Society, Sandwich, Marquesas, Low Archipelago (Pomotu ?), Cook's, Hervey Islands, &c., &c.
2. The Western Polynesians, inhabiting the Navigation, Tongas, &c., who are slightly touched with black blood.
3. Semimelanesians, such as the Fijians (N. Z. Maories ?), &c.
4. Melanesians, *i. e.* the New Caledonians, Solomon islanders, New Hebrideans, &c., &c.

Thus, having cleared our way, let us go back to our missionaries. The greatest schools I have come across are the Roman Catholics (of various " denominations," if I may be permitted the word), the Wesleyans, the emissaries—mostly "Congregationalist"— of the London Missionary Society, and those of the Church of England. The " Baptists," for reasons of their own, which I do not pretend to fathom, do not " work " the South Seas, sticking more particularly to the East and West Indies; in which, particularly the former, their success seems hardly to be worth the money expended, except to their missionaries, in spite of their quotation of Sir J. P. Grant, which, read by the light of the unregenerate, is anything but complimentary to them.

The Roman Catholic missionaries, of various denominations or sects, are widely scattered over the islands of the South Sea, more particularly in those wherein there has been some sort of civilisation already effected by another mission, which is very notable in the disgraceful affair (more to England than France,) of Tahiti. They play the part of jackal to the old English Missionary Lion, not leading him to his prey, but coming in to steal as much of the carcase as they can after the struggle is over, going noisily about with a few miserable bones in their mouths, to make all foolish animals believe that they killed the savage monster themselves. The success of any missionary efforts, so far as " religion " is concerned, is more than doubtful; but considering the early start of the Catholics in America (shall we say?), and its consequences, they have no right to crow over Protestants in the way they do. Moreover, they do not play fair. The other day some of theirs—all most honourable gentlemen—at Tahiti, distributed pictures amongst the natives representing the Crucifixion, and informed them that the figures standing round and mocking the Saviour were Protestant missionaries of all the different sects represented in the South Seas. The natives only laughed at them; and the Protestants, with a good sense that was hardly to be expected, contemptuously declined to take any notice of such an attack. Apart from Tahiti, which the weakness of England permitted them to occupy, their principal and

spocial fields of labour are :—Isle of Pines (where they
don't labour at all); the New Caledonia, where they
labour a great deal too much, to the great annoyance
of the Government of the former island, the Marquesas,
and the Gambier islands.　In the Marquesas I was informed by Admiral Cloué, they had not made a single
convert, had given up proselytising as hopeless, and
taken to cotton planting, " for the good of the
Church," of course.　One missionary was found there
so completely nativised as to have forgotten his own
language.　In the Isle of Pines the Roman Catholics
carry on as brisk an oil trade as the Wesleyans in
Tonga.

In the Gambier Islands their work has certainly been
very remarkable.　They have converted the natives
with a vengeance, and they bring them into the paths
of virtue in a style which reminds one forcibly of Tom
Hood's butcher, in the "Ode to Rae Wilson," "con-
ciliating " a sheep to make it go in the one direction
he wanted.　They rule the natives with a rod of iron.
They allow no woman to oil or decorate her hair, shut
lots of them up in convents (shade of Captain Cook!
imagine a Polynesian Nun), and have in fact bullied
them into such an unnatural state of virtue, that the
unfortunate people, who certainly do not seem to have
been created by Providence with an "ascetic (? acetic
or vinegary) tendency, have taken to make their
escape in canoes, preferring the chance of being
drowned and going to Hades to having their souls

saved by such very disagreeable processes. They are even reported, by the French, to have enlisted the dogs of the island in the cause of virtue, but the manner in which this is done would be difficult to describe in print. A stranger landing there is watched the whole time he is on shore, sent off forcibly if necessary to his ship at sunset, and on the slightest infringement of the missionary laws is imprisoned, and even flogged. This last they did to a Frenchman who published a pamphlet at Tahiti, exposing the severity of this fatherly priestly rule. It was answered in the usual fashion by the Roman Catholic bishop. If any one wants to know more of this extraordinary resuscitation of the sacerdotal tyranny of the Middle Ages in the Pacific, I cannot do better than advise him to get these two little books, and draw his own conclusions. One fact—if it be one—regarding the Roman Catholic missionaries all over the world, is worth mentioning, a fact which peculiarly regards the French missionaries. They are, if not from the beginning political, invariably followed by political movements. That most shameful Cochin-Chinese invasion (to say nothing of the equally shameful Tahitian one), was introduced by the French missionaries. And had it not been for the Franco-German war, France would have attacked China in defence of a class of men who set themselves against all settled authority.

Here I must make rather a lengthy digression about the Polynesian character, in order to air my views on this kind of treatment by whatever sect of missionaries it may be used.

He is brave, and, I have good reason to know, honest, generous, and good-natured to a fault, and possesses the most perfect manners I have met with in the world; natural, unostentatious, with an ever present kindly tact, and quiet generous consideration that make it impossible to associate with Polynesian men or women without feeling and acknowledging that nearly every one from the highest to the lowest is a gentleman or a lady. There is no such thing as a native snob, east of the Navigation and Friendlies (Tongas), where strange to say, the slight difference of race seems to produce a large quantity of most intolerable specimens of the great snob family, (a Tongan in particular being almost as insufferable and conceited a cad as a Jamaica negro). Yet these most charming and delightful people, who in many ways come nearer the Early Christian ideal of what men and women should be than any race in the world, have not the smallest idea of chastity whatever.

This fact presents at first glance a curious puzzle to a man accustomed only to civilised races. He naturally associates the idea of unchastity with degradation of character, and such qualities as courage, gentleness, courtesy, and honesty, with at least a tolerably high standard of female virtue. He must remember that " with the law came sin." Among civilised people want of chastity is a sin, a fall, a degradation, bringing

with it a shame and a depravity of character that tends
to destroy or annul whatever other virtues the sinner
may possess. But where there is no pain or shame
connected with unchastity or illegitimacy, there is no
fall and no degradation, and therefore little or no
injury to the other good points of the natural character.

The great question to be considered is, whether
" sin " is a term to apply equally to the same action
all over the world, or whether it is something relative
to surrounding circumstances.

There are, I believe, two great schools of philosophers. One, that declares ability or necessity to
be the source of all virtue; and another that holds
to a moral sense or original instinct of right and
wrong in the mind of man. Is it not possible that
both are partly right? That our earliest ancestors
had little or no natural instinct of virtue, but that finding certain things necessary for the good of themselves
and the community, they gradually developed certain
social or religious laws to enforce them; which laws
carried through many generations, gradually caused
an instinct or moral sense to arise on the subject of
right and wrong? In much the same way as the
original dogs who were trained to point game have
transmitted the accomplishment as an instinct to their
successors. Possibly in some such way what we call
conscience would spring up, rude and imperfect
enough in its birth, but developing and improving, as

it does, I believe, to this day, with the march of civilisation and advancement.

Do we not see different stages and developments of the moral sense in nearly all the races in the world, and is it not possible to trace the effects of natural circumstances and positions in the different ideas of the quality of virtue that they hold?

Supposing this theory of the origin of what we call sin, conscience, or right and wrong, had any foundation in truth, the character of the Polynesian is easy to understand. He has plenty of food, and no regular work is required to preserve life. Except when an occasional pinch comes, half a dozen mouths more or less make no very serious tax on the family purse. Moreover, his life is essentially a lazy one, partly from his natural disposition, and partly from the peculiar circumstances in which he is placed; he has no strong incentive to grow rich, and no profession or special occupation on which to concentrate his energies. In his case certainly it would seem that natural circumstances do not force him to develope a moral sense on the subject of chastity. If you tell him, You shall do no murder! or, You shall not steal, his sense of right and wrong makes him agree instinctively with the justice of the commandment, but when you tell him that unchastity is a sin, he asks why? it amuses me, and hurts nobody! There is no sense of degradation or sin on either side, and he follows it as he would any other natural appetite.

Amongst civilised people, of course, unchastity is a sin, and a most grave one, because, from the very fact of their advanced civilisation, and the laws which it has produced, it brings sorrow and misery, and being a sin, degrades and vitiates to a greater or less degree the whole natures of those who are concerned in it.[1]

Upon such grounds I venture to find fault with the tyrannical and terrifying mode of spiritual government when applied to these people by any sect. Many men use it, I am afraid (possibly unconsciously) from that intense love of power which is so often the failing of the priestly mind. Others, simply because they believe that what is a deadly sin in one state of society must necessarily be a deadly one in another, and that without exception such things are followed by eternal

---

. [1] My dear friends the Smell-funguses, on reading the preceding paragraphs in previous editions, of course remarked, with their usual kindness and keen discrimination, that I was directly upholding and approving the grossest immorality. Such a comment shows such carelessness both in reading and thinking that it need scarcely be noticed. I merely wished to show that "with the law came sin;" that the relative importance of certain manners and customs, altered according to circumstances all over the world, and to hint at a painful fact that is too little recognised, namely, that if, by terrorism or any unspontaneous method, you force upon a primitive and natural race a moral code above or unsuited to their nature, you not only do not improve them but you develope amongst them real crimes, such as professional prostitution, &c., which were utterly undreamt of in the times of their ignorant unsophisticated laxity.

damnation. I do not hesitate to say that if I believed what they do, I should act in the same way, and should not hesitate to make the poor Polynesians miserable in this life if I was sure that I was saving them from eternal misery in the next; but I do not, and I take the liberty to question the right of any set of men to tyrannise over others because their opinions do not agree.

It is common enough to hear the persecutors of the middle ages, men who ruthlessly condemned hundreds of fellow-creatures to death, spoken of as brutal and extraordinary monsters; but we should remember that it was their creed which made them what they were, and curse the creed rather than its simple believer. If I had lived in those days, and been a good churchman, steadfastly believing that the Almighty and Omniscient God would devote to a horrible and eternal punishment beings that he had created because they did not believe in the doctrines preached by a particular set of men; my reason would have told me (however much my *feelings* may have revolted against it) that to extirpate heresy in the most awe-inspiring manner, was but a common duty to humanity. The doctrine of exclusive salvation still remains amongst a large proportion of Christians, but the hearts of most of them are better than their heads, and they acknowledge instinctively that persecution is a wicked thing, without troubling themselves to see how far it is warranted by the dogmas they profess to hold. Whether the " Re-

ligious" particularly the "professional religious,"
would not roast each other to-morrow were it not for
a lay police, is another matter. I rather think they
would—joyfully!

If these races can be taught to appreciate the superior beauty of Christianity for its own sake, a nobler
purpose for a man to devote his life to can scarcely be
conceived, if not, are the enormous sums taken from
the relief of our terrible home necessities, wisely expended? and are the "Missionaries" to be looked
upon as working in their proper sphere?

I have never come in contact, personally, with any
members of the Wesleyan Mission, and therefore I am
bound to state that anything I may say about them
must be taken *cum grano.* I have *heard* a great deal
about them from white residents—from the white
residents in Samoa and the Fijis, and the evidence on
the whole is decidedly unfavourable. I have *heard*
them described as ignorant, fanatical, and extremely
inimical to all white men, but themselves; but this last
is not a peculiarity of their sect, and is neither an un-
common nor unnatural feeling amongst the island
missionaries generally. The missionary of one island
(not a Wesleyan) proposed to the king some years ago
to pass a law expelling every white man from his
dominions. "Very well," said the King, "but of
course you must go too"—which was a sell for the
missionary.

The cause of this dislike between the missionary

and the " white man " is simple enough. The beach-
man or white trader is in a great many cases of a
class with which the missionary can hardly be
" Hail fellow, well met," or of a moral character
which it would be possible for him to countenance
if he wished to improve that of the people. The
beachman is annoyed at " that missionary feller,
givin' himself such high and mighty airs," whilst the
richer trader turns up his nose at him as idle, luxurious, and useless. The most degraded runaway sailor
can pay off his grudge by sneering down the preacher
amongst his parishioners, or at least by setting them
an example of how little a white man cares for his
pastors and masters. And I have no doubt but that
the missionary does give himself airs occasionally,
and it is rather hard lines for the unfortunate
beachman, to be treated *de haut en bas* by a man
originally intended for a small grocer in a country
town. The fact is, that although there are plenty of
clever, liberal-minded, and tolerably well educated
men amongst them, there are not usually many of
what the lower-classes call gentlemen " born and
bred," and the aforesaid lower-classes are as quick as
anyone at finding out the fact. But there are exceptions to the rule, as at Raiatea in the Society Islands,
where the Congregationalist minister, Mr. Vivian,
spoke well of the white men on the island, and they
with great respect of him. The Wesleyans, as I said
before, are not much liked in the Fijis. And the

native teachers, who come trooping through Lavuka
of a morning, with clean white shirts and mighty
Bibles under their arms, still less so. It is curious
to notice how many of these men have acquired the
expression of the lowest and most fanatical class of
missionary, the real priest look, which by no means
enhances their originally very doubtful beauty. I
heard a story of a well-known and influential Fijian
planter and merchant who was continually bothered
by a lot of these gentlemen, who used to come and
steal his yams (there is no legal method of doing
anything in Fiji, and I suppose this was their way of
collecting tithes or church-rates), not being anxious
to quarrel personally with the mission, he went for a
constitutional and dropped a hint to his Solomon
island labourers that if they *did* happen to find any
one stealing yams they might break his or their heads,
and no questions asked. The " native preachers "
did come, but it was for the last time !

I had the misfortune once to find myself on board a
vessel that ran into a coral reef in Suva harbour, in
the Fijis. It was of the greatest importance to get
her off at the first high tide, before any wind or sea
arose, but one of these dusky missionaries actually
dissuaded his native flock from assisting to do it,
because it was Sunday. I thought to myself that if I
found that ass in a pit, I shouldn't care to help him
out even on a week day.

As I have already said, the Wesleyans seem to be

rather inclined to force Christianity on natives generally, whether they will or not.   Mr. Baker, who was
eaten in the Fijis, met with his fate through sheer
fanatical obstinacy.   In spite of the remonstrances of
the native chiefs, he insisted on penetrating into
" Tapùd " ground for the purpose of spreading his
doctrines amongst the " Devils," as the inhabitants of
the sea-coast politely designate those dwelling in the
interior ; but he would go, and not even alone, but
attended by " native assistants."   Good natured
" Devils " came and warned him, that if he would not
let them alone, they should be obliged to knock him
on the head ; and, after that, by way of utilizing him,
eat him.

But he would not listen to them, and so they did
eat him ; and one of those who partook of him, told
an acquaintance of mine in Fiji, that he was very good.
Better than usual ; for there is an idea amongst cannibals in these seas that white men " eat " abomi-
nably salt, which fancy probably arose from the fact
that they usually get hold of well " marinated " salt-
junk eating sailors.   Now, this is very dreadful ; but
suppose I trespassed on " Tapùd " lands in England,
should I not be—not " devoured " actually—but
very smartly dealt with ; and should I go to the
Church of the " Virgen del Pilar " at Saragossa, and
cast that well petticoated doll to the ground, should I
not be certain to be as full of knives in five minutes as
Mr. Rogers's shop ?—and would any English paper,

except possibly the "Record," deny that it served me perfectly right? This murder however, or whatever you like to call it, was not done solely on "religious" grounds. The "Devils" have a well-founded belief that the presence of a white missionary is too often followed by loss of land, either to the white settlers, or to the chiefs who protect them on the coast; and so they do their best to hold their own. They have not learned the wisdom of the Japanese, who have, or had, a French priest insulting their religion in every possible way, in order to gain admission into the noble army of martyrs :—"No," quoth the wise Japanese; "suppose we cut your head off, plenty too much French man-of-war come;" and so he will have to go to heaven by the ordinary route.

Whilst the Wesleyans range principally over the Friendly, Samoa, Fijis, and some Melanesian groups, the London Missionary Society extends its wings over the Society Islands, Cook's group, Loyalty Island, Samoa, &c. And certainly it has the very *crême de la crême* of the missionary position in that part of the world. It is true that the climate of many of the islands is very enervating, particularly for European women, and the children should be sent to another climate, say New Zealand, between the ages of six and twelve; but these are no greater hardships than those suffered willingly in India for one-half the comfort and position possessed by the missionary, and the question of "self-sacrifice is reduced to a minimum. From what I have

seen and have been told, the London Society seems to
be of a very liberal nature. It seems to care more
for "results" than for doctrines, and sends out its
emissaries with a free permission to teach almost any
form of Christianity best suited to themselves or their
natives. This very "easiness" tends to keep men of
very extreme or narrow ideas out of their ranks, and
is one great reason why they get on so much better
than most other sects. The Society seems to launch
their young missionaries much like a puppy that is
chucked into the water to teach it to swim. It takes
the young gentleman (figuratively) by the slack of
his reverend breeches, and pitches him all alone into
an island, saying unto him something of this kind:
"Learn the language, get up a school, improve the
people how you best can; teach them any form of
Christianity that is likely to suit them; keep clear of
native politics. God bless you!" They say that they
learn the language and people quicker this way than
if they were apprenticed to an older hand. Occasionally, however, they are found to be quite useless,
and have to be sent home again. Mr. Saville, the
minister at Huahine, told me that on his second
Sunday, he was able to preach his first sermon in the
native language.

I think that all the missionaries of this society that
I met with were "Congregationalists," and though of
course there are exceptions, they struck me as being
wonderfully good, intelligent, liberal, practical men;

not wilfully blinding their eyes to any imperfection in the success of their labours, or fanatically trying to force the natives all at once into their own groove, but patiently trying to make them peaceful and happy, and to instil into their minds a sense of the nobility and beauty of Christian morality, rather than any abstract and disputed dogmas.

"The young missionaries," said one of them to me, "have a new work to do. The old ones who first introduced Christianity captivated the minds of the natives by their superior accomplishments. 'These men,' cried they, 'can build ships without outriggers, make leaves speak (write), and many other wonderful things;—let us believe all they tell us, and we shall be able to do the same.' But after this first rush, there comes a re-action when they find that they do not gain all the advantages they expected; and we young missionaries will have to try and plant a *real* religious feeling in their hearts."

One of the best aids the Protestant Missionary has is his wife, whose example of fidelity and real affection must do more good than fifty sermons. In this he has an enormous advantage over the Roman Catholic priest, whose example is simply ridiculous in the eyes of his flock, if even they believe his celibacy is as real as he wishes it to be understood, which I take the liberty of doubting most exceedingly. I am not sure that marriage is positively required by the London Society, but it is encouraged at least, for I never

knew or heard of a member of this mission who had
not a European "helpmate"—and invariably one most
worthy of that honest old English term. I must not
mention names, or I would gladly publish that of a
"kindly Scottess" who, with rare good sense, abo-
lished, as far as she could, all the detestable European
"go-to-meeting" dresses worn by the women, and
induced them, yea, even by example, to return to the
modest, graceful, and most becoming muslin "sacque,"
—the prettiest dress, when its wearer rightly understands its mysteries, that a pretty woman can wear.
Talking of marriage, in some of the islands the native
chiefs have kept to themselves unlimited power of
divorce, which is good for themselves but bad for their
subjects, as it becomes a mere matter of dollars, and
makes the marriage-tie a decidedly loose one. One
missionary told me that when a couple came to be
married, he always said to the ardent bridegroom,
"By the bye, where's your other wife ? what has
become of her ?" or to the woman, "What have you
done with your late husband ?" He only asked on
spec., but he said that it generally turned out that they
had stray partners, either divorced or "somewhere
about." At the same island I knew a man who was
pointed out to me by the minister as an exemplary
character, rather a pillar of the church than otherwise.
He had run through seven helps-*meet* for him, and
was about to go in for the eighth. He must have had
rather a curious experience ; but as Touchstone says,
" Oh, sweet Audry," &c., &c. -

I cannot help admiring these missionaries for the honesty with which they disdain to conceal such little weaknesses in Polynesian Christianity, and the large-minded practical way in which they refrain from fanatical declamations against what to the natives is but a natural mode of life, and which, in their hearts, they regard much as Lieutenant Lismayhago's Indians did, in that memorable attempt at conversion narrated in "Humphry Clinker." I am myself by no means sure, though I scarcely expect that any of them would agree with me in this, that this easiness of divorce is not without its virtues in the present state of the Poly-nesian character, for it acts as a safety-valve to their almost incorrigible immorality; it is not much, it is true, but it is something more than they ever had before.

They begin their amourettes as soon as nature per-mits them, and like their cousins in New Zealand, sin, unreproved by their elders. Chastity is, in fact, un-known eastward of Samoa, where a chief's daughter, when heavily "tabooed," is supposed to be virtuous, until she is found to be otherwise. In one island I visited, the power of divorce, as well as that of mar-riage, was in the hands of the missionary. He was a young man, just arrived, and unable to speak the language; and the repeated applications for legal separations, were perpetually placing him in fresh dilemmas. If he granted their requests he felt that he was weakening the marriage tie; if he did not, tho

x

injured and disappointed applicants would go and break the seventh commandment all over the parish. Some of the missionaries have told me that they think that the general immorality of the people arises from their habit of sleeping all in one room, and that any other race would be just as bad under the same circumstances. I am inclined to think that there may be some truth in this, at least, as far as the immoral precociousness of the boys and girls are concerned; but, on the other hand, the Irish, who " pig " together literally, are remarkable for their " personal " chastity. Also, some missionaries regard these common sleeping rooms as rather good things than otherwise, as acquiring publicity and close relationship amongst the sleepers.

But, in fact, this question of personal chastity cannot for certain be referred entirely either to the religion or the domestic habits of a race. One of the greatest causes of South Sea immorality is, I believe, the universal system of " adoption," or of " birth-parents," and " feeding-parents," the origin of which I have been unable to find out. A very large proportion of Polynesian children have nothing to do with their real parents from the time they are weaned, being taken care of and brought up by some one else, who often bespeaks them even before they are born! Such a system must necessarily tend to weaken one of the strongest ties of matrimonial affection.

The Society Islands were never disgraced by can-

nibalism; but their old religion was a very bloody
one, and had something very ghastly about its method
of performing human sacrifices. I have stood on the
old " Marais " long, rampart-like place, formed of two
rows of great upright slabs, filled in with smaller
stones and coral, so as to form a kind of oblong stage
or platform, and felt a strong shudder as I thought on
all the terrible stories they could tell. Who can say
that the men who have changed such things for a mild
though lax form of Christianity have not done some
good ?

I am afraid that the " South Sea " natives are apt
to live two lives —a church and a natural one, —and
naturally the missionary reports the church one. I was
much struck with this in one island where I attended
divine service, and saw all the chief ladies of the land
dressed out to the nines, taking notes of the sermon
with big pencils on foolscap paper, and looking as
if butter would not melt in their pretty lips. I gazed
sadly on them, thinking what much better fun I should
have had if I had visited the island fifty years sooner;
but I was comforted the next day when I saw the
identical saintly creatures madly executing the most
improper gambadoes, all as wild, savage, and larky as
they were in the days of Captain Cook.

But I must not tell tales out of school; and, after
all, might not the same story be told of some much
nearer home. I once travelled on a steamboat with a
young lady, who used to lay in a tremendous stock of

piety every morning at prayers, worked it off gradually all through the day, and at about eleven p.m. ran short of it altogether on the " Fo'-castle "; she always laid in a fresh stock next morning, so I suppose the balance was about even.

The natives, to use one of their pastor's own words, " won't let the missionaries know too much ! " They keep their orange-rum drinkings, with the attendant highly improper dancings, and the other little diversions that accompany them, tolerably private. At one island, not long ago, a native drum was introduced from " abroad ; " and at the very first fingertaps, the little children of ten and twelve years old began instantly to dance the very naughty dances which were supposed to have been extinct for thirty years, showing clearly that there was a very efficient " Maître de danse " somewhere " in petto."

I hardly like to say that the older missionaries were guilty of deliberate lies when they reported that all the old native superstitions, immoral dances, and other improper excitements were entirely suppressed and forgotten : the wish was father to the thought, both in them and those they reported to. But such exaggerations, whoever started them, have placed the new generation of missionaries in a very awkward and painful position. As we said before, when the young missionary comes out, and honestly reports the real state of the case, they either entirely disbelieve him at home, or tell him that it is his own fault.

I heard from another missionary much the same story which I have already recorded. " The old missionary, who was looked on as a kind of god by the natives, because he was surrounded by the superior inventions and appliances of civilisation, which they had never seen before, and could scarcely understand, could alter, or at least keep down, anything he disapproved of. Now that the re-action has come, and the natives have discovered that the priest is only a man, and a person not more ingenious and wonderful in invention than a layman, but rather the contrary, the missionary has lost most of his power, and is puzzled how to act. In fact, the native wants to improve his body, which he cares a great deal about, and the missionary to save his soul, which he cares nothing about, even if he believes he has one. The missionary sees clearly enough that the old root and branch method will scare more birds than he can catch, and at the best is of very temporary advantage ; but if he honestly declares in favour of a liberal, gradual, moral influence and example, he is apt to fall into disgrace with—not only the " Hell-fire " fanatics at home, but, still worse, with those who make decent earnings out of the " Mission Platform." Every man is willing to pick holes in his coat from one side or another. If he goes on the old principle, every white man on the island is ready to cry out about his tyranny over the natives ; if on the new and more liberal one, they sneer at him for living a comfortable life (which he most

certainly does), and doing little or nothing to earn
it, not to speak of the abuse he gets from the Exeter
Hall-ites, for not supplying them with sufficient "flap-
doodle." If some of them get disheartened by such a
hopeless state of things, and let things slide, who can
wonder at it?

The crude truth is that nine-tenths of foreign mis-
sions are not got up for the benefit of the heathen
abroad, but for the good of the sect at home.

I only know one island of the London Society, where
the minister has both the power and the will to keep
up the old puritanical tyranny over the luckless natives
subject to him—subject to him by what right, except
that of blatant impudence?

This worthy allows no tobacco to be used on the
island, regulates the dress, habits, and manners of his
parishioners after his own sour-headed fancies, and on
one occasion, when he had been away for a short time,
and the women had taken the opportunity to buy some
pretty prints, he preached a furious sermon against
them the first Sunday after his return, and made the
women destroy them all before him. It is perhaps
needless to say that these gay and godless garments
were purchased from a worthless whaler, and not from
the store sanctified by the spirit of Wesley.

This kind of extraordinary missionary power, though
it may make the people very good as long as it lasts,
can only exist in spots which are but little frequented,
and when it is undermined by intercourse with the

outer world, it leaves few good effects of a permanent duration. The more isolated and unfrequented the island, the greater the power of the missionary, and when there are no more unfrequented islands, we shall have no more missionaries of the old ruling type—they will be improved off the face of the earth, like their flocks. The so-called demoralisation of the Polynesian by the white trader, really means the demoralisation of the influence of the missionary, and nothing more.

No amount of intercourse with white men could possibly make the Kanaka less virtuous than he was before—on the contrary, he has learned a new virtue —honesty, because he found out that it paid : as for disease, they had worse than we introduced before we found them ; and the diseases we introduced are infinitely milder than they are amongst ourselves. The only real mischief they have received is from the change of clothing, the forbidding of bathing, and the substitution of orange rum (thanks to the missionaries) for the wholesome kava.

The people who do the most mischief to missionary labour are the missionaries themselves. When one sect intrudes upon the field of another, the improvement of the native character comes to an immediate stand-still, as in the case of the Maories. The temptation to run down each other's faith, works, and power to the natives is usually too strong for the priestly mind to resist. Tahiti, Samoa, and New Zealand (though in the latter place there were other

causes) testify to this melancholy truth. Birds of a
feather may flock together, but when they do, they
usually fight over the carcase. In one island two different sects of so-called Christians did actually levy
war on each other, but I believe such a case is not
quite unknown in Europe.

These meetings of different sects on the same ground
should be avoided by mutual consent, if the conversion
or improvement of the natives is the great object to be
obtained; and in the matter of some islands, an agree-
ment took place, if I remember right, between the
London Mission and the Wesleyans. Of course, the
missionaries who belong to that most dogmatic and
conceited of religions, Roman Catholicism, will agree
to no such compromise; and I will back half-a-dozen
enthusiastic jesuits or marists, going the round of
Polynesia, to do more to demoralise the people, and
shake what small hold Christianity has upon them than
five hundred of the most dissolute sailors.

If you want real mischief done, place your cause in
the hands of a few "earnest" and "well-meaning"
men.

The London Mission has certainly had great success.
At the Society, Cook's Island, &c., the islanders, are
for the most part, nominal Christians, and although
their sexual morality be very lax, their honesty,
bravery, and general good feeling would compare very
favourably with many European races. They are lazy
—but why should they not be? They are very well

off without working, and wise enough to be contented. When one mixes with such generous, kind-hearted people—gentle without cowardice, courteous without humbug (it is difficult to imagine that so few years ago they could have been disgraced, some by human sacrifice, others by actual cannibalism)—and remarks how infinitely the virtue of common honesty has progressed since Cook's time, let us pay all honour to the missionaries, if they have wrought the change. But when any one who knows anything about the real nature and morals of the Polynesian, hears a report of them at a missionary meeting at home, he very naturally puts the resident missionaries down as a set of lying, or at least disingenuous humbugs. When he hears, for instance, how, in twenty years, the saving grace of Christ has descended on the souls of the heathen of ———, how dutifully they attend the churches and schools—how decently they dress—how they have entirely given up all their heathen customs, and immoral dances—and a like quantity of half truths, he feels inclined to insult the first missionary he meets. But the fault lies chiefly with the people at home, who snub the young resident teachers whenever they expose the opposite side of the picture, and oblige them to hold their tongues altogether, or to cook their accounts as prettily as they can. They have only to confine themselves to the meeting-going side of the native character—to omit all about the systematic orange rum meetings, with their accompanying orgies, and the in-

corrigible immorality and laziness,—and to dilate upon
the wonderful good temper, generosity, kindness, and
bravery of the race (natural characteristics little in-
fluenced by the change of religion, if the early voy-
agers are to be believed)—to make as pretty a report
as need be.

To put it coarsely, the home parsons must have a
good strong bait to catch their gold-fish with. If they
were to state, as they might do with truth, that three
women out of four, from the Island Queen downwards,
had not the smallest notion of chastity, shame, or common decency,—that the people were in the constant
habit of going off in groups of fifty or sixty for the
purpose of drinking themselves mad on orange rum,
and committing the most fearful bestialities,—that
their old immoral dances were as well known as ever,
and that five minutes' excitement turned church-mem-
bers into frantic savages, there might be a slight fall-
ing-off in the subscriptions. It is not fair to show
only one-half of the picture, though it may be very
convenient occasionally. Of course in some cases a
little actual lying is required to make things sound
nice, but I have only been referring to the better
specimens of Polynesian Christianity. It seems somewhat strange, at first sight, that the work of " conversion " should succeed so rapidly and effectually in
some places, and should fail so completely in others,
where the races are nearly identical. One great reason
for this is, the varying form of government. In

places like the Society Islands, where there were hereditary kings and queens, with nearly absolute power, the missionaries who then, as I have said, could easily acquire great influence, had only to convert him or her, and steadily use that influence, to gain over the great mass of the people, who naturally followed their leader.

In an essentially republican country like New Zealand, there was no such short-cut to success; the people being subdivided into numerous tribes, and absolute kingly power being, except in war time, nearly unknown. There was, in fact, no government strong enough to draw up a code in a copy-book, and fine its subjects smartly for their peccadilloes, as in the Fijis, for instance, where I have seen the luckless savage squeezed of his last dollar, the " native missionary " assisting in the operation with a sharky grin, which would have done honour to a jesuit at a death bed-side.

Christianity in New Zealand has also met with that hopeless death-blow, the contact of different sects of missionaries, which invariably inspires the native with a distrust of all of them.

But the most important reason of the utter collapse of the " faith " amongst the Maories lies in the peculiarly low and practical view they take of all religion. Like many of the Old Testament Jews, the Maori of thirty years ago looked on the divine power as a mere convenient aid to the great end of whack-

ing his enemies. Where the white man appeared he
naturally argued from their superiority in murderous
weapons, that their religion was "stronger" than his
own, so he turned Christian. When he found out his
mistake, and saw that a heathen could fight nearly as
well as a Christian, and that in spite of his Christianity
he was gradually going to the wall, he said—"Bother
Christianity," and used the leaves of his New Testament for cartridges; and invented a most bloodthirsty
and abominable religion out of the *old* one, a book
which, by its combination with the beautiful moral
laws of Christianity with the sanguinary superstitions
of Judaism, with its degraded, limited, and human
idea of the Creator, has been and will be the undoing
of many an earnest Christian.

This new form of Judaism, Hau-Hau-ism, is not
unlike the Taeping religion in China, and took its
origin in the same way—the missionary determination
to force very old wine into very new bottles. The
Maori, moreover, in spite of his Christianity, seems to
possess all the vices of both the western and eastern
Polynesians without any of their virtues, except their
bravery. He is as idle, immoral, and useless as a
Tahitian, without his perfect manners, unselfish generosity, and general kindliness. As snobbish, untruth-
ful, and avaricious as a Tongan, without his constructive and inventive power, he is a savage to the back-
bone, liking fighting better than any other occupation,
and living a much better life when he is fighting than

at any other time. In fact, I believe that Christianity in slipping off the Maories like water off a duck's back, in spite of the assertion in high quarters that New Zealand presents the most marvellous proof of the success of missionary work that the world has ever seen. The reports of the different men, employed to represent the real state of things to the New Zealand Government, are almost unanimous in declaring that Christianity is fast losing its hold on the people, and a Maori missionary stated, in a public lecture given at Otago in 1870, that he found a wide-spread hatred of the Gospel, with which the natives associate the many evils which afflict them, and which threaten their extinction. I have myself seen in a native church, raised at no small cost, an immense heap of Maori bibles, prayer books, and hymn books piled in the centre, crowned by two or three human skulls as a sign of desecration.

A traveller in the South Seas is often puzzled to define what "civilisation" really consists in. It is difficult for him to avoid looking upon the courteous Society Islander, with his refined but natural manner, as a civilised man ; but when he meets the Fijian, who is superior to him in constructive and inventive power, and has a far higher notion of female fidelity, he acknowledges instinctively that the man is a savage, and that the still more ingenious and subtle Tongan is a most absurdly vain and insufferable barbarian snob. " Tongans first," say they, " then white men, and then

all the rest of the world!" They hold that Wellington and Napoleon the First were both Tongans,
having drifted away in canoes to Europe. If a white
man laughs at this, they say, " They were great men,
weren't they?" " Certainly." " Then they *must*
have been Tongans! How stupid you are!"

The other day the Tongan Parliament held a debate
on the question of annexing the Fijis. One member
made a grand speech, in which he said, " Tonga is a
great power : so was the Roman Empire ; but she extended her conquests too far, and so fell. Let us be-
ware lest the same fate should befall Tonga!"

They were much disappointed that Prince Alfred
did not visit them ; but their absurd conceit would
hardly let them own it. They said the Queen would
not let him come, because the Tongese ladies were so
notoriously beautiful that he would be sure to marry
one of 'them. And they also wished that if Her
Majesty did intend sending a son to visit King
George she would send the Prince of Wales, not a
mere royal duke. On the declaration of war between
France and Germany, King George expressed his intention of preserving a strict neutrality.

I am inclined to think that the custom of making
native parsons ought to be very restricted, though no
doubt but that there are many good and useful men
amongst them. Those in Fiji have a very bad
name ; and, though Raritonga, a cannibal island, was
certainly first converted by brown preachers (I re-

member making the acquaintance of the old lady who
pluckily protected them on their first arrival), they
rather marred the beauty of their work, by intriguing
with the wives of the principal chiefs. In New Zealand they are looked on with little favour. One bright
and shining light.went to England to be made a fuss
over and shown at meetings : he employed his leisure
hours in learning how to make gunpowder to shoot
white colonists with ; but I am happy to say that he
blew himself up on his return to New Zealand while
prosecuting his scientific researches.

I was at first rather puzzled to understand why the
Roman Catholic missionaries gained ground so slowly
in Tahiti, when they have so many advantages over
the others, and the hold of any missionaries over the
natives is only skin-deep, and requires much "wheed-
ling" to exist at all.   Their faith, at first sight, seems
to be so much better suited to the easy-going, festival-
living, demonstrative Society islander, than the simple,
quiet form of the London Mission.   One reason is, because they hate everything French, and like everything English. Another reason is, that a Society
islander has a very strong sense of humour ; and,
though he is demonstrative, is seldom inclined to exaggeration in general behaviour. I have more than
once heard them sneer and make fun of Frenchmen
and Spaniards, "for talking plenty too much with
their fingers." The secret of the Kanakas' wonderful
good manners is his real extreme *good nature* · not in

that unnatural affectation of it which so often makes the civility of an Italian, Frenchman, Spaniard, or Hindu so repulsive to English feelings. This simplicity, combined with his sense of humour, inclines him to the belief that any hocus pocus, or affectation in dress or manner, particularly in religion, is out of place, and to be despised.

Of the English missionaries in Melanesia, I know very little. I understand that they have met with but little success amongst the mass of the people, who are mostly of a savage and ferocious disposition. Bishop Pattison has gradually collected about a hundred boys, whom he is educating at Norfolk Island, to serve as Christian teachers. Whether these boys will keep up, and spread their Christianity on their return home, remains to be proved. In New Caledonia and the Isle of Pines, the missionaries were mostly Roman Catholics, and were by no means popular either with the French officials or the settlers; the first declaring that they supplied the natives with arms and ammunition, and the second declaring that they " tapúd " the pigs and coco-nut oil for their own benefit. This " tapu " is performed by cutting a cross on the stem of a tree; and the sailor boy, who acted as my boatman in those parts, invariably chose a tree marked with this sign to steal coco-nuts from; and if they proved bad, he solemnly cursed the tree, saying, " that the parsons had tried blessing it, and that didn't seem no good, so he'd try t'other tack."

And now I must bring this article to a close. I have tried to give an impartial account of all that I have seen and heard concerning South Sea missionaries, and I have refrained from telling more than one anecdote against them, for fear it might be an invention or an exaggeration; but if I have trod unnecessarily on any body's toes, I beg most sincerely to apologise.

NOTE.

THE Maori notion of prayer reaches no higher than the thing we call an incantation. One day I was talking to an old Pakeha-maori (*i. e.* a white man who lives amongst the Maories) on the subject of missionary labour. At last he said, "I'll tell you a story that will establish your name for ever at Exeter Hall, only you mustn't tell it quite the same way that I do. I was here at the time when both the Protestant and Roman Catholic Missionaries were first beginning to make their way in the country; and the Maories of my tribe used to come to me and ask me which had the greatest 'mana' (*i. e.* fortune, prestige, power, strength)—the Protestant God or the Romanist one. I was always a good churchman, and used to tell them that the Protestant God could lick the other into fits. There was an old Irish sailor about five miles from me who used to back up the Roman Catholic God, but I had a long start of him, and moreover *was the best fighting man* of the two, which went a long way. In a short time I had about two hundred of the most muscular, blood-thirsty, hard-fighting Protestants you could wish to see.

"Well; it so happened that one day we had a little difference with some of our neighbours, and were drawn up on one side of a gully all ready to charge. I liked the fun of fighting in those days, and was rigged out in nothing but a cartridge-box and belt, with a plume of feathers in my hair, and a young woman to carry my ammunition for me; moreover, I had been put in command of the desperate young bloods of the tribe, and burned to distinguish myself, feeling the commander of the old Guard at Waterloo quite an insignificant person in regard to myself in point of responsibility and honour.

" Lying down in the fern, we waited impatiently for the signal to charge; had not we, on the last occasion worth speaking of outrun our elders, and been nearly decimated in consequence? Shall it not be different now? See! there is the great war-chief, the commander of the ' Taua,' coming this way (he was a real ' toa ' of the old stamp, too seldom found among the degenerate Maories of the present day). Little cared he for the new faith that had sprung up in the last generation; his skill with the spear, and the incantations of his ' Tohungas' (*i. e.* priests or magicians), had kept him safe through many a bitter tussle; his ' mana' was great. Straight to me he came and addressed me thus :—' Look here, young fellow! I've done the incantations and made it all square with my God; but you say that you've got a God stronger than mine, and a lot of our young fellows go with you; there's nothing like having two Gods on our side, so you fellows do the proper business with him, and then we'll fight.' Could anything have been more practical and business-like than this? But I was quite stuck up; for though I could have repeated a prayer from the liturgy myself, my worthy converts, who philosophically and rightly looked upon religion merely as a means to an end (*i. e.* killing the greatest possible quantity of enemies), were unable to produce a line of scripture amongst them.

" There was an awkward pause—our commander was furious. Suddenly one discovers that he has a hymn-book in his pocket. General exultation! ' Now!' cries the old chief, foaming at the mouth with excitement, ' go down upon your knees (I know that's the custom with your God) and repeat the charm after him. Mind you don't make a mistake, now, for if one word is wrong the whole thing will be turned topsyturvy and we shall be thrashed.'

" And then, having repeated one hymn word for word on our knees, I and my converts charged, and walked into the Amorites no end; but whether it was the hymn or the fighting that did it is of course an open question to this day.

Spottiswoode & Co. Printers, New-street Square, London.

MARION CRAWFORD

Price 6s.

Cecilia

A Story of Modern Rome

By

F. Marion Crawford

In his latest novel, Mr. Crawford has returned to Rome, the scene of some of his most famous works—**Saracinesca, Don Orsino,** and **Sant' Ilario.**

The story plays round the life and adventures of "Cecilia, the last of the Vestals." There is a mysterious connection between the lives of Cecilia and the heroine of the book—a young woman of modern Rome—which is worked out in the course of this remarkable novel with Mr. Crawford's accustomed skill. It would be unfair to the reader to explain the relation between the last of the Virgin Priestesses and events of the present day in Rome.

RHODA BROUGHTON

Author of

" Red as a Rose is She,"

" Foes in Law," &c.

Crown 8vo. Gilt Top

Price 6s.

Lavinia

By

Rhoda Broughton

"Lavinia" is a study in contrasted types of manhood seen through a woman's eyes. Sir George Campion is the father of two sons, and the uncle of the orphan Lavinia. One son has been killed in South Africa. The other, Rupert, who has always been betrothed to Lavinia, is wholly uncongenial to his rough, fierce old father ; he is a man of letters, with an aversion to all forms of violence. Lavinia acts as a buffer between the two, but when at last they are reconciled in a common desire for her marriage with Rupert, she meets a man of wholly different type, Captain Binning, the wounded soldier in saving whom the other brother has been killed. And between the two love springs up irresistibly, in spite of the barriers felt by them both. The book is occupied in working through the complications thus generated to a happy conclusion—only reached after much suffering.

3

G. & M. COLERIDGE

Price 6s.

Jan Van Elselo

**Being an Account of his Adventures
during the Reign of His Most
Catholic Majesty, Philip II.,
King of Spain.**

By

Gilbert & Marion Coleridge

"Jan Van Elselo" is a historical novel centreing round a lad who begins as a page to the Prince of Orange, in the days of the Spanish Inquisition of Alva and Philip II., and of war in the Netherlands —where the scene is principally laid, though it begins in France and shifts to England and to Spain. Nearly all the leading political figures of the time are introduced at greater or less length, and the book ends with an exciting picture of the siege of Haarlem. There is a great deal of carefully planned incident, and a happy close.

TIMES.—"The book has excellent points; it will be read with approval by many."
OUTLOOK.—"Told with spirit."
SUNDAY SUN.—"An excellent story, told with much spirit, and giving a capital impression of the period."

ROSA N. CAREY

Author of
" Nellie's Memories,"
" Not Like Other Girls,"
" Herb of Grace," &c.

Crown 8vo.   Gilt Top

Price 6s.

The Highway of Fate

By

Rosa N. Carey

" The Highway of Fate " deals with the fortunes of a young lady who is compelled to go out as a companion. Her employer is the kind-hearted, ill-educated daughter of a wealthy soap boiler, and the story is chiefly of the lady's kindnesses. A double love interest runs through the book, for, in addition to the companion's romance, Miss Dunstuth, her employer, falls in love with a handsome scamp whom her loyalty does much to redeem before the tragic and honourable death which ensures that he never shall deceive her.

WORLD.—"A story which will be read with much satisfaction by Miss Carey's large public."
OUTLOOK.—"A pleasant modern story. . . . The character-drawing—especially of the women—is clear; Miss Jim, in particular, is delightful."
MANCHESTER GUARDIAN.—"The natural grace and simplicity of Miss Carey's style, and the ease with which she tells a story, will make this story, like all her stories, very attractive to lovers of the domestic novel."

HAROLD VALLINGS

Price 6s.

By Dulvercombe Water

By Harold Vallings

"By Dulvercombe Water" is a love story of Somersetshire, in the year 1685, into which Mr. Harold Vallings weaves many incidents of the Monmouth rebellion. His hero, of illegitimate birth but gentle breeding, does his best to check the rising, and in an exciting moment saves the life of a suspected informer. But when the rising comes, his half-brother, the legitimate, to whom he is devotedly attached, joins the rebels and is taken, and Will Estcote, resisting the King's troops to rescue him from Kirke's men, becomes a rebel too. To help the brother's escape he personates him, is hunted, and finally taken and brought to the bloody assize at Taunton. Jeffreys in court, and Jeffreys in his private room sitting and taking bribes, is very forcibly presented by Mr. Vallings. The hero's adventures do not end even when he escapes from England by the aid of his sweetheart, but at last the Revolution of 1689 brings him back to a happy ending.

SUNDAY SUN.—"The story is freshly and crisply told. The hero and heroine are strongly drawn, and enlist one's sympathies from the outset."
ACADEMY.—"The story has a freshness unusual in modern historical novels."

"ELIZABETH"

Crown 8vo.   Gilt Top

Price 6s.

The Benefactress

By the Author of
"Elizabeth and her German Garden"

THE SPECTATOR.—"If 'Elizabeth's' satire is somewhat cruel, it is in the main justified by the situation and the results. For the moral of the story is as sound as the wit is mordant. 'The Benefactress,' in a word, combines the rare qualities of being at once wholesome, agreeably malicious, and in full accord with the principles of the Charity Organisation Society."
Mr. W. L. COURTNEY in the *DAILY TELEGRAPH.*—"It is difficult to describe by any single epithet the peculiar charm which surrounds the work of the authoress of 'Elizabeth and her German Garden.' . . . Quiet, tender, incisive, humorous. . . . Triumphantly successful."
LITERATURE.—"Fully equal to 'Elizabeth and her German Garden.' . . . Maintains its interest throughout, and is full of well-drawn characters."
STANDARD.—"Delightful from beginning to end. It is wholesome, full of charm and joyousness."
WORLD.—"The writer holds the reader, not to lose her hold while a line of the book remains to be read and read again. Every character is a living individuality, and every incident is a necessity."
MORNING POST.—"An excellent piece of work. . . . The most amusing reading which has come our way for some time."
DAILY NEWS.—"One of the most attractive novels we have read for a long time."

RUDYARD KIPLING

Price 6s.

Kim

By

Rudyard Kipling

TIMES.—"Treated with Mr. Kipling's amazing knowledge, insight, and sureness of touch."

MORNING POST.—"'Kim' is undoubtedly the finest Indian story that the author of 'The Man who would be King,' and a hundred other tales, has yet written."

PALL MALL GAZETTE.—"Mr. Kipling's varied and complex powers are seen at their strongest and best. . . . Kim is the creation of a great and true artist."

WESTMINSTER GAZETTE.—"Full, rich, and animated in every detail. . . . informed as before with a masterly intuition of Eastern modes of thought."

GUARDIAN.—"A series of wonderful kaleidoscopic pictures, ever shifting and changing. . . . May Mr. Kipling soon give us more of this kind."

DAILY NEWS.—"A wonderful procession of picturesque and interesting figures pass through the pages of the book."

STANDARD.—"By far the most successful piece of work Mr. Kipling has done for some time past."

ST. JAMES'S GAZETTE.—"It is beyond question the finest picture of Indian life which Mr. Kipling has yet made; it is the finest picture that has been made by any writer."

GLOBE.—"The pictures of persons and places in 'Kim' are among the best things that Mr. Kipling has done."

A. C. FARQUHARSON

"The story is absorbing."
—*The Athenæum.*

"Altogether worth reading."
—*The Westminster Gazette.*

Crown 8vo.   Gilt Top

Price 6s.

St. Nazarius

By

A. C. Farquharson

ATHENÆUM.—"It is a rare pleasure to find a book which is satisfactory in almost all respects. 'St. Nazarius' is such a book. The story is absorbing; its treatment is admirable, especially in restraint; and the tone is one of unusual distinction. . . . The deep thought of the book, its essential sanity, its presentation of a high religious ideal, interest us in the work of the author."

WESTMINSTER GAZETTE.—"A novel out of the common. . . . Altogether worth reading."

ST. JAMES'S GAZETTE.—"Should give delight to many readers who do not as a rule trouble themselves to cut the leaves of ordinary novels. The writer has dared to probe the depths and to scale the heights. . . . The story is clothed in language perfectly suited to its mysterious charm."

OUTLOOK.—"Mr. Farquharson has grip, and his story is well worked out."

SCOTSMAN.—"A striking story and one in which the reader's interest and admiration strengthen, from a somewhat formal opening, to an end which is unconventionally fine and sad."

S. R. CROCKETT

Price 6s.

The Dark o' the Moon

Being ·

Certain further Histories

of the

Folk called " Raiders "

SPECTATOR.—" Mr. Crockett's admirers will find plenty of his characteristic matter and manner to mystify and amuse them in 'The Dark o' the Moon.' "

TIMES.—" A rousing story, with plenty of love and fighting. . . . The story is told with unflagging spirit."

PALL MALL GAZETTE.—" The story is good Crockett from first to last, exactly what the author's many admirers will expect."

WESTMINSTER GAZETTE.—" A rousing book in the novelist's earlier manner, full of stir and picturesque movement. With a plot that is interesting and developed with skill. . . . It is in every way satisfactory to find Mr. Crockett on his native heath once more."

GLOBE.—" Should have a wide vogue and much appreciation."

WORLD.—" A stirring tale."

DAILY CHRONICLE.—" A romance, swift and compact, and told with spirit."

S. R. CROCKETT

" We should class this book as among the best of its author's recent works."
—*Athenæum.*

Crown 8vo.   Gilt Top

Price 6s.

The Firebrand

By

S. R. Crockett

ATHENÆUM.—" We should class this book as among the best of its author's recent works."

LITERATURE.—" A bustling novel. . . . Something is always happening in Mr. Crockett's books—generally something ingenious and unexpected. Not many writers can spin the web of a story better."

WORLD.—" The story of the ' firebrand,' Rollo Blair, a Scottish gentleman-adventurer, and his two incongruous associates, of the Abbot of Montblanch, the kidnapping of the Queen, the outlawry of Ramon Garcia, the outwitting of Cabrera by Rollo, and the doings of the gipsies, is decidedly good."

DAILY TELEGRAPH.—" A full-blooded tale of adventure."

DAILY NEWS.—" The story is a good one . . . Will be read with interest and pleasure."

GLOBE.—" Mr. Crockett is a born story-teller ; he has the knack of spirited and sentimental narration. In ' The Firebrand ' he runs to the length of 519 pages, and none of his admirers would desire that they should be fewer."

EGERTON CASTLE

Price 6s.

The Secret Orchard

By

Egerton Castle

GLOBE.—"The story, as a whole, is eminently effective, eminently readable, and can be recommended cordially to all and sundry."

WORLD.—"The persons are all well drawn, and the interest is great."

PALL MALL GAZETTE.—"A very clever and a very good book."

DAILY CHRONICLE.—"We expected much. . . . 'The Secret Orchard' does more than rise to our expectations. . . We follow the rapid development of the tragedy with a sympathetic interest which never flags."

DAILY MAIL.—"A novel of signal distinction and beauty."

ACADEMY.—"The style and manner of telling the story is of the easy luminous character that we associate with the authors of 'The Bath Comedy.'"

MORNING POST.—"There can be no doubt of the dramatic force with which it is told or of the interest it inspires."

THE TIMES.—"A finished piece of work."

E. F. POYNTER

Author of
"An Exquisite Fool,"
"Every Day's News,"
etc.

Crown 8vo.   Gilt Top

Price 6s.

Michael Ferrier

By

E. Frances Poynter

Michael Ferrier is the story of a young poet who loves and is loved by a beautiful girl, Helen Umfraville. In a moment of frenzy he kills, half by accident, the man who attempts to stand between them. The death passes for either accident or suicide, and no suspicion is aroused; but the girl sees her lover's trouble, questions him, and the turning point of the book is the scene when he confesses to her his act, and she takes the decision that seems to her right in consequence.

DAILY TELEGRAPH.—"There are so many real tragedies in life, and so few convincing ones in fiction, that the perusal of Miss E. Frances Poynter's little study is likely to make a deep impression on the reader. For here is real tragedy. . . . In her characterisation the authoress is most happy. . . . Miss Poynter possesses keen psychological insight and a not unkindly satire when she pleases, as well as the power to depict pathos and suffering, with the pen of the artist."

PUNCH.—"Miss Frances Poynter, though not a new novelist, is a fresh acquaintance of my Baronite's. If her earlier works are as good as 'Michael Ferrier,' they are worth looking up."

STEPHEN GWYNN

Price 6s.

The Old Knowledge

By

Stephen Gwynn

WESTMINSTER GAZETTE.—"It is long since it has been our good fortune to meet with a novel so fresh, breezy, and altogether charming."

SUNDAY SUN.—"A good book, very far above the customary novel of the day in all important matters. It has charm of manner, a delicate and indefinable melancholy—the inalienable melancholy of the Irish—and also a very welcome touch of Irish humour. . . . It introduces us to several very charming people."

DAILY EXPRESS.—"A very pretty story, wholesome and refreshing, with the sweet air of Donegal. . . . The humour, the prettiness, and the trouble of the story are all perfect in their lightness and harmony. Mr. Gwynn is among the most graceful and pleasant of Irish writers."

THE SPECTATOR.—"It is admirably written : it has an interesting theme, and its development in plot and characterisation . . . is in faithful correspondence with the facts of life. In a word, the book is both charming and convincing."

MERWIN & WEBSTER

> " Most remarkable story."
> —*Daily Mail.*
>
> "An interesting and amusing book."
> —*Scotsman.*

Crown 8vo. Gilt Top

Price 6s.

"Calumet 'K'"

By S. Merwin and H. K. Webster

" Calumet ' K ' " is a two-million-bushel grain-elevator, and this story tells how Charlie Bannon built it "against time." The elevator must be done by December 31. There are persons that are interested in delaying the work, and it is these, as well as the "walking delegates," that Bannon has to fight. The story of how they tried to "tie up" the lumber two hundred miles away, and of how he outwitted them and just "carried it off," shows the kind of thing that Bannon can do best.

DAILY MAIL.—"Most remarkable story. . . . The story makes an epic—the epic of a sleepless, tireless man who can never be beaten. Every young man who is to-day starting out on the business of life should read it."

SUNDAY SPECIAL.—"No romance of the Middle Ages surpasses this story in stirring interest, virility, and strength. It is a moving picture of the resistless American of to-day, and, as such, is worth a hundred average novels."

SCOTSMAN.—"It is an interesting and amusing book, and once taken up will be read to a finish."

SPECTATOR.—"The story will delight readers who combine mechanical taste with the spirit of practical enterprise."

UNA L. SILBERRAD

Price 6s.

Princess Puck

By

Una L. Silberrad

THE PILOT.—" It is unspeakably refreshing to come upon a book so bubbling over with life and love and character and humour as 'Princess Puck' that to notice it forthwith is an imperative duty and pleasure. This is a novel to read once so that you may find out how good it is, and then straightway over again because it is so good that you must enjoy it more leisurely."

THE SPECTATOR.—" Miss Silberrad's exceedingly clever, fresh, and wholesome story. . . . *Bill* Alardy is a delightful creation: she bubbles over with life and goodwill, humour, energy, and affection ; and everything she touches turns to romance."

THE ACADEMY.—"The whole story is in the aggregate so pleasing and entertaining that we have little inclination to pick holes. Let it go as fresh and recommendable."

PUNCH.—" . . . the exceeding charm of the creation of *Wilhelmina Alardy,* commonly known as *Bill.* In her freshness, her unconventionality, her keen insight, and her honesty, *Bill* is delightful."

THE DAILY CHRONICLE.—" Miss Silberrad's book deserves a high place in the fiction of the moment. The story is interesting and rattles along to the end without a pause ; there is originality in the construction of the plot, and perception as well in the way the characters are conceived and presented. *Bill* herself is a charming conception. . . Altogether, ' Princess Puck ' is a book to be read, and to be read with discrimination."

EVELYN SHARP

Price 6s.

The Youngest Girl in the School

THE ATHENÆUM.—"Told with much humour."

THE ACADEMY.—" A most amusing story."

LITERATURE.—" A vivid picture of a girl's school."

THE PILOT.—" . . . . its raciness and humour."

PALL MALL GAZETTE.—" Extremely diverting to the average man."

THE GRAPHIC.—" Very fresh and natural."

THE SPECTATOR. — " Shows a wholesome and humorous grasp of life."

THE DAILY CHRONICLE. —" Miss Evelyn Sharp has scored a brilliant success in a *genre* where success has been attained by few. Schoolgirls have suffered rather more than schoolboys at the hands of writers of fiction. Miss Sharp possesses an endowment of humour, rich, sensitive, radiant, that pervades her book like a joyous elemental spirit. And with this frolic spirit, ever alive to the humorous aspects of life, the subtlest apprehension is revealed of the psychical depths beneath the exuberant manifestations of healthy aspiring youth."

14

15